In a Relationship

By

Ross Hawse

    I fell in love with reading when I was quite young and I owe that to my mother. She always found a way to support not only my passions, but also those of my siblings. I'm not sure where she found the money but she managed to enroll me in a science fiction book of the month club and that was the start of a journey that has brought me here, to the publication of my first book. Thank you mom, you have always been there for me.
    There have been others along the way that have inspired, supported and challenged me to be more, to do more, and to live more. I couldn't possible thank them all by name but they know who they are.
    My three children, Shaedan, Sheridan and Holden have not only listened to my stories but have lived through many of them. They are my real world and I love them completely. My brothers and sisters, you were, and are, always a safe haven and solid foundation that I have jumped from often.

In a Relationship

Copyright © 2016 Ross Hawse

All rights reserved

ISBN 978-1-539644446

No part of this publication may be reproduced, distributed, or transmitted in any form or by any means including electronic, mechanical, photocopying, recording, or otherwise without the prior written consent of the author.

This book is a work of fiction. Names, characters, places, and incidents either are products of the author's imagination or are used fictitiously. Any resemblance to actual events or locales or persons, living or dead, is entirely coincidental and beyond the intent of the author or publisher.

Editor:
Patrick Beckerton

CHAPTER 1

It was one of those rare sunny days in the middle of a Pacific North West Winter – the kind of day that you had to take advantage of by getting outside to enjoy it before the mist and rain moved back in to cover the sun and darken your mood. Jake Jensen was looking out his bedroom window watching his son walk up the sidewalk. After he disappeared from view, Jake went to the bedroom door and waited until he heard the sound of the front door closing before he sat down at his desk and turned on his computer.

In today's social media world with Facebook, Twitter, Instagram, Snapchat, Tumbler, and all the rest, nothing became official until it was posted for everyone to see. With that in mind, Jake brought up his web browser, logged into Facebook and updated his relationship status to "In a relationship". *Funny*, he thought, *it really does seem official now.* More than that, it actually felt pretty damn good.

Jake Jensen was a 42 year old, two time divorcee with a 12 year old son. There were days Jake felt a lot older than 42, but those were rare. He had aged well; while some people aged prematurely, that wasn't Jake. He had a full head of light brown hair, deep blue eyes and a way about him that put anyone he met at ease. That was one of the things that had made him a great team leader and allowed him to advance so quickly in his career. He genuinely liked people. Finding women willing to date hadn't been a problem – his demeanor and good looks attracted plenty of women, but his heart and head weren't into it. He was focused on raising his son and building his career.

On paper, having two divorces sounded a lot worse than it really was – at least Jake had pretty good stories behind both failed relationships. After the second marriage ended he had taken some time off from dating. Following some good advice from friends, he sought out counseling to make sure he didn't repeat any of the mistakes from the past as he tried to move forward with life. He decided that picking Dave Grohl, front man for *The Foo Fighters*, as his therapist probably wasn't the best choice, but iTunes downloads were less expensive than traditional therapy.

He remembered how shitty he had felt when he realized that his ex-wife had changed her status from *married* to *single* after they had split up. It had been like a kick in the balls. He hadn't really cared that she had stopped wearing her wedding ring; that was something only their friends and family noticed, one or two people at a time. But to change your status on Facebook – that told the whole world all at once, and it wasn't long before the close (and not so close) friends were quick to add their two cents.

"For Christ's sake! How painful is it to see your mother-in-law and sister-in-law click 'Like' on your soon-to-be-ex-wife's 'single' status?" he thought to himself when he first saw it. *"I mean come on, at least un-friend me first so I don't have to see it!"*

It would have been equivalent to taking out a full page, color ad in the local community newspaper. Assuming, that was, people even remembered what it was like to have a local newspaper.

It shouldn't have really mattered to him seeing as the entire city had found out about their break up at the same time. He and his ex-wife Ashley had worked together at the city's local TV station. Jake was the sales manager and Ashley the co-host of an afternoon talk show. They had worked there together for about five months.

Prior to that, Jake had been working as sales manager for a competitor station in the same city for five years. He loved that job; he had developed a great relationship with his boss and was working for a company that was really good to him. Unfortunately, Ashley couldn't get any other TV station in the city to hire her because of where Jake worked, and his employer wouldn't hire her because he already worked for them.

When a new TV Station began hiring prior to signing on the air, Ashley had applied. As with everywhere else, while they really liked her, they wouldn't hire her for the same reason: her husband worked at the competition. They had asked if Jake would have considered leaving his employer to join them as well – hiring both of them. Not many companies – let alone TV stations – would hire a husband and wife, and Jake felt a sense of obligation to give it a shot so that Ashley could work in the field she had gone to college for. She was quite good at what she did, and the new company offered him a lot of money to make the switch – "Baseball Player Money!" as Jake's old boss put it, when he found out how much they were going to pay.

Once they started working at the new station, their already fragile marriage began to quickly unravel. Ashley started spending all of her time at work or meeting with her co-host to plan for the show. It turned into a lot of evenings and weekends.

Jake remembered the night they agreed the relationship wasn't working for them anymore, and that they should split up and move on separately while they were still friends. Ashley had suggested she could use their relationship, separation and impending divorce on her program. It was compelling television during sweeps week, and would have made for a great show. Jake was adamant that their private life stay private. There was no way he wanted his family, friends, co-workers, boss and everyone else finding out about their split on her TV show. He hadn't even had an opportunity to tell his son yet.

The next day, he'd had a packed afternoon of client calls with his sales staff, and didn't get a chance to watch Ashley's show or even get back to the office. He had finished his last call at five in the west end of the city, and then driven straight home to feed their two dogs. They were actually Ashley's dogs as she had picked out both of them and brought them home as separate surprises. She felt the golden retriever, the first they'd adopted, needed a buddy to keep him company when they were out. He had agreed because frankly, it did make them feel better when they had to be out late.

He got in the house, greeted the dogs and fed them. He had really grown to love that about dogs – it didn't matter how long you were away, five minutes or five hours, they were always happy to see you when you came in the door.

Once he'd had a chance to sit down and relax, he checked his phone and saw he had received an email from his old boss.

"Hey, bud. Just wanted to say that I've cleared my schedule tomorrow if you want to talk or grab a drink."

Jake had thought that was a bit strange, but nice. Then he received another email, this one from Jim, a sales rep who had worked with him at his old company.

"Dude, I just heard the news, call me."

There were more, but before he could read any of them, his new boss had called from head office.

"Hi Jake," he said. "How are you?"

"Fine," Jake replied. "Why?"

"Were you out on sales calls all afternoon? What's going on?"

His boss calmly told him that Ashley had done a segment on her show, using her own experience to share with the audience what it was like to work in the same building as your ex. Half way through the segment she and her co-host had announced that Ashley was separating from her husband and would be filing for divorce. Then they took calls from viewers sharing their experiences of working with their exes.

"Fuck me," was all that Jake could spit out into the phone. Other than that he was speechless, and for Jake that was rare, he always had something to say. It certainly explained all the strange emails and text messages he had been receiving. His boss went on to tell him that the Station Manager had taken Ashley and her co-host aside after their show and expressed the station's displeasure with such a personal matters being discussed on-air without prior approval from management. They had concerns about how it may affect not only Jake, but the rest of the staff and the station's clients. He told Jake how sorry they were that it was happening and that the segment had aired without his knowledge or permission.

Needless to say, the entire debacle created quite a bit of a work shit-storm for Jake. The owner of the company who had been on vacation in the Caribbean flew back the next day and took Jake out for dinner. The owner was a smart, kind and generous man who had been through his own divorce. He advised Jake to take some time off, offered to fire Ashley and pay Jake his bonus early so he could get away for a break if he needed too. Jake told him firing her was unnecessary – he couldn't believe they actually offered to terminate her employment – and he also turned down the advance on the bonus.

Of course, the next day at work, his bonus check was sitting on his desk. The company didn't fire Ashley and her co-host right away, but a month later they were both let go for-what seemed to Jake-bullshit reasons. Jake wasn't happy about it, but it did make things easier for him at work not having to see them come and go every day. It would have made for a messed up Christmas party, he thought.

That was three years ago, and he hadn't really dated all that much since then. It had really screwed him up for quite some time. Initially Jake took the normal route that most men take when trying to get over the love of their life taking everything they could from them both emotionally and financially. He moped around feeling sorry for himself for a couple of months, got very little sleep, felt like every break up song ever written was about him, and it had his family and friends freaked out. They would try and get him to go out; dropping by to make sure he had food, invite him to their homes for the important holidays. They were as good friends should be, they were there. He just wasn't into it.

Ashley had fallen in love with her co-host and kept it from him for a good six months before she called up one day to ask him to meet her for coffee at the Starbucks just around the corner from their old house. He could remember that day like it was yesterday. It was a couple of weeks before Christmas when she had sent a text and asked him to meet her. Jake had arrived first and found a seat in the crowded coffee shop. When Ashley walked in she took his breath away. She looked like she had just finished a photo shoot for Vogue. Her long dark hair was partially covered by a red hat and a matching scarf was wrapped around her neck and tucked inside her black jacket. Under her arm was a green and red Christmas tin she had brought that was filled with homemade cookies for Mathew. Mathew was Jake's 12 year old son from his first marriage. When his mother and Jake, who had married young, realized it wasn't going to work out, he had asked if he could live with his father. His mother wasn't thrilled about it but Jake knew it would be good for both of them, and eventually Mathew's mother relented. Mathew could spend most of his time with his dad and it would help keep Jake focused so he wouldn't go crazy and hit the booze and the bars. At 12, children could decide where or which parent they wanted to live with. Jake was actually quite happy to have Mathew come and live with him. He was a bright, funny and quite an intuitive young man who he saw a lot of himself in.

Jake hadn't seen Ashley for a while, not since she had stopped over in early October to visit and had ended up drinking two bottles of wine with him and staying the night. She had this way of always coming back into his life just long enough to keep him from getting over her. Ashley had told him she had some news and wanted to tell him in person. Jake had immediately felt his stomach churn and had felt like he was going to throw up. Ashley skirted around the real reason she had asked him to meet with small talk about Christmas, the weather, and how the world wasn't doing enough to solve the world's refugee crisis. Discussing world political issues and deeper subjects were one of the things he enjoyed most about his relationship with

Ashley, she always found a way to tap into things that were important to him. Jake could tell she was delaying the delivery of the real reason for the meeting. After a few minutes he finally interrupted her and asked her to spit it out. Ashley paused, then slowly and quietly told him that she and Ryan were going to move into together; Ryan, of course, being the co-working son of a bitch that Jake had been accusing her of having a relationship with over the past six months. Jake was dumbfounded and shocked. Quite frankly, it fucked him up. Not finished with her news Ashley started to softly cry and then told him between sobs that there was something else.

"What else can you possibly have left to say? Let me guess- you're pregnant." He didn't really think she was, but he threw it out there.

Upon hearing those words, Ashley broke down completely and the tears streamed down her cheeks. It took her a few minutes to pull herself together, but she finally managed to whisper a yes.

It was a moment that made Jake feel like he was in the movie *The Matrix*: You know the scene where Keanu Reeve's character is standing in the line of fire, dodging bullets, before realizing that his power had miraculously slowed down the world enough to make such things possible. This was Jake's moment. It was like time stood still. He could hear the conversations around them stop, he could see the snowflakes falling outside the window and he must have counted a hundred flakes before he realized Ashley was asking him if he was ok. "Say something," she was whispering.

He stood up, reached for his jacket, put it on slowly, fixed his scarf and looked at her without blinking. He stared at her stunned and said, "You promised me you would never hurt me."

He didn't cry. In fact, he didn't show any emotion at all. He was numb, empty. He had nothing left to give her, not even a tear. He pushed the green and red tin of Christmas cookies back across the table, stood up, pushed in his chair and walked out the door without looking back. Ashley had been the woman who had helped him through the breakup of his first marriage and they had been through so much good and bad over the previous seven years. He had never known anyone like her, and really believed that they were meant to be together forever. Even though they had been separated for six months, he had still hoped that they would get back together. But that wasn't going to happen now. She was moving in with Ryan, and they were having a baby.

CHAPTER 2

Jake took a trip to Cuba with his best friend Darryl in the spring following his break-up with Ashley. He had originally booked the trip for him and Ashley, but with her new boyfriend and impending motherhood, she obviously wasn't going to be making the trip.

Jake and Darryl had a decent time; at least Jake thought they did. Darryl would disagree. He made the mistake of borrowing Jake's iPod for an hour at the beach the first day, and threw it back at him saying it was too depressing (it was Jake's musical therapy). Darryl had been divorced for a year at that time, and though he too wasn't quite over his wife, he was certainly further along than Jake. He had already started dating and was working on dragging Jake back into the dating world. Jake wouldn't have anything to do with it.

When they had arrived back from the trip, Jake had decided that he needed a change of scenery, a fresh start. Darryl lived in Seattle, working for a company that Jake had worked for before he had met Ashley, and suggested he call them to see if there were any openings. Jake made a few calls and before he knew it, the president of the company had called him and talked him into flying out for an interview. Everything fell into place, and the next thing he knew he was running a TV station in Seattle and restarting his life with Mathew in tow. Having grown up in Seattle, Mathew was pretty excited about the move. His mother's new boyfriend had just purchased a summer home on the water just outside of Seattle, so he would still get to see her a lot – especially during holidays and over the summer break from school.

Life was good for the two of them. Jake got his shit together by getting back into the gym, eating better and – after a lot of complaining from Mathew, he even quit smoking. Jake had been in for a little therapy as well, and it had helped him put a lot of his relationship issues into perspective. He still hadn't taken the plunge back into the dating world, but he felt like he was getting close.

Mathew had become quite the online gamer. When he wasn't doing his homework, he would spend countless hours playing against other kids on various gaming sites. Jake had done a lot of research to make sure everything was on the up and up with the different sites Mathew enjoyed playing on. He was worried that it was a venue for pedophiles or freaks and weirdo's who were looking to make contact with young kids, but they all checked out. Mathew had developed a pretty close relationship with a couple of other players his age and they would play for hours at a time. One particular player, *Rudy2*, had become his favorite and they would not only play, but they would chat back and forth at the same time. It turned out *Rudy2* was a young girl who also lived in Seattle, and from what Mathew told him, she was a pretty good player. Jake could tell Mathew liked her because whenever he played her he didn't yell at the computer. It was kind of cute, and Jake figured it was all pretty harmless.

One night he overheard the two of them talking about dating. Mathew being only 12, Jake was curious. After Mathew finished his game, he brushed his teeth and then stopped by to watch the sports hilights on TV with Jake.

"Seahawks play tomorrow dad, against the Bronco's."

"I know," Jake replied, "they're going to kick their butts!"

Mathew smiled and then leaned in to give his dad a hug goodnight. Before he could leave, Jake told him to sit down for a moment because he wanted to talk to him about something. Mathew rolled his eyes with the here we go again look.

"You're not dating yet are you?" Jake asked him.

Mathew blushed and quickly said, "No."

"Well what were you and *Rudy2* talking about tonight then?" Jake pressed.

Mathew laughed, "You can just call her Rudy dad. You don't have to call her *Rudy2*. Her mom just signed up on this internet dating site. Her dad died a few years back and her mom hasn't dated since."

Jake was relieved and reached down to tussle Mathew's hair. He wore his hair a bit longer than Jake preferred but it wasn't as long as Jake's was when he was young so he didn't push him on it.

"You should think about dating again too, dad. You're not getting any younger," he said with a smile.

"You think so?" Jake grinned back. Mathew hugged his dad and headed for bed. "Hey," Jake yelled after him.

Mathew stopped at his bedroom door and then turned back towards his dad, "What?"

"Why does your friend use *Rudy2* as her game name?"

"I'm not sure," Mathew said softly, "but I think it has something to do with a puppy she had once or wants to get. She doesn't like to talk about it."

With that he was off to bed and Jake was left to wonder about what Mathew had said regarding not getting any younger. He hadn't been on a real date in close to five years and maybe Mathew was right, maybe it was time to start dating again. Jake grabbed his cell phone and sent a quick text to Darryl. If anybody could give him the low down on the transition back into the modern dating world it was Darryl.

They had been pretty good friends for close to 10 years. Darryl had moved out west to start a new sales division for the same company Jake was working for at that time. He would never forget the day the company president introduced Darryl to the management team at their AGM. He was about 28 at the time but you would have sworn he was 18, if that. He was the Doogie Howser of TV sales. But he was so confident in himself and his abilities that he just didn't give a shit what any of the old bastards in the room thought, and you know what, he was good. Jake and Darryl became close friends pretty quickly, along with a couple of the other younger managers who had joined the company around the same time, and they all stayed close. They weren't quite the "get together a couple of times a year buddies", but they all stayed in touch even though they had all ended up living in various cities across the country.

Darryl's wife had cheated on him and it had rocked his life. As much as Darryl loved the world of sales, he had loved his wife even more, and it really messed him up when he found out she was having an affair. It didn't help that they had a four year old son and a two year old daughter. Over the past two years, Jake and Darryl had spent a good deal of vacation time together and had gotten to know each other even better than they had before. Darryl could call Jake on his shit (and he was usually right) so much it pissed Jake off, but he liked that Darryl was always straight up and honest with him.

Jake appreciated Darryl more than he ever told him – kind of a guy thing Jake supposed, but he had helped him through a dark time in his life and never judged him over some of the mistakes he made, even when they pissed him off. Once, despite his buddy's objections, Jake moved into the same neighborhood as Darryl's ex-wife's boyfriend even though he knew Darryl didn't want him living there because he didn't want to risk running into his ex-wife. It was stupid of Jake to do, and it really pissed off Darryl, but it never derailed their friendship.

Jake was hoping that things had improved from Darryl's early dating days, and in particular, one double date they had shared that they didn't talk about anymore.

IN A RELATIONSHIP

Jake was going out to Portland for a job interview and Darryl had invited him to come and spend the weekend at his place. It sounded like a nice break and Jake was getting the itch to get out of Vancouver even though he wasn't crazy it was Portland. He flew into Seattle and Darryl lent him his Jeep to drive down for the interview while he hung out at the house and got things ready for a little back yard BBQ. Darryl loved to cook.

While Jake was in the middle of his interview his phone started to go off like it was possessed – to the point where he had to actually put it in his pocket because the blinking red message light and the vibrating was driving him nuts. After the interview was over, he checked his phone and noticed that Darryl had been texting him about this girl he had met on a free dating sight. Jake found out later was actually more of a hook up site. He had said to Darryl later, "What did you think you were going to get? It's a FREE site!"

It turns out this girl had a friend and they weren't doing anything that night so Darryl had invited them both over to his place for a BBQ. He wanted Jake to change his return flight to Vancouver from that night to the next morning and barbeque with him and his "fish dates" as Jake would call them. He had also text messaged Jake to stop and pick up some beer on the way back to the house and to hurry up.

Jake thought he should have interrupted his interview with his potential future employer to tell him he had a hot double date set up, and then laughed out loud at the thought of how that would have went over. It did sound like it could be fun though, he thought. It had been a while, what the hell. He changed his flight (it cost $350 dollars to change a $99 dollar flight – he hoped it would be worth it), picked up some vodka, wine and beer and headed for Darryl's house. When he got to the house he could hear music and voices coming from behind the house on the deck so he headed straight back.

There was Darryl, standing there with his apron on, drinking wine and cooking up a storm. He really was a great cook and he enjoyed entertaining the ladies with some great dishes and chilled wine. Jake surveyed the other items on the menu and tried to stay cool.

Darryl's guests seemed nice; they were a couple of nurses from Idaho who had moved out to Seattle for work. They were as you would expect two girls from the heartland to be: sweet, honest and straight forward. No bullshit to these girls, and no trouble dropping the f-bomb. In fact, Jake learned a few new ways to use the word in everyday conversation along with some very interesting tidbits about Idaho. Aside from the fact that Idaho produces 27 billion *fucking* potatoes annually, the state is also home to the world's largest *fucking* potato chip at 25 inches by 14 inches, has the only football field with blue turf known as "Smurf Turf", has a "Bra Tree" at the base of McCall Ski resort that skiers throw their bra onto from the chair lift (that Jake thought Darryl would be all over) and has a town named Pocatello where it's against the law to not *fucking* smile. They could be tour guides for an adults-only tour, thought Jake. He drank three vodka sodas in about 30 minutes and then sent Darryl a text as he worked away on the barbeque. It was six short words.

We're going to need more booze.

For the record, they were very nice girls. So nice in fact, that Darryl decided after they had eaten that he would take one upstairs where he preceded to role play some fantasy that included what sounded like a lot of spanking. Darryl hadn't realized that his bedroom window was open and Jake, along with nurse2, spent the next hour listening to them. Darryl never brought up that plane ticket Jake rebooked.

That was Jake's first and only experience with dating up to that point, but Darryl had been sharing a lot of his experiences, and he seemed to be doing alright. Most of the time he had two, three, or even four different girls on the go, and he had pretty good taste too, Jake thought, with that one exception from the state of Idaho.

It was dark by the time Darryl knocked on the door and Jake had already put back a couple of vodka and soda while waiting for him. When he opened the door Darryl was standing there with a six pack of beer and a big grin. Jake noticed he was still in his work clothes, but he had sunglasses sitting up on his head like he had just come from the beach.

"What's with the sunglasses?" Jake asked him. "It rained all day today."

"Well, I've been thinking lately that I need a thing. You know, something to be known for. Some guys wear black, some guys wear hats, some guys wear white sneakers. My thing is going to be shades on my head. It's going to be my thing."

"Really," Jake said, "it's your thing? So, middle of winter, blinding snow storm and you're going to be the guy wearing sunglasses on his head because it's your thing?"

"Yup," he stated smugly. "It's my Smokey and the Bandit, my Burt Reynolds so to speak. Just like Burt, I only take them off for one thing, and you know what that is!"

Jake loved this guy, but there were times he reminded him a lot of the character Quagmire from *Family Guy*. He swore sometimes he actually could hear Darryl laughing, "giggedy giggedy."

"You have a thing," Jake replied. "Your thing is you don't have a thing."

They opened a couple of beer and Darryl shared some of his experiences with internet dating and dating in general over the past twelve months. For the most part he had met a lot of different women but had only spent any real quality time with a couple of them. One he had really liked a lot but she broke it off with him; and one that he really got along well with and could booty call whenever he wanted – a friend with benefits relationship – but he didn't connect with her on every level like he was looking for. Jake was still skeptical about the dating thing and Darryl could tell that he wasn't going to be as quick adapting to it as he had been. Darryl always liked a good challenge.

After another hour of debating the merits of joining one of the many dating sites, Darryl gave up and asked Jake to throw a copy of their Cuba pictures onto a memory stick so he could have a copy for himself. Jake put a memory stick into his laptop and dragged the Cuba folder on to it and tossed it to Darryl as he walked down the hall way.

"See you tomorrow," Darryl said with a mischievous grin as he grabbed it and walked into the dark with his "Burt Reynolds" on top of his head.

CHAPTER 3

Jake woke up a bit later than he had planned, mostly due to hitting snooze four times. Drinking half a bottle of vodka the night before may have also been a contributing factor. This sure wasn't like his younger days when it was only a matter of popping a couple of Advil before making his way through a hangover day with ease. Now it took four Advil, a day of dragging his ass, and a mental fog that lasted into the next evening.

Jake was so out of sorts that he didn't even notice that he had 12 new messages on his phone. Rushing into work, he was relieved to remember that it was mercifully a Friday. Fridays were great because they were the one day of the week that Jake kept his schedule open. He could put out any fires that had developed over the week or plan late last minute client calls or if needed have one on one sessions with the staff. Friday was like his spare class in high school and he was so grateful for that today.

After he managed to make a cup of arguably the worst coffee he had ever tasted he sat down. Jake flipped open his laptop and while waiting for it to power up, he began checking his phone for messages.

IN A RELATIONSHIP

Twelve new messages? Interested, Jake opened up his email folder to examine the stream, wondering what this was all about. Twelve new messages from 12 women he had never heard of before.

He opened the first one and just about shit his pants. It was from a woman named Hilda: 58 years old, 5"9", 150 pounds, long black hair and looking like she smoked while she slept. Her message stated that while she realized she was a little older than what he was looking for, she had hoped that he didn't mind, and that she was up for any kind of "**Fun**". Jake quickly deleted the note before any co-workers came into his office and saw what he had up on the screen. It was definitely NSFW.

They went on and on, every one of them with some scantily clad or supposed sexy, intentionally posed picture; each e-mail had invitations ranging from coffee or drinks to whip cream and strawberries. Having just read through the final message, Jake's office phone rang. He picked it up and heard Darryl on the line asking if he had changed his mind about signing up for dating?

Something sounded a little suspicious in Darryl's voice. The string of emails started to make a little more sense even in his hangover driven fog, and Jake had a bad feeling that he'd just figured out who was behind this string of mysterious invitations.

"No," he said.

"Oh," Darryl replied, "how's your morning going, anything interesting going on…?"

"You bastard," Jake whispered, "you know exactly how my morning's going and I don't know what or how you did this but you need to make it stop! These women are scaring me!"

Darryl laughed, "No, it's good - it takes a few to sift through before you find a good one. But it's alright, you'll see. Just give it a few days and then we'll go through them together."

"Not a chance," Jake shot back. "What site is this and how did you put me on it?"

Darryl explained to Jake how he filled out a profile for him on the free site that he was on and then uploaded the photos from Cuba that Jake had copied for him the night before. All Jake had to do was throw in his address and presto, he'd be back in the game. After a short but somewhat animated discussion, Darryl promised to turn the site off if Jake agreed to meet him at lunch and sign up on a site for real. Reluctantly, Jake agreed.

When Jake got to the restaurant Darryl had already ordered two beers and set up his laptop. It was a trendy little spot that Darryl frequented enough that every waitress knew him by name along with what he liked to drink, without him even having to order. Whenever his beer ran low there was another delivered before he had to ask. They all wore the same outfits; tight black skirts and tight white tops and they were stunning, each and every one of them. They flirted with Darryl constantly and he gave it right back. They were working on a good tip, but that didn't bother Darryl, he loved the attention.

Jake slid onto the stool beside Darryl and told him he still wasn't sure about this dating thing.

"Look, we made a deal and you're going to stick to it. It's time you got back in the saddle and there's no easy way to do it. At least this way, you don't have to approach them in person like a cold call. You can screen them, and then only contact the ones who you at least have something in common with," Darryl stated. Jake still wasn't buying it.

"The only way I am going to close down that other site is if you do this," Darryl said. "Come on, what do you have to lose? I'll tell you what, go on 12 dates in 12 weeks and if you don't find a spark with any of them, then I'm out. I won't bring it up again. Ever!"

"Ever?" Jake repeated back to make sure Darryl meant what he had said.

"Ever," Darryl said emphatically.

Jake thought about it for a minute and took a big drink before he agreed with a slight amendment, "Make it six dates in six weeks and you have a deal."

"OK," Darryl said. "Deal!" and they shook on it.

The two of them spent the next hour and a half filling out Jake's dating profile and loading pictures to set up the new account. As usual with Darryl, it became a bit of a production as he had to have every waitress get involved in choosing which pictures to load. When it became clear Jake didn't have enough good pictures, Darryl grabbed his iPhone and had Jake pose for a couple of half and full body shots to add to the profile. Jake thought the pictures actually seemed like the easy part compared to all the questions they asked in the profile section.

Jake really struggled with the pet question. Not whether he liked dogs or cats – that was a no brainer, he was a dog person, period. The problem was he had struggled through the process of finding homes for the two dogs he and Ashley had when they split up, and that process had taken a lot out of him. Ashley loved the dogs. She treated them more like her children than dogs, and while she hadn't spent a lot of time with them over the last six months of their relationship, they meant the world to her.

Jake had kept them for five months on his own, but because he wasn't home much during that period, it had become extremely unfair for the dogs. He developed a lot of guilt for leaving them home alone all day when he was at work, even though they had a dog door from the garage into a large back yard. Ashley didn't come to see them very much, and though she had promised to find a place where she could take and keep them, she had moved into a swanky apartment downtown that didn't allow pets. That left Jake with the responsibility of having to come home every evening right after work to feed them, walk them and give them some love. It also meant he had no life in the evenings or the ability to stay out late if he did. He had left Ashley voice messages and emails about helping him find them good homes and she had agreed that they should. Unfortunately, she didn't help at all and Jake had to search on his own.

He found a nice couple through one of the girls he worked with – their sheltie had passed away and while they really wanted another dog, they didn't want a puppy to house train. Cooper was a three year old black and white sheltie that Ashley had brought home to keep Oscar, their golden retriever, company. Cooper was a perfect little gentleman who would play catch with his ball for hours at a time and constantly keep Oscar on his toes. Jake wasn't sure Oscar actually liked Cooper, but he tolerated him, and it certainly made him and Ashley feel better when they had to be out for an extended amount of time knowing that Oscar had a buddy to hang out with.

When it came time for Cooper's new owners to pick him up, it became very emotional, and Jake had fought off tears until they drove around the corner. He had sent Ashley an email telling her that he had found Cooper a new home and that if she wanted to see him before his new owners picked him up she should come to the house. She never showed up, and Jake never heard anything back from her. It left him angry that she hadn't bothered to help find them homes, and then couldn't even be bothered to show up to see them go.

Oscar was a bit harder to find a home for. He was a big dog, about 90 pounds, and four years old. He was a beautiful dog though, a true golden retriever, and Ashley used to call him a sexy dog because he was simply that beautiful. He wasn't that smart though, and apparently – as they had found out as he started to grow up, retrievers weren't known for the size of their brains. In fact, the vet told them that retrievers usually took about four years to grow into their brains and out of the puppy phase, but once they were through it they were great. Oscar did chew through quite a few shoes, as well as a lamp, a Christmas tree, a vacuum cleaner, a lot of Christmas ornaments, and any toilet paper ever put into the garbage. It's also likely he ate the crotch out of at least a dozen pairs of underwear; he didn't care whose underwear it was, he liked them all. He was a simple dog, but he was loyal and he loved Ashley. She had pretty much raised him from a puppy like he was a child. As Ashley wasn't working full time and could be home by 10am every day, Jake would often come home during Oscar's first year with them, and find Ashley and Oscar sleeping together on the couch.

Jake had delayed finding Oscar a home because he knew how much he meant to Ashley, but again, she didn't return any of his messages or help to find him a home even though they had agreed it would be best for both dogs. Jake had listed the house and needed to find Oscar a home before it went on the market so he wouldn't have to race back every time the realtor wanted to show it. He put an ad on *Craigslist* and interviewed about a dozen candidates before settling on a nice family who lived just outside the city. They owned a big house on two acres that was completely fenced with a large garage and three young children. Best of all, they already had a golden retriever, and while their dog was older, he would be a great companion for Oscar. The day they came to the house, Jake brought them into the back yard to make sure Oscar and the kids got along. They had an eight year old son and he and Oscar played for about an hour nonstop. It was perfect.

Jake asked them to leave for a few minutes to give him a chance to say good bye to Oscar. He spent the time gathering all of Oscar's things together – his dish, brush, leash, collar, nail clippers, treats, dog food, toys and a big pillow he slept on. The half hour went by so fast that Jake didn't have time to really think about Oscar leaving. They had spent the last two weeks together, just the two of them, since Cooper found his new home. Oscar had spent those two weeks listening to Jake go on and on about life's problems and he never complained. When the time had come for Oscar to go with his new family, Jake walked him to their van and Oscar hopped right in with the kids in the back eager to go for a ride. Jake passed them the bag with all of Oscar's belongings, gave him a pat on the head, and leaned in so Oscar could lick his face one last time. They promised to send pictures and told Jake he could visit Oscar anytime, but he knew he would never see him again. As they drove away that day, Jake remembered how the tears had started running down his face and just didn't stop. He had sat on the front steps and cried for what must have been an hour before he could gather the strength to go back inside the house. It took him weeks to get over how empty the house seemed without the dogs. He would find dog hair on his suits, or bits of chewed underwear Oscar had left under the couch and it would break his heart. He had vowed that he would never have another dog.

Ashley was pissed that he had given Oscar away, even though she had agreed to help and then gone MIA. When she had sent him a text and asked if she could visit Oscar some three weeks after he had been gone, he simply sent a text back saying Oscar doesn't live here anymore. She didn't talk to Jake for quite a while after she found out that Oscar was gone, but Jake didn't care. He was so mad at her for making him give the dogs away on his own.

Darryl, who had heard Jake tell the dog stories a few times, suggested that they look for someone who doesn't want or have pets. Especially if they were only looking at six dates, it cut down the chances of Jake having a melt down with some dog lady.

Jake thought the questions in the profile were more in-depth than the questions his therapist had asked, and there wasn't a lot they left uncovered. He really wasn't sure he even knew if the answers he was giving were honest except on the age questions. Darryl was adamant that he look for someone between 20 and 40 even though Jake was thinking more between 30 and 40. He made the point that if Jake didn't like them, he didn't have to date them, but it just widened the pool. It seemed like a good point, but again Jake made Darryl compromise and they used 28 to 45. Jake punched in his Credit Card number and hit "Confirm".

IN A RELATIONSHIP
32

CHAPTER 4

Sarah Stone hit the power button on her laptop and waited for her computer screen to come up. The sun was shining in through her bedroom window as she sat on her bed cross-legged watching her daughter Emma run across their front lawn, laughing as if she didn't have a care in the world with a puppy nipping at her heels. As the computer came to life a picture of a golden retriever puppy popped up. That made her smile. She logged into her Facebook account and clicked on edit profile. Under relationship status, she made the change to "In a relationship" then saved her changes, smiled again and looked back out the window at Emma.

Sarah could be described as the girl next door all grown up. She had dirty blonde hair, hazel eyes and a slim figure that would be the envy of many women, both younger and older than she was. Her smile made others smile back and her voice was a melody you never got tired of.

Sarah lived in the perfect neighborhood. Sure, she and her daughter Emma lived in the smallest house on the street, but her late husband had always said it was better to be in the smallest house in a good neighborhood than the biggest house in a bad one. She had used that advice when she purchased the house with the life insurance payout money after his accident. It hadn't been easy adjusting to life as a single mother, but she was determined to give her daughter the best life she could, and the other great thing about this neighborhood was it was only two blocks from Catherine's house.

Catherine was Sarah's best friend; they had been close since they had met in university, which seemed like a million years ago. She had been there through the dark days that had enveloped Sarah's life after her husband had died, and Sarah was pretty sure that even if Michael hadn't been Catherine's brother, she still would have helped with all that needed to be done in the aftermath of the accident.

Catherine and Sarah were the same age, and while they had celebrated Catherine's 40th birthday earlier in the summer with a big party and lots of friends, Sarah had told Catherine that under no circumstances did she want a big 40th Birthday party. Her birthday was the next day and Sarah just wanted to spend a quiet night with Emma. It had been five years since Michael had died, and Sarah still wasn't interested in meeting anyone new. She had been using Emma as an excuse to not go on dates, but now that Emma was 12 (going on 16) the excuse was starting to wear thin – Catherine had been trying to set Sarah up on dates for the past several months with no success. Catherine had always been the one to push Sarah out of her comfort zone, to get her to try new things. When they were in university, Catherine was the one who said *yes* for both of them, and many of those *yes*'s led them to all-night parties and spontaneous weekend getaways.

Catherine was still a very attractive woman, and you could tell when you met her that she looked after herself both physically and mentally. She didn't wear her hair quite as long as she use to, but she swore she would never have it as short as some of the other mothers in the neighborhood. She said the minute she cuts her hair short, she would become just like the rest of the moms. The next thing you know, she would be wearing sweat pants and running shoes and driving a mini-van. Whenever they went out, she would spot a mini-van and say, "Show me a woman driving a mini-van, and I'll show you a woman who wants an SUV."

She was always dragging Sarah to some new workout or nutritional seminar. That was one of the things that Emma had enjoyed most about spending so much time at Aunt Catherine's house – there was always fresh fruit and lots of vegetables. Sarah was pretty sure it was Catherine that had turned Emma into a vegetarian.

The latest workout craze Catherine was into was Hot Yoga. Sarah had started going to a weekly yoga class with Catherine and had really enjoyed getting some exercise and it had also helped her clear her mind from work. When Catherine signed them up for a hot yoga class, Sarah went along thinking it couldn't be any harder than what they had been doing for the past month. She was wrong. It should have been called *Hell Yoga* because it was probably that hot in hell, and regardless of what kind of shape you were in, nothing prepares you for 60 minutes of yoga in a sealed off room with the thermostat set at 120 degrees. It was ridiculously hot. The first session had nearly killed her, and 20 minutes in she tried to leave but was told you couldn't leave or open the door until the session was over. She had tried to just lie on her mat and rest, but the instructor switched to partner poses and matched up with Sarah herself so there was no escape. When the hour was up, Sarah felt like she had just stepped out of the shower: her hair was soaked, her yoga outfit was dripping and mascara was running down her face. She couldn't wait to get the hell out of that class and told Catherine she would rather sumo wrestle than go through another hot yoga class. She hadn't been back since.

Catherine had two children of her own, a thirteen year old daughter named Jessica and a nine year old son named Ben. Emma had spent a lot of time at their house in the early years after Michael had died. The kids were quite close back then, but over the past year Emma had started to stay home on her own after school and was spending a lot of time playing online computer games. Emma looked a lot like her father, Michael. She had long blonde hair with natural hi-lights, dark blue eyes and a smile that would brighten Sarah's worst days. Sarah and Emma had always been close but Michael's death had brought them even closer. Emma was protective of her mother; it was almost as if no one was good enough to replace her father and she enjoyed the amount of time they were able to spend together, just the two of them. Sarah knew that she should do more adult things on her own but she didn't want to let Emma out of her sight for any longer than she had to, and actually quite enjoyed taking Emma to fancy restaurants for dinner and getting dressed up and going to see live community theatre productions. There was only one area where the two didn't see eye to eye and that was over the one thing that Emma wanted most in the entire world, a puppy.

    Sarah pulled the car into the detached garage at the back of the house, turned off the lights and shut off the engine. She liked her car, it was the one thing that she had spoiled herself with and the guilt she had felt when she first drove it home was long gone. The used black Volvo suited her and it had more than enough room for her and Emma. The first weekend she had the car, she and Emma decided that they would load up her iPod with 12 hours of music and then drive until it had played exactly six hours. Where they were at that time would be where they would spend the weekend. They had made it to a little town in Washington State that at first glance seemed like it was going to be boring, but turned out to be quite the opposite. It was filled with friendly locals, unique little shops and the best waffles they had ever tasted. They had a terrific weekend in that little town and had hated getting back in the car to leave when Sunday afternoon arrived. Emma had started putting pictures up in the garage from all of their road trips, and the picture from that first trip was always the last thing Sarah saw when she turned off the garage light and went into the house. She liked that. It always put her in a good mood before she stepped through the back door and started dinner.

IN A RELATIONSHIP

As she stepped into the hallway she could smell something cooking and it brought a smile to her face. She and Emma had been spending more and more time in the kitchen these past few months, planning and cooking dinner together. She knew Emma was trying to make things easier for her when she got home from work and she appreciated it. She was a bit worried though, because Emma had never attempted to cook dinner on her own before. It was either going to be great or a disaster.

Sarah put her coat away and rounded the corner into the kitchen to see what was cooking. The table had been set with the dishes she and Sarah had purchased when they took that first little trip in the car – blue plates with yellow flowers, matching glasses, and napkins set beside each plate with a knife and a fork. In the center of the table she had placed butter, syrup, whip cream, fresh strawberries and a carton of milk. Standing over the waffle maker was Emma wearing the apron that Michael had given Sarah the last Christmas they had shared together. It was covered in puppies of every kind.

Emma turned around and smiled at Sarah and said, "It's a backwards day today Mom, so we are having breakfast for dinner."

It was Sarah's turn to smile. "I love backwards days," she said and sat down at the table. They chatted about each other's day as they ate the waffles Emma had made, which had turned out pretty good for her first time. Sarah told her daughter she would clean up since Emma had made dinner, and she could go wash up and start on her homework.

After she had cleaned up the kitchen Sarah went upstairs and peaked into Emma's room. "I'm just going to check my email Emma, then have a bath, please do your homework before you play any online games tonight ok?"

Emma looked back over her shoulder startled by her mom's comments and quickly switched her computer screen from the game she was currently playing to her math homework. "Of course, mom," she replied with a tone of innocence.

"I mean it," Sarah said sternly and then smiled as she closed the door and took off for her bedroom.

IN A RELATIONSHIP
40

CHAPTER 5

Sarah sometimes thought she was too hard on Emma; after all, she was only 12 years old and hadn't had a father figure in her life for over five years. Over the past year she had spent a lot more time in her room during the evenings and after school, and it was starting to worry Sarah. She knew Emma was online playing games, but she had checked them out quite thoroughly and felt comfortable that they were ok. A friend of hers had shown her how to track websites that Emma visited and she had put software on the computer that wouldn't allow adult or X-rated sites to be accessed. She had installed the same software on her computer as well, just in case. Quite often Emma would use her mom's computer when she wasn't home because it had a bigger screen and was faster. Kids today needed everything right now - if it didn't load in 2 seconds they were on to the next thing. Sarah could only imagine how frustrated Emma would have been in the old dial up internet world her mother had grown up in. Emma didn't even know what dial up meant; they had never even had a house phone.

Her laptop was not in its usual spot on her desk in the corner by the bedroom window, so Sarah knew that Emma had been on it earlier that day. She flipped it open and powered it up. When the screen came up it was a picture of a beautiful little golden retriever puppy with a little red bow. It wasn't her usual screen saver and it caused Sarah to pause and sit back staring at the picture. A rush of memories came flooding back to her and with shaking hands she quickly closed the laptop and yelled for Emma to come to her room. Emma took her time coming into her mother's bedroom and just peaked in around the door concerned about the tone of voice her mother had called for her with.

"What's up mom?" she asked quietly.

Sarah was visibly upset and on the verge of crying but was doing all she could to remain calm and not get emotional, "Why did you change my screen saver, Emma?" she asked.

Emma could clearly see her mother was not mad, just very sad. She looked close to tears and Emma suddenly felt remorse for what she had done. "I thought you might like the change, mom. It's been over 5 years -" but she didn't finish the sentence. Her mother broke down in tears and told her to change it back as she got up and ran into the bathroom.

Emma changed it back as quick as she could and then softly walked over to the door of her mother's bathroom. "Mom?" she quietly whispered through the door.

Sarah didn't answer but she heard Emma. She was trying hard to stop the tears from running down her cheek. Emma could hear her through the bathroom door and started to cry herself.

"I'm sorry, mom. I just thought it would be ok. I didn't mean to make you cry."

Sarah hated it when Emma cried. She had spent months lying in bed with her when Michael had died holding her while she cried herself to sleep. Then she would lay awake until the early morning fighting back her own tears. It had taken them both a long time to work through the pain of losing Michael, and whenever Emma cried now – which wasn't often, it would bring back memories of those long nights they had worked their way through. She opened the door and wrapped her arms around her daughter whispering to her that it was ok, everything was alright.

Emma looked up at Sarah with her eyes swollen from crying and asked, "Can we get a puppy mom? I just think it would help and we could put our name on the adoption list with the shelter again just like dad -".

Sarah cut her off by putting a finger to Emma's lips.

"I can't yet, princess. I wish I could, for your sake, but I just can't yet," she whispered. Emma, unable to hold back the tears, buried her head into her mother's chest and started to cry again.

It took a while for the two of them to compose themselves and their usual hot-chocolate-and-American-Idol evening dragged by without a word spoken. After Emma had brushed her teeth and gone to bed, Sarah ran herself a hot bath. She added some bath oil and made sure the water was as hot as she could possibly stand it before she slid in. It was hot alright – so hot it nearly burned her, so she turned on a little cold to even it out. Once she had it just right, she poured herself a large glass of Pinot and climbed in. The water felt great, and she let it cover her entire body. She took a drink of her wine and tried to get her mind off of the events of five years ago but she couldn't shake it.

CHAPTER 6

When Sarah and Michael first met they were both in their final year of University. Michael was studying law and Sarah was majoring in Psychology. They both knew the minute they met that they were meant for each other. Sarah had never really had a serious boyfriend, either in high school or in university. She had dated, she just hadn't found what she was looking for and wasn't prepared to settle. When she and Catherine became friends, Catherine had told her she should meet her brother. Catherine thought they would be perfect for each other, but Sarah had always told her she didn't have time for a boyfriend.

Then one weekend, she and Catherine had gone on a weekend road trip and their car had broken down in the middle of nowhere. They hitched a ride into the nearest town where Catherine phoned Michael to come and rescue them. That's what Michael was like; he would drop anything to help out a member of his family or a close friend. He was the most unselfish person that Sarah had ever met and not only that, he was extremely handsome. When he had shown up in his old truck to pick them up she had nearly had a heart attack when he got out of the truck. He had dark hair under an old Seattle Mariners baseball cap, a blue plaid shirt with a white t-shirt underneath, and a pair of old jeans that made his ass look divine. His blue eyes locked on hers for what seemed like an eternity and at that moment she knew she had met the man she was going to marry.

They hooked up Catherine's car so he could tow it with his truck and they all jumped in for the 2 hour ride back. It was one of those old trucks with just one long bench seat and Catherine made sure that Sarah sat in the middle with the gear shift between her legs. That 2 hour drive back felt like 2 minutes to Sarah and she hadn't wanted it to end. Both she and Michael were too shy to ask each other for a phone number let alone a date, but that's when Catherine stepped in sensing that neither of them were going to say anything.

"Hey, Michael," Catherine said, "Sarah and I were going to see Pearl Jam this Friday, but I have to work now. Maybe you could take her". Catherine was smiling like the proverbial cat that ate the canary.

Sarah started to stumble out a "you don't have too", but Michael was faster.

"Sure! I'd love to." The rest as they say was history.

Other than classes, Michael and Sarah spent pretty much every minute they could together. They got married soon after they graduated in a private little family ceremony in Michael's parents' back yard, and took off for a week's honeymoon in Mexico. When they returned, they bought a small condo and agreed to work on their careers for a few years before they started a family. That plan didn't quite work out as Sarah found out she was pregnant shortly after they returned from their honeymoon. Michael decided to take a job as a realtor in his father's real estate office rather than continue his pursuit of a career as a lawyer, and they quickly sold their condo and bought a little house in a nice neighborhood. Emma was born 6 months later, and her arrival brought the two of them even closer together. It was a fairy tale, pure and simple.

A week before Emma's seventh birthday, Michael had told Sarah of his plan to surprise her with a puppy as a present. Not just any puppy – it had to be a rescue puppy and a Golden Retriever; the same dog he had been given when he was a child. He was so corny that way with tradition, but it was one of the many things about him that Sarah loved. She agreed, but wanted Emma to pick out the puppy herself. Michael was persistent though, and would not give up. He debated it with her every night the week prior until finally, the night before Emma's birthday, Sarah gave in to Michael's wish to surprise her with the puppy sporting a little red bow and sitting on her bed when she got home from school.

It still tore Sarah's heart out when she thought about that day. It was a blur really, and she never knew all the details until months later when she went back and read the news stories online. Michael had picked up the puppy and was on his way home when he came across a vehicle with a flat tire on the side of the road. He couldn't just drive by, he had to stop and see if he could help, that was who he was. While he was changing the woman's tire, a semi-trailer struck his and the woman's vehicles. The truck driver survived, but Michael, the woman, her two children, and the puppy all died. It turns out the truck driver had been up for 24 hours without sleep and had dozed off when he struck them. When Emma made it home from school that day, she had gone to her bedroom and seen the little puppy bed and water dish with the name "Rudy" on it, but she couldn't find her mother. It was only after searching the house that she found Sarah curled up in a little ball in her bedroom crying. Catherine had arrived minutes later and took them both to her house where they stayed for weeks.

CHAPTER 7

Morning came far too quickly for Sarah. Her eyes were bloodshot from crying the night before and she could tell the puffiness around her eyes wasn't just from sleeping. Her reflection in the mirror caused her to feel all of her 40 years of age. She was relieved that she didn't have a big birthday party to go to tonight, just a family dinner at Catherine's. She turned on the shower and waited a few minutes for it to get hot enough before she stepped in and let the warmth cover her. As she started to get dressed, her focus turned to Emma. She probably hadn't slept that well either. She quickly finished dressing and then put on some makeup. She normally didn't wear much make up, but this morning she felt like she needed it, and she had a hard time leaving the mirror. Finally, she stood up and looked at both her right and left profile, sucked in her tummy, took one last look, and wished herself a happy 40th birthday.

When Sarah got downstairs, Emma was already sitting at the table with a bowl of oatmeal and raisins. *She seems to be in a pretty good mood*, Sarah thought to herself. When Emma spotted her mother, she jumped up and hit the power button on the microwave and told her mom to sit down.

"Happy Birthday, mom!" she shouted with a smile and then ran over to give her a kiss on the cheek and a big hug.

"Thanks, princess," Sarah said. "I thought you might have forgotten".

"No way," Emma replied, and then jumped up when the microwave chimed that it was finished its task. Emma pulled out a steaming bowl of Oatmeal and raisins and set it down in front of her mother. Sarah was just about to put her spoon into the bowl so she could cool off a spoonful, but Emma stopped her.

"Hold on Mom", she said urgently "It's not ready".

She pulled out a two large candles, a number four and a zero, and placed them into the oatmeal. Then she pulled the long BBQ lighter out of the drawer and lit both candles. Once they were going, she flipped open the laptop that had been sitting on the table and there were Catherine, Jessica and Ben on Skype.

"Three, Two, One" counted down Emma, and they all started singing happy birthday to Sarah. They were awful at the singing, but it was so cute, Sarah could feel the tears beginning to form in her eyes again – only this time they were tears of happiness. When they were finished Sarah wiped her tears and thanked them for the perfect start to her day.

"It's just started, birthday girl," Catherine shouted. "I'll see you at lunch, and don't be late."

"I don't know if I can make it. I have a super busy day today," Sarah stated.

"Too bad. Meet me at Earls at twelve sharp, or I'm coming to the office," declared Catherine.

"Ok, ok," Sarah gave in. "I'll be there."

"Good," said Catherine. "Now say goodbye, kids."

"Goodbye, Auntie Sarah! We love you! Have a happy birthday!" they yelled before the Skype screen went blank.

"You put them up to that, didn't you?" Sarah asked Emma who was sitting at the table with a big smile on her face.

"You only have one 40th birthday, mom," Emma replied. "You have to make it special."

"Well thanks, princess. I appreciate it, although this morning I feel more like I'm fifty," sighed Sarah. "How are you feeling this morning? I'm sorry about last night. It wasn't fair of me to react the way I did."

Emma feigned a smile and told her mother everything was okay. Then she placed another quick kiss on Sarah's cheek, slipped on her boots and jacket, and headed for the door. "Not so fast!" Sarah yelled at Emma as she grabbed the door knob. "You forgot your backpack."

Emma ran back into the hallway and picked up her backpack. "Thanks, mom," she said as she smiled across the table. She took a step, stopped and then placed the backpack on the ground so she could open it.

"What's the matter?" Sarah asked.

"It feels too light, mom. My lunch is missing," she muttered as she rummaged around inside the backpack. Then she paused before pulling a 20 dollar bill from the bottom and holding it up. "What's this?" she asked with a scowl.

"Well, I just thought you could buy some lunch at the cafeteria today instead of eating another PB and J sandwich," Sarah offered with a sheepish smile.

"That's guilt lunch money, mom," Emma shot back with a straight face, then smiled. "But I'll take it." With that, she was off and down the hall and out the door.

CHAPTER 8

Working as a grief counselor for pet owners having a hard time with their pets passing wasn't something that Sarah had planned to do when she was studying psychiatry in university, but it felt like the right thing to do after Michael had passed away. It allowed her to help others go through the grieving process while she and Emma worked through their own loss. It had taken her a good six months to figure out what she wanted to do after the accident, and once she made the decision to open her own practice, she had thrown all of her free time into building it up. That had been four years ago, and not only was the business doing well, but it was allowing her to heal as she worked. The first two years she had worked alone, but as things had gotten continuously busier, she had realized that she needed help to keep her organized and allow her more time to spend actually counseling her patients.

A young girl had come into her office one day, devastated by the loss of her Yorkshire terrier. The girl didn't have any money, but Sarah, much like she was with strays, took her in. Mary, it turns out, had just broken up with her boyfriend and desperately needed a job.

Everyday Sarah would arrive at work and Mary would be sitting on the front step waiting for her. It was only a matter of time before she hired her and the two had become a pretty good team. Emma and Catherine couldn't understand how Sarah could help complete strangers deal with the loss of their pet's but not be able to move on to the point where she and Emma could get another dog of their own.

The morning flew by for Sarah, which was great because it didn't give her time to think about Emma, her birthday, or any of the lingering black cloud issues from the night before. She had purposely scheduled two early appointments for this morning weeks ago, knowing that her 40th birthday might be a difficult day. Michael had always made her birthdays special and every year since his death it had been a real challenge to get through the day without crying. Last year had been the first year she had been able to work through the entire day, and this year seemed to be going pretty well, too.

Her last appointment before lunch was an emergency for Mrs. Worthington. She had lost her iguana several weeks ago, and was having a difficult time dealing with the loss. Sarah had thought they had turned a corner on her recovery the previous week, but had scheduled an emergency session when Mr. Worthington called and said his wife had had a relapse of sorts. When they arrived, Mrs. Worthington was in hysterics, sobbing uncontrollably, and Sarah's assistant Mary quickly ushered her into the private office while Sarah took a minute to speak with the husband before going in.

"What happened?" Sarah asked him. "She seemed to be doing so well last week."

Mr. Worthington looked up at Sarah sheepishly and just held out a plastic bag. "What's this?" Sarah asked.

Mr. Worthington opened the plastic bag and pulled out a little clutch purse. "I thought she'd appreciate the fact that she could take him with her everywhere she went, so I had this made from his skin," he mumbled.

It took Sarah a good half hour to get Mrs. Worthington calmed down, and then another 20 minutes before she could get her to talk to Mr. Worthington. Finally, they made up and left with their iguana purse.

Sarah barely had time to get to the restaurant to meet Catherine for lunch, but she made it.

IN A RELATIONSHIP

CHAPTER 9

Catherine had replaced Michael as Sarah's birthday lunch partner, and while at first the annual lunch date was emotional, the last few years they had become something that Sarah looked forward to. She knew the lunch meant a lot to Catherine as well. In a way, it helped keep the good memories of Michael alive. Over the past few months, Catherine had been starting to push Sarah into getting back into the dating world, but so far she had been able to hold her off using the *Emma's not ready for me to date* excuse. Sarah knew that was not going to work much longer, and honestly speaking, she had been thinking about starting to date again. It had been five years, and Emma was old enough to understand that Sarah wasn't replacing Michael, but rather, her mother needed to find a man to spend some adult time with. The thought of dating excited Sarah a little, but at the same time scared her to death; the world had changed a lot since her last date.

As she walked into the restaurant, Sarah spotted Catherine sitting at a little table against the window near the back of the restaurant and quickly made her way over. She had eaten there once or twice before and always enjoyed it. There was plenty of light from the wall of windows and the staff was always so pleasant – it was like they truly enjoyed their job. Today they seemed extra nice as they greeted her when she got close to the table, and she knew why once she got around the bar. There was a huge birthday balloon bouquet tied to her chair with the largest balloon sporting the number 40 on it.

Catherine looks great, thought Sarah. *Hard to believe she's older than I am.*

Sarah pulled out her chair and sat down. Catherine had already ordered them both a glass of wine, and hers was sitting on top of an envelope with Sarah's name written on it.

Sarah could feel her face starting to warm up from the blushing the balloon and attention were causing. She picked up her glass of wine and said "You look terrific, Catherine. I wish I looked as good as you do."

"You can, but it's a lot of work, believe me. Maybe I'll tell you the secret next year, you don't need the help right now," smiled Catherine. Then she paused and looked at Sarah with concern, "I take that back. You look like shit Sarah. What's going on?"

"I know," whispered Sarah, "I was up late. Emma and I had an argument last night and it was a disaster. But thanks for noticing," she added sarcastically.

Catherine's expression changed from puzzled to concern. "What was it about this time? No, don't tell me, let me guess. She wants a puppy?"

Yes, it's always the same. It's always about a stupid puppy and I just can't do it," replied Sarah. "Do you think I'm being unfair?"

"Look, sweetie, I know it still hurts, but I really believe you need to let it go and maybe getting her a puppy will help you both move on," assured Catherine. "I mean, you spend your entire day counseling strangers on how to grieve and move on after their pets die, and yet you can't even move on yourself". Sarah could feel the tears beginning to come again, and she really didn't want to do this, especially here in the restaurant.

"Thanks, Catherine. For everything. This morning, lunch, the card, the past five years. I don't know what we would have done without you and Peter," Sarah blurted out in an attempt to change the conversation.

"Oh don't be silly. We love you, Sarah, you know that. And this morning was Emma, not me. Now open that card," she said with a mischievous grin.

She's up to something, thought Sarah as she picked up the envelope and opened it. Inside the envelope was a corny yet mushy 40th birthday card. Sarah read it out loud even though she knew Catherine had read it a dozen times before and probably even read it to Peter, Jessica and Ben a dozen times as well. Sarah thought it was funny too, even though it implied that her female parts were going to stop working if she didn't use them soon. Inside the card was a gift card to Victoria's Secret and a small piece of paper with a password and username. The username was Stone40 and the password was

Birthdaygirl40. Catherine could tell Sarah was confused, but she just stared at her with a big smile on her face.

"Do you remember our bet last year on your birthday, Sarah?" she asked. "Don't tell me you forgot?"

As Sarah tried to recall the events of last year's 39th birthday party, Catherine pulled out her iPhone and put it in front of Sarah. "Now I know you had a lot to drink that night, but a bet is a bet and I videotaped it just in case you forgot."

The video started to play, and there was a very drunk Sarah agreeing that if she hadn't gone on a date by the time she turned 40 then she would agree to let Catherine enroll her in an online dating service.

CHAPTER 10

It had been another mundane fall day for Emma, the kind of day that she wished she had a dog to hurry home to so she could take him or her for a walk. There were leaves everywhere on her street and she loved to push them into a big pile in her yard and then run and jump in them. It was really a beautiful time of the year, and while the weather was getting colder, she had no problem bundling up and enjoying the change in seasons.

She hesitated for a moment as she walked up her sidewalk contemplating a quick run through the yard, but ignored the colorful swirling leaves and instead went inside, grabbed a granola bar from the pantry and headed upstairs to her room so she could go online. She had told Mathew that she would battle with him after school and she didn't want to be late. She had talked her mom into buying some more game credits so she could upgrade her armor and weapons and she was eager to try them out against Mathew.

Before she could bring up the gaming site she needed to log into her SPCA account and see if there was any news regarding her puppy adoption status. She felt bad that she hadn't been able to tell her mom that she had put her name on the waiting list for a puppy. She had signed up over ten months ago as they said it could take up to a year and Emma had hoped that her mom would change her mind during the waiting period. That's why she had put the screen saver up on her mom's computer the night before – in hopes that she would give in and say yes to them getting another puppy. Emma just knew that once her mom saw the puppy she would never make her give it back and it would help them both get on with their lives. Her mom had gone back to work and was doing okay, but Emma sensed a layer of sadness about her mom that she wanted to make go away. Sarah wasn't crying at night anymore, not for a few years now, but she wasn't dating and rarely went out, even with Aunt Catherine. Emma logged in and checked her SPCA adoption status but there was no news. *Oh well, maybe tomorrow,* she thought as she logged into the gaming site and got ready to battle Mathew.

Mathew had gone straight home from school in anticipation of getting a little practice in before he took on *Rudy2* in another battle. She had kicked his butt the last couple of times they played and he was really getting tired of her talking smack. He had stopped on the way home and picked up a gift card with the lunch money his dad had given him, so he could upgrade his character.

This is going to be so sweet, he thought as he deliberately launched his character into an existing battle and starting working on his new weapons and moves. It wasn't long before he saw Emma logon as *Rudy2* and he accepted her challenge to battle. They played a couple of games, and while he was doing better than the last time they had played, she was still kicking his butt and it was making him mad. He remembered what his dad had told him about what he did to throw off Darryl when they played poker: he always brought up topics that got Darryl off focus – usually women with Darryl, and then he would lose concentration and focus and start to lose.

Mathew typed in, "How's the search for a puppy going?"

Emma typed back that she hadn't heard any news from the SPCA yet but she was getting close to the one year wait period that they had said it would probably take.

"Do you have a name for the puppy yet?" Mathew asked, and then quickly switched his characters weapons and pounced on Emma's, sending her to a bloody death. He smiled to himself.

Emma sent him a message. "Well played Mathew... well played...no more puppy talk; I know what you're doing."

They played for a while longer in silence and then decided to just chat for a while before they both had to start doing some homework.

"What are you going to call your puppy?" Mathew asked.

"I'm not sure. I'd like to use the same name that my dad was going to call our puppy but I think that might be hard on my mom."

"Why's that?" asked Mathew.

"It's a long story. My dad died 5 years ago on his way home with a puppy for my birthday, and it was really hard on mom and me. Harder for my mom because I was so young. She won't let me get a puppy and I haven't told her I'm on the wait list. I tried to tell her last night but she started crying again and I couldn't finish telling her."

"What are you going to do when you actually get the puppy?"

"I don't know", replied Emma. "I haven't really thought about it too much. I just keep thinking that once she sees me with one she'll be ok and we'll all be happy."

"Well, I hope it all works out for you, Emma. I love dogs too. My dad had two when he was married to Ashley, but he had to find homes for them when they split up, and it was really hard on him. Maybe one day we'll get another one as well. I have to get to my homework now before my dad comes home, so I'll message you tomorrow and maybe we can play some more."

"Ok" said Emma, and then added, "I have to get ready to go to my aunt's for my mom's birthday dinner. You better practice some more tonight, though, or I'm going to have to find some harder competition☺" she typed back.

CHAPTER 11

Sarah and Emma decided to walk over to Catherine and Peter's rather than drive. They only lived a couple of blocks away, and Sarah knew there was a good chance that the evening could end up a repeat of the last couple of years, and she would probably not be in any shape to drive home. Now that Emma was older, she also had someone to help her navigate back down the side walk and make sure she made it home safely – not that Catherine and Peter would let her walk home if she had a little too much to drink. The other good news about this year's birthday was it was on a Friday night, which meant she wouldn't have to go to work hung over. It was a cool crisp fall evening, and the neighbors' yards that had been busy with kids playing and families working on flower gardens earlier, had now been replaced by the sound of leaves blowing from yard to yard. The trees were almost completely bare now, and you could tell from the smell in the air that winter's first storm was getting closer every day. Sarah liked this time of year. She always looked forward to the change of seasons and the inevitable blanket of fresh snow that would cover the mountain tops. It was like turning over a blank page in her diary. Emma seemed quiet on the walk, and while Sarah wanted to go back to last night's conversation, she thought it was best to steer clear of it for a while – at least for the night. The last thing she needed was an emotional cry at Catherine's over her birthday cake.

As they walked up the sidewalk to the front door, Sarah could see Catherine through the kitchen window and she smiled as she caught Catherine's eye. She could hear Catherine shout to Peter that they were here and to go get the door for them. Before Emma could ring the bell, Peter pushed the front door wide open, and with a big smile asked Sarah if he could help her with the bag she was carrying.

"What did you bring?" he asked.

"Oh just a little wine for the evening" Sarah replied.

"Why did you go and do that?" Peter shot back. "If there's one thing we never run short of here it's wine and hugs." He sat the bag down and swept Sarah into his big arms, giving her a warm comforting hug that almost made her cry. Peter had been so good to her and Emma since Michael's death; she could never begin to thank him enough for everything he had done over the years. She had started to not mention things that were wrong with her house to Catherine because every time she did, Peter would show up the next weekend and fix it. He finally let her go and leaned in and kissed her on the cheek.

"Happy Birthday Sarah," he smiled. "We made up the spare room for you and Emma just in case you can't make the two block walk home again this year". Then he looked at Emma. "I know you can make that walk, kiddo, but I was hoping you'd stay over and help us make breakfast again this year. I hear you're getting pretty good at it," he said and then winked at her. Emma blushed saying she wasn't that good, but Peter picked her up and hugged her as well. "Don't be so modest. I'm sure you're a very good cook, just like your Aunt."

At that moment Catherine bounced her way into the hall way from the kitchen holding two glasses of wine. "Here you go birthday girl – a little Pinot Grigio, your favorite. And for you my little princess, help yourself to whatever you like in the fridge. Jessica and I went shopping today so there are lots of choices, Pepsi, Coke, 7 up, whatever you like."

"Thanks Aunt Catherine, but I am not drinking pop anymore. I'm trying to cut down on my sugar intake. Our teacher at school said that we should drink eight glasses of water a day and if we need something sweet to drink we should have natural fruit juices, but only before 7pm."

"Really," said Catherine. "Does she live at home with her mother and a house full of cats?"

"I don't think so – about her mother, I mean. Though, she really does like cats," Emma said quite seriously.

"Why don't you find some juice in the fridge?" Sarah told her, and then gestured for everyone to move along into the kitchen.

They spent the next couple of hours drinking wine and eating dinner while discussing everything from Sarah's work to Emma's online gaming skills. Ben was quite impressed with how high her scores were, and they left the table to go to his room so she could show him some of the moves she had developed for her warrior. Jessica went to do her homework, and Peter knew it was time for him to leave Catherine and Sarah alone, so he made up an excuse to go work on some project for his job. Catherine called his bluff and told him not to fall asleep watching sports again because she would be up later for her dessert. Peter blushed and walked upstairs.

"All right. Now that we're alone," said Catherine, "let's get you set up so we can start picking some guys for you to date."

"Do we have to? I mean, I know we made the bet last year, but maybe we could give it another year?" Sarah replied.

"No way! A deal is a deal, and you turned 40 today so it's time." Catherine was really excited about the whole project; it was like she was going to use Sarah's dates as her own personal form of entertainment over the next few months.

"Ok, ok. Let's do this and get it over with. But I'm going to need some more wine. A lot more."

Catherine was a machine; she filled Sarah's glass and left the bottle on the desk so she wouldn't have to keep going downstairs to get more while they entered all of Sarah's information. It became apparent that she had done some advance prep work, as Sarah found out when Catherine opened a folder on her computer that was pre-filled with pictures of Sarah. Not all of them were current – in fact some were from her college days, and a few were pictures of her and Michael that Catherine had cropped him out of for the purpose of posting them to her profile.

"You can't use some of those old pictures, Catherine," Sarah told her. "Those are over 5 years old and I've changed a lot since then."

"I realize that" Catherine beamed, "but you don't smile much in any of the new ones I have, and you know men want to see that you have great teeth. A person that doesn't smile in their pictures usually means they're hiding bad teeth".

"That's not always true," Sarah smiled back. "Remember, Michael didn't smile a lot either and he had great teeth".

"He was shy, sweetie, but he always smiled around you." she smiled back and gave Sarah a hug. "You're right, we won't judge any of your potential dates by whether they smile or not. We need a close up of you, a head shot, we also need a waist up shot so let's use this one, and then we need a few pictures of you doing things you enjoy. Those will be tough to find."

"What is that supposed to mean? I do fun things."

"You're right: work, Emma, more work. That does sound like fun. Hmmm. Here's one of you bowling at Emma's birthday party! And this one, when you were playing with Emma in the leaves."

"Those are all good, but I don't want to use any pictures that have Emma in them. Can we crop her out or something?" asked Sarah.

"Sure," quipped Catherine as she went to work on the computer and soon had removed Emma from the pictures. "How does that look?"

"Good enough," said Sarah as she filled up her glass again. "What's next?"

After finally agreeing on the pictures, they moved onto filling in the rest of her profile. Catherine was a bit of wiz at filling everything in, and it made Sarah wonder if she had done this before so she asked. Catherine replied that she had a friend who had been using this same online dating site for about 3 months, and she had spent some time with her each week at work going through her matches. "There are some really cute guys online. I kind of wish I could go out on just one date," she whispered to Sarah.

"That's just the wine talking, Catherine," Sarah whispered back. "Peter is an awesome man. He adores you."

"I know, I know," Catherine smiled, "but sometimes I just wonder what it would be like to spend a night with one of these young guys. I'd never do it, but thinking about it always makes for a great night with Peter, so in a way, it actually helps our relationship. I'm sure he sometimes fantasizes about Kelly Johnson next door – her and her perfect fucking lulu lemon ass. Wait until she has a couple of kids. We'll see how good her ass looks then," Catherine declared. She then reached for the bottle of wine and groaned when she realized it was empty.

"I'll go get another bottle," Sarah said. "I want to check on Emma anyways."

Sarah got up and grabbed the empty wine bottle and went down the hallway towards the stairs. She stopped at the last bedroom door before the stairs, and quietly opened it to peak in on Emma. She was curled up in the bed with Rex, Catherine's chocolate lab. Rex lifted his head and looked towards the door at Sarah, but clearly wasn't interested in leaving his warm comfy spot on the bed beside Emma. Sarah quietly walked over to the bed and stroked Emma's cheek and then Rex's head.

Maybe Emma's right, thought Sarah. *Maybe it's time for us to get a puppy.* She leaned in and kissed Emma, and while she was kissing her daughter, Rex licked her cheek. She smiled and kissed him on the head too.

"Look after my princess, Rex", she whispered.

Sarah slipped out of Emma's room, closed the door and made her way down the stairs to the kitchen, a task that was made more difficult from the two bottles of wine she and Catherine had drank so far. She set the empty bottle down on the kitchen counter, then opened the fridge and took out a new one. She paused for a moment, and then realized she had a bottle that would need a cork screw. *Damn*, she thought and started rummaging through the kitchen drawers looking for the wine opener.

"Are you looking for this?" she heard Peter's voice and it startled her so badly she almost knocked the bottle of wine off the counter.

"Why yes, I am." Sarah slurred slightly as she saw the cork screw in his hand.

"Here, let me open that for you," Peter offered, taking the bottle and methodically opening it for Sarah. As he pulled the cork out, he turned to Sarah. "Are you sure you want to do this online dating thing, Sarah? You don't have to do it just because Catherine wants you to, you know."

"I know," Sarah said, "but she's having so much fun with it, and you know me – I'm a giver. And, after all, I'm 40 now. Maybe I should meet some guys and have some fun. If I meet the right guy – someone who's handy around the house – then maybe you can have a few more weekends off to work on your own house." Sarah reached out and punched Peter in the shoulder, missing completely.

Peter smiled back at her "I don't mind helping out, Sarah. Michael would have done the same for Catherine. And I enjoy coming over, it gives Emma a chance to hang out with Rex."

"She's a dog lover, that's for sure," smiled Sarah as she reached out rather clumsily to grab the two glasses of wine that Peter had filled.

"Here, why don't I bring those up for you and Catherine," he said, and quickly grabbed the glasses from Sarah before she could leave the kitchen with them.

Peter made sure the two women were comfortable with their wine and then left to go to bed. Catherine couldn't resist another reminder that she would be still hungry for dessert later, so he better not be asleep. Peter just laughed and bid them goodnight. He gave Sarah a hug and wished her a happy birthday before slipping out of the room and closing the door behind him as he left. Catherine had turned on her iPod for some music, and was just about finished loading all of Sarah's information into her online profile.

"What song are you listening to?" Sarah asked Catherine.

"It's a new song by Bob Schneider. It's called *40 Dogs and Cigarettes*. I really like it," she said and then turned it up.

The two of them sat and drank their wine, listening to the song. It was nothing like the tittle indicated; it was a song about a man sharing with a woman how much he loved her, and how he didn't want to wait any longer to tell her how he felt. It reminded Sarah of Michael, and she could feel the tears start to run. It wasn't a sad song – it was a happy song about living happily ever after – but before she knew it, she couldn't stop the tears from streaming down her cheeks. Catherine turned, and without saying a word just wrapped her arms around her.

"This song makes me think of you and Michael, too. You know he would want you to find love, sweetie. He'd want you and Emma to move on."

"I know," whispered Sarah. "I know. I just think it's a miracle if you find that kind of love once, but twice? I don't know if that's possible."

IN A RELATIONSHIP

CHAPTER 12

It had been a long day at work and the last thing Jake felt like doing was going to the gym, but he knew he had to stay disciplined with his workout routine. It was nice having the gym in his building complex because if he had to go home to change and then drive to a gym he would probably never go. It was also convenient for him to be able to check on Mathew before he went for his workout. Sometimes Mathew would go to the gym with him, and ride the bike or play with his PSP, but lately he just preferred to stay at home to do his homework so he could play online with *Rudy2* when he was done.

Jake changed into his gym clothes and then poked his head into Mathew's room on his way down the hall.

"Hey, buddy. How was your day?" he asked.

"It was good, dad," Mathew replied. "How was yours?"

"Same old, same old," Jake said back. "Did you learn anything new today?"

"No, nothing new," Mathew answered.

"How can you spend the entire day at school and not learn anything new?" Jake shot back.

"Well, dad, some days we just review material we've already learned, and that's what we did today," Mathew said matter-of-factly.

"Well, what did you review today?" Jake asked, still looking to validate why Mathew had gone to class if he wasn't learning anything new.

"Photosynthesis," Mathew stated as if he was bored with this conversation.

"That's about plants and stuff, right?" Jake asked, trying to sound like he knew what he was talking about.

"Yeah, dad. It's about plants and stuff," Mathew said sarcastically. "What did you learn today?"

Jake paused for a moment. It was a fair question, he just wasn't sure if he had learned anything new himself. "It was a review day today," he said back with a smile.

"What did you review dad?" Mathew asked, now with a big smile as he knew he had his father squirming.

Jake paused and then he replied, "Stuff. You know, work stuff."

"Weak answer, dad. What are we having for dinner tonight? And don't say chicken again. We've had so much chicken I feel like I'm going to start growing feathers," stated Mathew, changing the subject.

"I was thinking we could order in a pizza tonight. How's that sound? You can order it now for delivery in an hour, okay? And order one with chicken," he laughed before running out the door and off to the gym.

Jake had really started to enjoy his time in the gym working out. It gave him a chance to unwind after his stress filled days at the office, and helped him keep the spare tire off his waist. He had filled his iPod with a ton of music and would usually spend about twenty to twenty-five minutes on the elliptical machine before spending the last twenty-five lifting weights. On this particular day there weren't a whole lot of other people in the gym – just Jake and a couple of the female University nursing students who lived in an apartment complex close by.

About 20 minutes into his aerobic workout, he was so deep in thought about the whole online dating thing that he forgot he wasn't alone in the gym and began to sing along with the song streaming from his iPod. He was only one line in before remembering, but by then it was too late. The nursing students had heard him and were giggling. Singing out loud wasn't that bad, but singing Rihanna's *Make Me Feel like the Most Beautiful Girl in the World* wasn't good. He realized he may never be able to come back to the gym again after his karaoke performance. Jake ended his aerobic workout and did a couple of sets with the free weights before he snuck out and back to the house.

Jake got back to the house just as Darryl was pulling his jeep into the driveway.

"I thought you were coming over at seven?" Jake asked as he walked up to Darryl's window.

"I know. I was bored, though, so I thought I'd come over for pizza," Darryl smiled.

"How did you know we're having pizza?" Jake asked.

"Mathew posted his status on Facebook," replied Darryl, "and let me quote, 'Yay, no chicken tonight. Pizza is in the house!'"

Jake looked at Darryl with a silly smile, "Stupid Facebook. I really hate that Mark Fuckerburg."

"You mean Mark Zuckerberg," corrected Darryl. "He invented Facebook."

"No," Jake replied, "I meant Fuckerburg. Are you going to sit here in the driveway, or are you coming in for pizza?"

"I am down for pizza, dude. But before we go in, I want you to check out this new app I downloaded for my iPhone. It's called *Drivesafely*. It's super cool. It reads out my text messages and emails through my Bluetooth so I don't have to check them while I'm driving. Go ahead, send me a text. I'll show you how it works," he begged Jake.

Jake pulled out his phone, typed a quick message, and then hit send. About ten seconds later, the song that was playing on Darryl's stereo was interrupted by a sexy British female voice.

"Text message from Jake Jensen: *Hey Darryl, why don't you come over for pizza? Oh yeah, bring some cash it's your turn to buy.*"

"Ha, ha, ha. Very funny," Darryl shot back. "But it's cool right? And you can pick any accent you want – British, Australian, American or even a Chinese one."

Jake was smiling now, "Why am I not surprised. That is so you."

Just then the song playing was interrupted and the sexy British voice once again came on. "Text message from Nurse Naughty: '*Hi sexy, how was your day. Are you coming over for your exam later tonight? I have some new lube for you to try.*'"

Jake burst out laughing. "You're going to want to be careful who you have in the car with you if you're using that app."

Darryl had been desperately trying to turn off the Jeep, and failing that, turn the stereo down, but it had been too late. He was a little embarrassed, but still proud of his new app.

After the pizza delivery man had come and gone, and the three of them had finished eating, Mathew left to finish his homework and play online with *Rudy2*. Jake and Darryl logged into Jake's computer so they could check his online dating profile and see if he had any potential matches. Darryl set his beer down and adjusted the sunglasses sitting on his head as he waited for the site to open up.

"This is a nice computer you picked up. What size is this screen?"

"It's a 17 inch HD. The guy at the computer store said it's the best picture you can get on a computer, just as good as an HD TV. In fact, you can run your cable through it and use it as a TV," Jake replied proudly, like it was his baby.

"Yeah, it's nice. Should be good to check out the ladies," Darryl smiled back.

At that moment the site came up. Darryl typed in Jake's password and then clicked on the 'New Matches' icon. Darryl was like a kid at Christmas – he was so excited about the prospect of finding Jake a good match, or at worst, finding him a few ladies to go out and have a good time with. He opened up the first one and clicked on her picture.

Both of them said nothing. They looked at each other and then back at the picture. Darryl was the first to speak.

"She seems ok. It says she's divorced and likes cats."

"You can't be serious. I mean, come on, Darryl. I think she ate her husband and the cats! No bloody way," Jake stated emphatically.

"She's curvy," smiled Darryl." But I agree. I don't think she's your type."

"I don't understand, though," Jake replied, "in the profile, we put down that I was in shape and active and was looking for the same. Why would they send her as a match?"

"I don't know. Let's open the next one," said Darryl as he closed her profile and clicked on the next one. They both liked her a lot better, at least the picture. She was pretty, and had a nice smile.

"What do you think?" asked Darryl. "Let's look at her profile and see what sort of things she's into."

He clicked on her profile and they both started to read it.

"I am passionate about cats, book clubs, movies, reading, crafting/handicrafts, scrap booking, cats, spiritual pursuits, fishing, camping, personal improvement and cats. The most important quality is someone who can accept me as a human, wants to

participate in life - build a partnership. Going with the flow and seeing where we end up is very important to me - that's how the best things happen."

It was apparent to both of them that this was going to be a lot harder than they had first thought.

"I should have gone with 'Likes Dogs'," Jake chuckled as Darryl closed out number two and clicked on number three.

She was super cute. Smiley555 was the name she had filled out for her profile. She was blonde, 5'5" and had a nice smile and bright warm blue eyes. They looked through the 5 pictures Smiley555 had posted in her profile and she looked fairly attractive in all of them. Jake pointed out that she didn't show her body from the waist down in any of the pictures, but Darryl was quick to say that you could see that her face was pretty. Her shoulders and arms looked pretty good, too so they moved on to read her profile.

"The things that I am most passionate about are my family, art, music, exploring life and living healthy. The most important thing I am looking for in a person is confidence, character, passion, loyalty and honesty."

"Winner, winner, chicken dinner!" Darryl gleamed. "I think this is going to be date number one. What do you think, Jake? Let's email her."

"I don't know, do you really think so?" replied Jake.

"Yup, let's do it. Ok, we need to send her an email, something short but funny, just enough to get her attention and a response."

"*Hi,*

I thought of about ten different ways to start this email but once I wrote them out, none of them seemed good enough to send. Hope you're having a great weekend. Your profile seemed really honest and straightforward and I liked that. Let me know if you would like to grab a coffee this weekend?

Jake"

Darryl was quite pleased with himself for coming up with the email but Jake thought it came to him far too quickly to be the first time he had used it.

"You've used that email before haven't you?" asked Jake.

"Well, not exactly. But I have used various forms of it, and it has worked quite well. It's true though, and honest. Let's go grab another beer and then we'll send out a couple of more emails to try and line you up a date for this weekend. You'll have new matches sent to you overnight so we can wait a few days and then go through them and line up a second date for the following weekend."

"What if the first date goes well and I want to see her again?" asked Jake.

"No, no, no. You can't start dating the first one you see on a regular basis. You need to sample some of the other ladies out there. It's ok, they're doing the same thing, believe me."

Darryl went downstairs to grab another couple of beers and Jake worked through some of the other matches, none of whom caught his attention or piqued his interest. In fact, he couldn't understand how or why they were even sent as matches as he had nothing in common with them. He was getting quite disillusioned with the quality of women who were on the site. With most of them, he didn't even get past the picture to read the profiles. If he didn't find them attractive he just closed the file and moved onto the next one. He was so engaged in working his way through the matches that he didn't notice that he had an email back from Smiley555 until Darryl returned. He just about dropped his beer; he was so excited that she had already sent a reply back.

Hi Jake,

"Lovely it is to hear from you today, as I was going to send you a quick and cheeky email as I read your profile earlier (curiosity got the better of me) but my day of busy got the better of me. Thanks for the compliment on my profile. It is honest and genuine, which are traits I do value in others. I look forward to getting to know you a little better, perhaps we can meet this Saturday night at 7pm at Starbucks for a coffee."

Smiley555

IN A RELATIONSHIP

CHAPTER 13

Sarah could feel something wet pressing against her cheek and the warmth of someone's breath as she struggled to open her eyes. Her head was killing her and as she rubbed the sleep from her eyes she started to remember the events from the night before. The light from the morning sun was streaming in through the bedroom window and she took a moment once her eyes were open to take in her surroundings. Rex, Catherine's chocolate lab, was pressing his nose against her cheek urging her to wake up so he could get outside and do his morning business. Sarah pulled back the sheets and sat up. She immediately knew it was not a great idea as her head started to spin. She lay back down and nudged Emma who was sleeping on the other side of the bed, oblivious to the morning light and Rex's need to go outside. Emma was not a morning person either, but today Sarah really needed her to get up and let Rex out, and then find her some Tylenol. Fast. She nudged her again, and this time Emma rolled over, opened her eyes and said a groggy "what?"

"Rex needs to go outside, Emma, and I need you to do a big favor for your mom. Can you go get me some water and Advil from Auntie Catherine's medicine cabinet? And I need you to do it now please, princess."

Emma smiled a big grin and looked at her mom for a second before she pulled back the covers on her side of the bed. She climbed out of the warm of the bed, and looked back at her mom when she got to the door. Rex was at the door jumping up and down in anticipation of getting outside and emptying his bladder.

"Are you feeling 40 today, mom?" Emma asked with a big grin before heading out the door in search of Advil.

Emma always gave her mother a hard time when she was hung over. It didn't happen that often, but when it did happen it usually meant a day on the couch watching movies with her and ordering in food. She loved that part, but still couldn't understand why her mom would drink if it always made her feel so crappy the next day. *Adults are weird*, she thought.

As she came out of the bathroom with the Advil, Rex was still jumping up and down waiting to be let outside, so she went downstairs and let him out into the back yard. Emma then headed for the kitchen to get a bottle of water for her mom. As she walked down the hallway towards the kitchen, she could smell breakfast, and it smelled delicious. She rounded the corner and was startled to see Uncle Peter doing the cooking. He spotted her at the same time and a big grin came across his face when he saw the bottle of Advil in her hand. He opened the fridge and grabbed a bottle of water and passed it to her.

"Looks like your mom is suffering from the same thing as Aunt Catherine," he smiled, "the Wine Flu."

Emma smiled back, "I don't know why people drink wine if it makes them feel so bad, Uncle Peter?"

"Well, it's one of those things that you do even though it's not good for you because you forget how bad it made you feel once you feel better. I'm not sure if that makes any sense to you right now but it will when you're older."

"I'm never drinking when I'm older, Uncle Peter. I tried some of mom's wine once and it did not taste good. It was gross. Breakfast smells good, though!" she smiled up at him.

"We're having waffles, sausages and hash browns so hurry up and get that to your mom so you can come back and help me. I don't think your mom or Aunt Catherine will be up to doing any cooking today, or tonight for that matter."

"I don't think mom's going to be up to doing anything today, Uncle Peter," Emma grinned. "I'll be right back. Do you have any whip cream and strawberries?" she asked before she scampered down the hallway towards her mother's room.

Peter had taken on the father figure role in Emma's life when Michael had died, and Sarah had been grateful for that. Sarah took two of the extra strength Advil and washed them down with the large bottle of distilled water Emma had brought her. The drugs kicked in about 20 minutes later, enabling Sarah to start feeling human again. She could hear Emma and Peter busy chatting away as they made breakfast. Emma was telling Peter all about school and her online gaming friend *Seahawk17*. Sarah jumped when she felt someone slap her butt from behind. She turned around to find Catherine smiling at her through blood shot eyes.

"Looks like we got rolled by the same wino last night" Catherine complained with a raspy voice.

Sarah smiled back, "We never learn, do we?" The two of them walked into the kitchen and sat at the island.

"Look who's finally joined the living," Peter said with a little grin on his unshaven face. "Would you two like some coffee?" he asked.

"Please!" Sarah and Catherine said at the same time.

"Emma, two coffees," ordered Peter like he was placing an order at the coffee shop. Emma jumped up from her chair at the end of the island, got two large coffee mugs from the cupboard and then picked up the coffee pot filling up both mugs.

"Did you feed Rex?" Catherine asked Peter.

"I fed him after I let him out this morning, Auntie" piped up Emma.

"Oh you are such a good girl," Catherine smiled over at her, "and Peter, I love you honey, you're the best husband ever." she purred as she took a sip of the steaming hot coffee. Catherine looked over at Sarah and before she would allow Sarah a moment of self-pity, she quickly added, "And you, miss 40 year old, are going to hit the computer after breakfast and see what we caught in our web last night."

After they had finished Peter's fabulous breakfast, Catherine and Sarah started to gather up the plates and clean up, but were abruptly stopped and ordered out of the kitchen by Peter. "Emma and I will clean up, and then were going to take Rex for a walk so you too can have a shower and check out what's in your web!" Peter chuckled.

Catherine was still moving pretty slow as she and Sarah made their way up the stairs and into the computer room. The previous evening was now coming back to Sarah and she was apprehensive about checking her dating profile. Catherine on the other hand was excited to see if Sarah had any messages from prospective dates.

She turned on the computer and logged into her account. Sure enough there were several messages that had come in overnight and she clicked on the first one. He seemed nice enough on paper. He was in his Mid-forties, a local realtor who had been divorced for several years and not altogether un-attractive.

"Hi Stone40,

I enjoyed reading your profile. It seems like we have lots in common. Let me know if you would like to grab a coffee sometime.

Mitch"

Catherine was quite impressed and urged Sarah to email him back in response to his request to meetup with her for a coffee on the weekend.

"Tell him Saturday at Starbucks – the one down by the market," she urged.

"I don't know, Catherine," Sarah replied. "That seems pretty fast. I don't even know this guy. He could be a serial killer, or a rapist, or worse yet, a Republican" she laughed nervously.

"Oh, don't be silly," Catherine chided her. "It's Starbucks. You'll be around lots of people and you might as well get the in-person part over with right away. You don't want to go back and forth messaging for days."

"Oh shit, I don't know," Sarah muttered. "Do I have to? Seriously?"

"Yes, you do. Come on, it'll be fun. What's the worst thing that can happen? You make a new friend?"

"Ok, all right. I'll do it, but you're watching Emma and you need to call me after 20 minutes in case I need an excuse to bail, OK?"

"Deal" Catherine beamed back at her.

CHAPTER 14

Jake was super nervous about meeting up with Smiley555. It wouldn't have mattered with who the date was – this was, after all, his first date in a long time. Sure, he had been set up on a couple of double dates through some work colleagues, but this was a solo date and a blind date to boot.

Mathew had been pretty funny with him as he had been getting ready. Joking about looking forward to meeting his future step-mom and asking him if he had brushed his teeth as he went out the door. All kidding aside though, Mathew was glad his dad was finally starting to date again. Besides potentially finding someone to make his dad happy, it also meant it distracted him from paying attention to how much time he spent on the computer or whether or not his homework was done. *Breathing room,* he chuckled to himself as he grabbed a root beer and went up to his bedroom for a little online dueling with Ruddy2.

Jake pulled into the Starbucks parking lot, turned off the car and sat there for a moment. He had purposely arrived 15 minutes early to make sure he wasn't late. He was nervous as hell, but committed to going through with this date. He knew that he needed to get out and meet some new people. As he sat in the car he noticed an attractive woman across the parking lot sitting in her vintage Volvo and it looked like she was talking to herself. He assumed she was talking to herself, as there was no way that year of Volvo had Bluetooth he thought to himself. She was beautiful though, and he wished she was Smiley555.

As he was deep in thought wondering what her story was, his phone vibrated with a new message. He picked up his phone and saw a message from Smiley555. She was inside Starbucks waiting for him. He checked himself in the rear view mirror, took a big breath and got out of the car and walked over to the entrance. He was so caught up in his own nervousness that he hadn't noticed that the woman in the Volvo was also walking up to Starbucks. They arrived at the same time and Jake opened the door to let her in. She looked into his eyes and held them for a second, just long enough to make it more than a casual glance. She broke the gaze and offered a shy "Thank you," and then stepped past him into the coffee shop, making her way to a table where a man got up from his chair and greeted her.

His attention quickly turned to scanning the room for Smiley555. He didn't see anyone who looked like the picture he had from her email, but there was a table at the back with a woman sitting with her back to the door. Jake made his way to the back of the coffee shop and approached her table. As he arrived, she turned around and he recognized her, barely. She was a lot older in person than what she had appeared to look like in her pictures from the dating site. He tried not to look surprised, but he was stunned. What happened to the hot woman he had seen on the internet?

She had been a total liar about the way she looked; either that or the pictures were way out of date. Not wanting to be rude, and having gotten over the initial shock, Jake introduced himself.

"Hi, I'm Jake, you must be Smiley555."

Smiley555 didn't get up – that would have been too much work. She simply raised her hand and said, "Hi, I'm Carmen. Could you get me a slice of cake and tall café mocha with whip cream and caramel, please, dear?"

Still reeling from the differences between her profile pictures and what she looked like in person, Jake made his way to the counter and ordered her cake and coffee and a green tea and muffin for himself. He had been hungry when he first arrived, but not so much now. All he could think of was how could he get the hell out of this place. He returned to their table and they made some small talk about her mom and her cats and how much she enjoyed working at the bingo parlor. They were interrupted by the barista who had stopped at their table to pick up Carmen's empty plate. Once the barista was out of earshot, Carmen leaned forward and whispered to Jake, "Do you think he's a terrorist?"

Jake, uncertain as to why she would think that, turned and looked back at the barista who had returned to making a latte behind the counter. The man couldn't have been more than 25 but was obviously of Middle Eastern decent. Jake looked back at Carmen.

"Why do you think he's a terrorist?" he asked, knowing full well what her answer would be.

"You know, he looks like he's from ISIS."

"You know ISIS isn't a country right?" Jake replied. "And you know not all Muslims are terrorists? That would be like saying all Caucasians are serial killers. This country was built on immigrants from all over the world. It's what makes us strong, unique, and special. Where are your ancestors from?"

"Denmark."

"Denmark. So your ancestors were Vikings. Should we be worried you're going to rape and plunder the neighborhood?" Jake asked.

Carmen didn't answer Jake, instead she reached over and grabbed what was left of his muffin and asked, "Are you going to eat that?"

As she finished off the muffin, Jake looked around the room and saw the woman from the Volvo. She was sitting facing him, and had a pained look on her face as she listened to the man who had greeted her when she first came in. He was a decent looking man. He looked like the kind of guy who spent a lot of time at the gym, wore too-tight *Affliction* shirts, well-tanned, and spoke quite loud as he talked about himself and how much he could lift. If it wasn't for the pain of his own date, Jake may have found this amusing.

Unfortunately, Jake didn't have time to take in anymore of what was going on with her table as Carmen was wiping crumbs off the plate and onto her spoon so she could get the last bit of the muffin into her mouth. Jake had had enough. He made an excuse about picking up his son and got up to leave. Carmen asked if she could see him again, and he blurted out that he was moving soon as he had been recently transferred, and then bolted for the door. Once outside, he hastily made his way to his car, unlocked the door, climbed in and breathed a huge sigh of relief.

My god, he thought. *That was absolutely horrible.*

As he sat in his car contemplating phoning Darryl, he saw Carmen walk out the front door and make her way to one of those tiny smart cars. He couldn't help but laugh out loud as she poured herself into the driver's seat. Somehow she managed to close the door and drive away.

Sarah had been trying her best to pay attention to the incredibly self-absorbed man who was not at all as advertised on his profile. He wasn't an unattractive man but all he wanted to talk about was himself.

For crying out loud, she thought. *Had no one ever told him how uninteresting he was?*

Thankfully, it was only a coffee. She had watched the man she met at the doorway abruptly get up from his table and leave the coffee shop. It was apparent that the meeting he had with the woman who was at his table had ended awkwardly. Sarah was trying to figure out how they knew each other, but kept being drawn back to her own coffee date with Mister Personality. Mitch was now lecturing her on the benefits of a high protein diet, and was offering to be her personal trainer. It was at that precise moment, 20 minutes into the date, when her phone rang with Catherine on the other end. *Thank God,* Sarah thought to herself as she picked up the phone.

"Hello," Sarah answered quickly into her phone.

"How is the date going?" Catherine asked.

"Oh, that is terrible," Sarah replied back. "I totally understand, though," she added. "No, it's ok. I understand. I'll be there in ten minutes."

"What the hell are you talking about?" Catherine asked, confused.

After pausing for a few seconds, Sarah replied, "its ok. He totally understands. We can do this another time. Thanks for calling. Bye." She hung up the phone and turned to Mitch as she put her phone back in her purse, telling him that her daughter was sick and she had to pick her up from the babysitters.

"I'll text you later," she said as she walked out the front door and practically ran to her Volvo. Once safely inside her car, she started it up, put it in gear, and pulled out of her stall without looking, cutting another vehicle in her haste to get the hell out of the parking lot. Sarah had to laugh to herself as she made the drive back to Catherine's to tell her about the first date.

They can't all be like this, she thought. She wasn't sure she could continue this dating experiment if they were all going to be like this first one. *How do single people do this?*

As Sarah pulled into the driveway Catherine opened the front door and hurried down the driveway like a kid at Christmas.

"Well, that was a short date," she blurted out, opening the car door for Sarah.

"I don't think I can do this, Catherine," Sarah whined as she climbed out of the car and closed the door. "I mean, he was nice looking but he couldn't stop talking about himself. Thank God you called. That was so painful!"

"Don't worry. That was only the first one. You've got your feet wet now, back in the game so to speak," Catherine chuckled. "Let's go upstairs and find a second one. I've been looking through the emails on your account, and I think you'll like some of the new prospects."

As they walked through the front door, Peter looked up from the couch where he was watching the football game with Emma, and smiled at Sarah.

"Well, that was a short date," he stated with a slight smile. "Not Prince Charming I take it?"

Sarah blushed slightly and recounted the brief coffee date, being extra careful in the words she chose to retell the story as Emma was listening intently.

"It's ok, mom. Sometimes you have to kiss a few frogs," she giggled.

"I don't want to get warts though," Sarah muttered.

Catherine grabbed her arm and dragged her up the stairs. "Come on. Let's see if we can't find someone a little better suited to you."

Catherine sat down behind the computer and pulled up a second chair for Sarah. Catherine had signed in to Sarah's account, highlighting a few new candidates for her to check out. As they rolled through the potential suitors, they joked about her brief first date. While he hadn't been what she was looking for, it had allowed her to gain a little confidence in herself.

About ten minutes into their scanning of potential candidates, they came across an absolutely gorgeous man. He was into restoring old cars, claimed to be into all kinds of music, including classical. His profile wasn't filled with pictures of him with his shirt off or multiple pictures of old cars. He seemed like a dream candidate. Catherine insisted they send him a message and so Sarah agreed. Deep down, Sarah secretly hoped that he wouldn't respond. That first date had made her a little gun shy.

It was a little after 9 in the morning when Jake heard Darryl's Jeep pull into the driveway. Darryl let himself in through the unlocked front door and strolled into the kitchen with a drink tray containing two cups of coffee and one hot chocolate.

"Where's Mathew?" Darryl asked as he put the tray of drinks down on the kitchen counter.

"He's probably upstairs on the computer" Jake responded. "He's addicted to that stupid online game he's been playing the last month or so."

"I brought him a hot chocolate. Mathew!" Darryl yelled up the stairs. "Come on down, I brought you a hot chocolate."

"He can't hear you. He has headphones on so he can talk to whoever he is playing against," Jake explained. Darryl grabbed the hot chocolate and headed up the stairs. As he opened the door to Mathew's bedroom he could see him intensely working away on his computer, headphones on, and in deep concentration. Darryl tapped him on the shoulder, startling him.

"Hey, Uncle Darryl. What's up?" Mathew asked after a quick glance, but not taking his focus off the game. "Just give me a second; I'm almost done this game."

Darryl waited a minute while Mathew made a few quick plays, and then put his hands in the air exasperated, "Shit...I mean shoot. Sorry, Uncle Darryl. I didn't mean to swear."

"It's ok, kid," replied Darryl. "I won't tell. Is the game not going well?"

"No, she beat me again. She always beats me" Mathew mumbled.

"Hey I got you a hot chocolate, buddy," Darryl told him and placed the drink down on his desk beside the computer. Mathew picked it up and moved it to the far side of the desk, away from the computer.

"Dad hates it when I put drinks near the computer."

Mathew got up and went to the back of his bedroom and picked up a pill container, popped it open, and took two tablets.

"What are those for?" Darryl asked.

"I'm lactose intolerant. I have to take two of these if I want to eat anything with dairy in it."

"Well that sucks," Darryl replied. "All Dairy? Even ice-cream?" asked Darryl.

"Especially ice-cream. Dad and I went to Baskin Robbins and I had a big bubblegum flavored milkshake. I couldn't even make it home. Dad had to stop at a gas station so I could use the washroom. It was like a barking spider. Do you know what a barking spider is, Uncle Darryl?" Mathew asked.

"No, what's a barking spider?"

"Well, it's like when you have diarrhea and it just explodes when you go. Not pretty. Especially if someone is in the stall beside you," Mathew explained.

Darryl laughed out loud. "Yes, that would not be good. A barking spider, huh? I'll have to remember that one," he chuckled. "Good thing you have those pills. Good luck on your next game, I'm going to go back downstairs and see how your dad's date went last night."

"I don't think it went well," Mathew smiled. "Dad was home a little early."

Darryl turned and went back down the stairs into the kitchen. It was bright, the sun was shining through the big bay windows lighting everything up. Jake was putting the dishes into the dishwasher and cleaning up. He grabbed his coffee when Darryl sat down at the island and joined him. Darryl had a big grin on his face as he spoke.

"So…Mathew said you were home early last night. I am guessing she was not your soul mate?"

"No," Jake replied. "No she was definitely not my soul mate. She didn't look at all like her pictures. They had to be ten years old."

"Well, one down and five to go. After all, you did promise six dates, so let's get started on finding number two," Darryl said and then pulled out his laptop and turned it on.

It didn't take them long to find number two. Her name was Marcy, and she seemed good on paper. Jake didn't put up a fight as he had resigned himself to the fact that he would have to go on five more dates before Darryl would get off his back. They sent an email to one of the potential dates, and then Darryl turned off his computer and packed it up.

"I'll set up something for you to do this Friday with Marcy," Darryl told him as he put his jacket on and moved towards the door.

"Shouldn't I be the one who sets up the dates?" Jake asked.

"You're busy, trust me. I'll filter this one through, and let you know when and where to meet her," Darryl smiled. "Come on, I have lots of experience with this, and it's fun for me." With that, he closed the door and was off into the fall evening.

IN A RELATIONSHIP

CHAPTER 15

It was Friday night and Sarah was busy getting ready for her second date. The first one had not been a whole lot of fun but she knew that if she wanted to find another Michael she would have to put herself out there. Sarah's second date was with James. He arranged something pretty impressive for their first date. He said he would pick her up and take her to an Italian restaurant, and then to a club for some dancing. Sarah thought it sounded wonderful and couldn't wait for the night to arrive.

Sarah, Catherine and Emma were sitting in her living room waiting for James when he showed up in his 69 Camaro. When he stepped out Sarah was impressed. His pictures did not do him justice. He was gorgeous. She kissed Emma goodnight, hugged Catherine and then opened the door and floated down the sidewalk where James warmly hugged her and then opened the passenger door. Sarah slid into the passenger seat and James closed the door behind her. While he walked around the back of the car Sarah waved a nervous smile back to Emma who was peeking through the blinds with Catherine's head just above hers.

IN A RELATIONSHIP

James didn't say much on the drive to the restaurant; he seemed preoccupied with the music and was driving far too fast for Sarah's liking. He was speeding and swearing and blasting his metal tunes as loudly as he could to avoid having any kind of conversation. The only things he muttered were things about metal music and how it's the only genre of music that matters. Sarah had been hanging on to the arm rest the entire drive and was relieved when they finally pulled into the parking lot at the restaurant. She had been tempted to just call a cab and end the date then, but James reverted back into his gentleman routine when they arrived and opened the door for her, apologizing for scaring her on the drive saying his Friday had been hectic. She gave him the benefit of the doubt and decided she would see how dinner went before making a final decision.

The restaurant he had chosen was quite impressive – lit just right, soft Italian music playing and the waiter had a beautiful big smile that made her feel completely at ease. He asked them to follow him to the back of the restaurant and sat them at a small table in the corner. James didn't offer to pull her chair out for her but the waiter did and as she sat down she glanced around the crowded room. She noticed the same guy from the Starbucks sitting at the bar beside a different woman from the one she had saw him with the previous week. *What a coincidence*, she thought. She was interrupted by the waiter who was asking her what she would like to drink. After ordering a glass of white wine, Sarah regained her focus on James. He began asking inappropriate questions such as if she would sleep with another woman for money. Sarah was a bit taken aback by his directness. At this point she thought to herself, *I would sleep with Rosanne Barr to get away from you*! He had no idea what anything on the menu was and kept staring at Sarah making her feel uncomfortable.

"Why are you staring at me?" Sarah finally asked after the third long uncomfortable stare.

"Just to see what you do" stated James. That was followed by more awkward silence. They eventually ordered and the rest of the meal was much the same with more inappropriate questions and more uncomfortable staring. Dinner couldn't end soon enough for Sarah and as they passed the bar on the way out she noticed that the couple she had seen earlier at the bar had already left.

As they drove to the club Sarah was contemplating whether she should make up an excuse and bail or stick it out a little longer. James made the decision easy for her with more speeding, more awful music, and acting like he was in high school doing things like punching her arm and more stares. As they pulled into the parking lot at the club, James turned on one of his songs especially loud and announced, "Listen! This one's about DATE RAPE! Probably not the best song to be playing now, huh? Ha!"

Well that sealed it for Sarah. She turned the music down and told James that she was tired and the wine had given her a headache. "Would you mind taking me home?" she asked.

James tried to talk her out of it, but after Sarah offered to take a cab he finally relented. He insisted on driving through a Wendy's on the way, and as they drove through he told her this was where he stopped all the time when he gets the munchies after getting stoned. As they pulled into her driveway Sarah started opening the door to the car before James had even finished putting it into park. She didn't want to give him a chance to kiss her goodnight or ask for a second date. She politely thanked him for dinner and told him she would text him later. They both knew that wasn't going to happen. James cranked up his music and squealed his tires as he roared down her street. Sarah looked to the neighbor's houses to see if they noticed her getting dropped off, but no one was looking out their window. Well, no one except Catherine. Sarah walked up the stairs and sat on the front steps. Catherine opened the front door and came out to sit down beside her. She put her arm around Sarah and didn't say a word. They looked at each other, and then Sarah burst out laughing.

"That was probably the worst date of my life," she spat out between laughs. She told Catherine the details and then hugged her good night. The house was quiet when she entered although she could hear faint music playing from Emma's room. She quietly opened Emma's bedroom door, tiptoed over to the dresser and turned off her stereo. Emma was curled up with her arms around her stuffed retriever. Sarah leaned over and brushed Emma's hair away from her cheek and kissed her.

Darryl had gone back and forth during the week, working on setting up Jake's second date with Marcy. He had arranged for their first meeting at the bar inside a quaint Italian restaurant downtown. It was packed with people, but they had found a couple of stools at the bar and ordered drinks. After some basic small talk they decided to take a stroll outside along the waterway. They grabbed a couple of coffee's and after walking for about ten minutes sat down at the base of a statue on the steps below the art gallery. Jake offered to put his jacket down for them to sit on.

Marcy seemed sweet; she was an assistant at a Law office, divorced and mother of two young girls. Jake was feeling good about this date. *Maybe Darryl knows what he's doing,* he thought to himself. He noticed a homeless fellow saunter up the stairs behind them but thought nothing of it. They continued to make small talk and Marcy began to open up regarding her past relationship. Apparently she was not divorced but separated. He husband had an affair and had then left her and the girls 3 months ago. She started to cry and told Jake that she was still in love with him. *That's great,* Jake thought to himself. What was she doing on a dating site if she wasn't over her ex and why had she said she was divorced when she clearly wasn't.

It was at that moment that an older model Camaro drove by with the music blaring so loud everyone on the street could hear it. Jake and Marcy both looked towards the noise and the car. Jake noticed that same beautiful woman he had seen at Starbucks sitting in the passenger seat, trying to hide her face as the car drove by with heavy metal music blaring. Marcy resumed her crying and Jake thought it would be best if she went home so he decided to stand up and offered to walk her back to her car. As he stood up, he reached for the jacket he had put down for them to sit on and discovered to his surprise that it was soaking wet. Jake wondered if perhaps he had spilt his coffee. He decided to keep quiet as they started walking; meanwhile discreetly checking out what he took to be coffee on his fingers. He put his fingers to his nose and almost gagged. Totally 100% piss. Somebody had relieved themselves nearby during their conversation and it had run down the stairs and soaked into his jacket. They still had a ten minute walk back to her car. It wasn't just the jacket, his pants were soaked too and the very thought of it all made him nauseous with disgust. He knew Marcy would be able to smell it soon to. He looked at the back of her dress and he could tell it was wet as well. Crazy thoughts were running through his head. He wasn't sure what to do. He could make a sudden excuse and leave, find a washroom for an emergency clean up or tell the truth.

    He didn't get a chance to act on any of his options. Marcy had noticed the odor and was staring at him with a funny look on her face - the look when you smell something foul but can't figure out what it is or where it is coming from. There was no hiding or avoiding it now. Jake tried to explain to her that it must be from the homeless fellow relieving himself, back when he had gone up the stairs behind them while they were sitting beneath the statue at the art gallery. Marcy put her hands to the back of her dress and could feel the wetness. She shrieked and started to dry heave. At that point there was nothing Jake could do. Marcy threw up all over the sidewalk as she attempted to make it to the garbage can. Seeing Marcy throw up sent a wave of nausea over Jake, and he let fly, too.

It took a while before they could both recover, and eventually they had nothing left to expel from their stomachs. He knew Marcy didn't believe him. She probably thought he had wet himself while they were sitting on the steps. He offered to walk her back to her car, but she told him it wasn't necessary and thanked him for the drink and the coffee as she hurried down the street. To make matters worse, Jake had decided to take the bus downtown. Parking was limited and it was only a 15 minute bus ride from his house. What had seemed like a good idea then was making a bad situation even worse now. His jacket and the back of his pants were soaked in urine. He threw the jacket into the trash can and thought about ditching the pants as well, but that would have meant riding the bus home in his boxer shorts.

He walked to the bus stop and stood way back from the other passengers while they waited for the bus. Once it pulled up to the bus stop, he waited to board last and looked for an empty seat. It was Friday night and the downtown was busy, so the bus was crowded. He would have to stand. That was good and bad he thought. If he stood with his back to the side of the bus no one would be able to see how wet his pants were but they would be close enough to smell him. By the time the bus pulled up to his stop there was no one standing near him and he had endured countless dirty looks and joking comments from the group of teenagers that had been standing at the back of the bus with him. When he exited the bus, a small round of applause erupted.

Jake marched straight for the laundry room to strip off his pants and underwear, and then threw them into the washing machine. He couldn't believe he had actually sat in hobo piss, and to top it off his date had thought he had pissed his pants. He called Darryl and told him what had happened. Darryl burst out laughing.

"You must have really been pissed off," he squealed. "Look, what are the odds of that happening? Don't let it get you down. It sounds like it was a good reason to end a date that wasn't going anywhere anyways. Let's take a leek - I mean let's take a look at your account in the morning and find you another date," he joked. Jake hung up the phone and turned the washing machine on. He then pulled on his sweat pants and went upstairs, stopping at Mathew's bedroom door. He could hear Mathew on his computer, so he knocked and walked in. Mathew looked up once he noticed his dad standing behind him.

"What is that smell?" Mathew asked. *Shit,* Jake thought to himself, *I forgot to shower.*

"Nothing. I just sat in something when I was out."

"Nothing?" Mathew asked. "Smells like something to me. You're stinking up my room dad."

"Yeah, well, do your homework and don't stay up to late," Jake replied in an attempt to change the subject. Then, as he smelt the urine wafting up from his pants, he closed the door and took off down the hallway for a long hot shower.

CHAPTER 16

Mary greeted Sarah with a big smile when she walked into the office the next morning. Sarah was suspicious that she knew about last night's disastrous date.

"I don't want to talk about it," Sarah said sternly to Mary as she walked into her office and hung up her jacket. Sarah turned her back to Mary as she took off her scarf, threw it over her jacket and then sat at her desk. Mary set a cup of coffee down for Sarah and then stood in front of her, waiting for her to acknowledge that she wasn't going to leave until Sarah gave her some details.

"Mary, I mean it. I don't want to re-hash it. I'm sure Catherine filled you in, and the two of you had a good laugh."

"Actually, I just wanted to reassure you that there are still good guys out there and you shouldn't give up. I'm sure you will find someone special. Oh yeah, and Metallica is playing in town this weekend if you want to go," she blurted out with a cheeky grin on her face. Then she giggled, turned and left, dodging the pen Sarah threw at her as she closed the door behind her.

Sarah turned on her computer and opened up her calendar. As she looked through the schedule of appointments she had for the day she came across the name of Nancy Weninger. Nancy had lost her dog and had been coming in to see Sarah every other week for well over a year, but then suddenly stopped coming in. Sarah picked up the phone and buzzed Mary.

"Are you ready to tell me all the details?" Mary quipped into the phone.

"No, stop asking," Sarah snapped back. Then in a concerned voice, Sarah asked Mary if she had heard back from Nancy Weninger.

"No, not yet Sarah. I've left three messages and I also sent an email, but I haven't heard anything back. Do you want me to try again?"

"Hmmm. That is so strange," replied Sarah. "Yes, keep trying please. Do we have an address? Maybe I'll stop by over the holidays and see how she is doing."

"I'll call again today and I'll find an address and send it to you. Is there anything else I can help with this morning?" Mary asked.

"No, that'll be good. Thanks, Mary. Oh, if Catherine calls, tell her I'm busy," she stated coldly and then hung up the phone.

It had been a busy morning for Sarah but she was grateful for that. It meant she didn't have to think about the disastrous date she had last night or worry about what new date Catherine was setting up for her. She hadn't given much thought to lunch when noon rolled around and Catherine walked into her office unannounced.

"Look, you should know better, Sarah. If you ignore my calls I'm just going to come over in person. Besides, it's time for lunch and I just so happen to be free. Grab your jacket, girl."

Sarah smiled back at Catherine, "Alright, I'll go for lunch with you on two conditions: one, we don't talk about last night's date, and two, you pay."

"Deal," Catherine smiled back, "but I'm picking the location."

Sarah grabbed her jacket off the coat stand in the corner of her office along with her scarf. As she wrapped it around her neck and put her jacket on, Catherine stood waiting patiently and stared at her.

"What are you doing?" asked Sarah.

"Is that what your date was doing, just staring at you like that?" inquired Catherine.

"Yes, that is exactly what he was doing. It was super creepy - and I told you I didn't want to talk about it," smirked Sarah. "I'm serious."

"That is creepy," smiled Catherine. "Ok, no more talk about last night's date, we have a new one to plan," she giggled. Catherine put her arm through Sarah's and they went out the door.

"Bring me back a salad," shouted Mary as they left.

IN A RELATIONSHIP

CHAPTER 17

When Jake woke up the next morning, he could swear he still smelled piss from the previous night's date. He had hoped that it had all been a bad dream, but no such luck. He reached over to the night table and picked up his phone that had been charging all night. He skimmed through the spam and noticed he had a message from Darryl. It was a text.

"Hey, let's meet for lunch today. I have a new hottie for you to check out."

Jake groaned to himself and rolled his eyes. *Right,* he thought, *I still have 4 more dates before he lets this stupid thing go.*

He sent a short text back to Darryl. *"Can't do lunch today. Too much to do at work. I'll give you a shout later."* and then hit send. He made his way down the hall and into the kitchen where Mathew was sitting at the counter playing on his computer. Jake grabbed a coffee cup from the shelf and placed it under the Tassimo machine, threw in a coffee pod and hit start. Mathew hit the pause button on the game he was playing and looked up at his dad.

"Well, you smell a lot better today, dad," he smiled.

"Thanks, I was hoping that was a bad dream," Jake smiled back. "Do you have any homework to do kid?"

"Yeah, I did it all last night. I'm just killing time waiting for you to give me a ride to school," Mathew replied.

"Alright, let me have a quick shower and then we'll get going," Jake responded as he took a big sip of his coffee. "I have a busy day today, so you'll have to take the bus home ok?"

"Really, dad. I hate the stupid bus. It takes so much longer to get home."

"Sorry, buddy, I can't today. I'm getting a haircut after work, so heat up some of the left over spaghetti when you get home, and make sure you clean up when you're done."

Things were hectic at work; it seemed to get busier every year with the pre-Christmas programming and sales. A lot of clients still waited until the last minute to commit to their Christmas advertising campaigns. Most of the office staff were exhausted from the long days and tempers were reaching the boiling point. Not many of them had time to get out for lunch, including Jake, so it was a very pleasant surprise when Darryl showed up at his office with food.

Darryl could see Jake through his office window. He knocked and then opened the door just enough to peak around the corner. "Are you hungry?" he asked.

"Starving," Jake exclaimed as he looked up from his computer and waved for Darryl to come in. Darryl walked over to Jake's desk and placed the bag down after pushing some papers to the side to make room. Jake got up and walked around Darryl, opened his office door and told his secretary to hold his calls as he would be busy for the next 30 minutes. Darryl had removed the contents from the bag and set everything on the desk.

"Don't bitch, but I grabbed you a salad," Darryl smiled as he pulled the lid off of one container and passed it over to Jake.

"A salad. You got me a salad?" Jake asked. "I think you had plans for lunch with one of your lady friends and she was unavailable, so you brought it to me so it wouldn't go to waste. Am I warm?" Jake inquired.

Darryl laughed out loud, "You know me so well. She already had plans for lunch, and well hey, why let it go to waste? Besides, we need to talk about your next date, so sit down and eat it. Here, you can have some of my chicken sandwich, you big whiner," he said, pushing over half of his sandwich.

"Her loss," replied Jake, and he happily took the sandwich. "Thanks, I do appreciate it. The sandwich, not the dates."

Darryl took Jake through some of the messages he had received on the dating site and stopped when he got to one from a school teacher named Liz. Her profile seemed pretty normal and her pictures were ok.

"She looks a bit tall for me," Jake said.

"It's hard to tell with these pictures," Darryl commented as he scrolled down her profile. "She says she is 5'10". That's not that tall. And hey – it says she likes Mexican food and so do you!"

"Darryl, lots of people like Mexican. And Italian, and Thai. That does not make it a perfect match," Jake replied with a look of annoyance.

"I think she is number three dude. Leave it with me and I'll set something up for this Saturday at the Mexican joint over on 5th street."

Jake let out a long sigh and then, as if he had no other choice, he agreed to the Saturday night date. *Three down, three to go*, he thought to himself, *Halfway there*.

"Oh, one condition. And yes, I am full of conditions today. It needs to be an early date because Mathew and I are going to the Thunderbirds game at 7," Jake added.

"Hockey? You spent way too much time in Canada, but ok. An early Mexican dinner it is," Darryl confirmed and then started cleaning up from lunch. Jake helped him sort what was garbage and what could be thrown into the recycling bins. Darryl wasn't as concerned with protecting the environment as Jake was. As Darryl stood up and started putting on his overcoat over his suit jacket, he remembered the other thing he had meant to cover off with Jake.

"Hey, you're still good for Sunday night's poker game right?" asked Darryl.

"Right, I almost forgot," Jake responded. "It's at your place right?" Jake asked Darryl.

"Well, that's why I brought it up. It is my turn to host, but my place is a mess with the kitchen renos, and I was wondering if you would switch nights with me? I'll take your turn next month, and you have everyone over to your place this Sunday. What do you say pal?" Darryl asked with a pleading look.

"Why not," Jake caved in. "But you need to bring some snacks."

"Awesome," Darryl beamed as he put his sun glasses onto the top of his head and headed out the door.

"I'll set everything up with Liz for an early Saturday evening fiesta, and I'll see you Sunday night for poker. Make sure you have some cash on hand. You're going to need it," he shouted as he made his way towards the elevator.

This is going to be an interesting weekend, Jake thought as he closed the door to his office and sat back down behind his desk. *An interesting weekend indeed.*

IN A RELATIONSHIP

CHAPTER 18

Sarah and Catherine waited patiently as the hostess cleared and wiped down a table before she escorted them through the busy restaurant and to their spot by the window. The sidewalks were busy with the downtown office workers scurrying along looking for a quick bite, or trying to find some place to pick up a takeout order so they could get back to their offices and eat. Sarah did not miss working downtown – she preferred the quiet little neighborhood she had built her practice in. Downtown always seemed hectic. Everyone was either head down typing into their phone, or they were holding it to their ear and talking to someone at an audio level that made her think they were trying to convince those who could hear that it was super important. No one was enjoying the moment – the crisp autumn air, the tree's changing color or the street musicians playing enthusiastically along the sidewalk. Catherine spoke Sarah's name out load and it snapped her out of her thoughts.

"Where were you, Sarah?" Catherine asked. "I said your name three times. Are you ok honey?"

"Sorry, I was thinking about work," she lied.

"Well stop. Figure out what you want to eat and then let's focus on date number three," Catherine smiled as she brought out her iPad and opened up Sarah's messages.

"Look at this one. His name is Geoff. I think you'll like him," Catherine whispered enthusiastically. Sarah turned the iPad so she could have a better look. He seemed alright. He was wearing a snappy tux and looked really good to Sarah. He liked animals, was employed, had done some traveling, and enjoyed spending time outdoors. *No alarm bells so far*, thought Sarah.

"He seems nice," Sarah softly replied after checking through all his photos.

"He is nice. I've been messaging him on your behalf, and he would like to take you for dinner on Saturday night. I said yes, so you're committed. Good thing you like him too, but I knew you would. Oh this is so much fun," Catherine giggled.

"Saturday night works I guess. It will have to be after 6 though, because Emma and I are going shopping Saturday afternoon."

"I'll set it up for 6:30pm so you're not too rushed then ok?" asked Catherine.

"I don't know why I let you talk me into these dates, Catherine. None of them feel right. Maybe online dating isn't for me," pondered Sarah.

"Nonsense," interrupted Catherine. "You're busy, men are busy, and this is the way of the future. Just have some patience. Besides, you have to."

"I know, I know. You have to kiss a few frogs, yada yada yada," Sarah broke in and finished the sentence.

They finished lunch and Catherine picked up the bill before Sarah could even look at it. "I promised I would pay, and a promise is a promise. Just like you promised to go on six dates," she smiled as she handed her credit card to the waitress.

Sarah and Catherine put on their jackets and walked back out onto the busy sidewalk. Sarah took in a big breath of fresh air and thanked Catherine for lunch.

"You're welcome, honey," she replied.

"Don't forget to pick up this month's book club book and some wine for Sunday's meeting. It's at my place so you can walk over. And you should bring Emma. The kids can watch a movie downstairs with Peter."

"I don't have time to read the book before Sunday, Catherine. There is no way, especially if I'm going out on Saturday night," lamented Sarah.

"Darling, no one reads the book – at least not the whole thing – except maybe Sheila. I have a summary I'll send you," Catherine smiled. "You know we just drink wine and chat anyways."

IN A RELATIONSHIP

CHAPTER 19

"Dad, you should go workout before your date tonight," Mathew said as they drove back from the grocery store. He was intently looking at his phone as he read an online story about the benefits of exercise before going out. "This article says your skin will look better and you will have a glow," he laughed, "and you'll feel more confident."

Jake looked over at him as he drove and smiled. "Really. I'll have a glow," he restated.

"Yeah, and you'll be more confident. I read somewhere yesterday that confidence is one of the main things women are attracted to."

"Why are you reading up on dating and what women like?" Jake asked him, looking over at Mathew but keeping his eyes on the road as he waited for the reply.

"Dad, I'm going to be 13 soon. A guy has got to be ready for the ladies."

Jake laughed, "You can't believe everything you read on the internet, but confidence does come from feeling good about yourself, and being in good health certainly helps with that. Maybe you should spend less time on the computer and more time outside," he added.

Mathew looked up at his dad and smiled back. "Maybe you should spend less time on your dating site and more time dating," he laughed.

Fortunately for both of them, they rounded the corner and pulled into their driveway so they could let the conversation go. Jake opened the garage door remotely and pulled inside. Mathew's bike was partially in the way so he hopped out and moved it so Jake could pull the car all the way in.

"You always leave your bike in the way," Jake complained as he got out and to hit the garage door button. The wind was blowing leaves inside the garage.

"Not always, dad. Always means every time and sometimes I don't."

"You know what I mean – more times it's in the way than it's not. Why do you always have to argue?" Jake asked.

"Why do you always have to be right?" Mathew asked.

"Why do you have to answer a question with another question?" Jake asked back.

"Dad, we could do this all afternoon, but I think you need to go to the gym before your date," Mathew laughed as he grabbed a few bags from the trunk and took them into the house.

Darryl had set up Jake's date with Liz for 5pm. An early dinner meant that he would have time to get back to the house and pick up

Mathew before they had to get to the hockey game. Jake showered, and then took his time picking out something to wear from his closet. He went back and forth to Mathew's room asking him for his opinion on each outfit, and Mathew was starting to lose patience. Jake resorted to his old standby, and after putting on his favorite shirt walked into Mathew's room for one final vote of approval. By now, Mathew was getting tired of the continuous interruptions from his gaming.

"Dad, you look fine, ok? It's just a date, not a wedding. Don't over think it. They all look good so just pick one and get going. That one is good."

"I know, I know. I really don't want to go to be honest with you," muttered Jake.

"Then don't go," Mathew stated without looking up from his computer screen.

"I have to. I already agreed to go. I should go. I need to go. I mean, I can't cancel now, can I? Maybe if I told her you were sick, I'm sure she would understand," mused Jake.

"Dad, you're always complaining that you have nobody to do anything with. You drag me to farmers' markets and crappy grownup movies. Think about your son. Think about what you're putting me through. Don't be so selfish," Mathew said as he actually took a break from his game and looked over at his dad with a big smile on his face.

"You're right. I am so sorry. This isn't about me, it's about you," Jake retorted sarcastically. "I'm sure once I'm there it'll be fine. It's just getting there." Jake smiled back. "You'll be good here on your own, right? I'll be home around 6:30 so be ready, and we'll head straight to the hockey game."

"I'm fine, Dad, get going. And yes, I'll be ready to go." Mathew was back focused on his game and getting annoyed again.

Jake closed the car door and put on his seatbelt on as the garage door opened. More leaves blew into the garage and he muttered to himself about how the breeze always blew his neighbour's leaves into his yard. The wind never seemed to blow the other way. He reached down and turned the heated seats on high as well as the heated steering wheel, and then backed out of the driveway and onto the street. As he pulled onto the freeway heading over to 5th avenue to meet Liz for dinner, his Bluetooth kicked in and he turned up the music in an attempt to calm his anxiety. It took him a little while to find parking – he forgot to give himself extra time for that. It was always hard to find parking downtown, especially Friday and Saturday evenings. He checked his phone and Liz had sent him a message saying she was inside and waiting at the front doors. As he walked into the restaurant he was greeted by the delicious smells from the kitchen and the warmth of the cozy Mexican Cantina. He had never eaten there before but had seen some great reviews online. He was glad he hadn't taken Darryl up on his Groupon offer though – he hated using coupons.

Liz was sitting on the bench just inside the doors and to the right of the hostess counter. She looked close enough to her pictures that Jake was able to recognize her without a problem, and as he extended his hand to greet her, she ignored it and instead stood up and wrapped her arms around him for a hug. Jake was taken aback by how tall she was. There was no way she was 5'10", she had to be 6'3" at least and she was not wearing heels. He felt like he was in a bear hug and took a moment to catch his breath once she had released him from the embrace.

Liz looked down at Jake and sensually spoke, "You smell wonderful, and you are just as gorgeous in person as you are in your pictures."

Having caught his breath and still taking in how tall she was, Jake started to reply that she looked great as well, but was interrupted by the hostess asking if they had a reservation. Jake quickly shifted his attention from Liz to the hostess and confirmed that they had a reservation for five o'clock under his name. The hostess called a waiter over and asked him to seat them at a table along the wall next to the fireplace. The waiter introduced himself as Pedro, and then motioned for them to follow him over to the table. Both Liz and Jake noticed at the same time that their waiter had only one arm. Liz seemed apprehensive about following Pedro but reluctantly started to follow as more customers entered through the front door and it started to become crowded. Jake was confused by her hesitation but assumed it was just nerves. He took a moment to survey his surroundings. To the right of the door way was a small stage with a mariachi band playing that added some life to the little Cantina, and the walls were brightly painted in yellow and orange and covered in pictures of past celebrations.

Once they were at their table, Pedro pulled out Liz's chair so she could sit down. He started to push it in to help her get seated, but Liz rudely stopped him and told him she could do it herself. Jake sat down in the chair across the table from her, and after thanking Pedro made a comment on how nice it was to be by the fireplace. Pedro gave him a friendly smile back, then read them the evening's specials and asked if they would like anything to drink. Liz, who was still acting uncomfortable, asked for a lime margarita and Jake asked for the same.

When Pedro was far enough away from the table that he wouldn't be able to hear their conversation Liz leaned in a little closer to Jake and said, "I probably shouldn't say this, I mean we just met, but I really hate handicapped people."

Jake was shocked. He had been working on getting over the fact that Liz was an amazon, but her newly revealed hatred of the physically challenged blew him away. He didn't know whether to laugh or get up and walk away. While Jake was considering his options, he heard a burst of laughter erupting from the table across from them. There were four teenagers sitting at the table, laughing and having a great time but not really conscious of the fact that they were being so loud.

Liz, apparently not one to be shy, leaned in to Jake again and whispered to him how much she disliked kids. *But you're a teacher,* thought Jake to himself.

She went on to explain that she had to deal with hundreds of teenagers all day, and the last thing she wanted to put up with after school was more teenagers. "I work from 7am to 4pm, putting up with all their crap and I certainly don't need more of it when I leave the school," she went off, adding, "y'know" at the end of her diatribe, looking for consensus from Jake.

Before Jake could respond, Pedro was back with their drinks. Liz took a break from expressing her disdain for the handicapped and teenagers just long enough for to take a big sip from her margarita, and then she was back at it. She started going on about how too many teenagers were from single parent families and had been raised by TV and video games. At this point Jake couldn't take it any longer. He was either going to have to get up and leave, or he was going to have to say something and then get up and leave. He looked across the table at Liz and asked her why she was a teacher if she hated kids so much.

"I don't hate them," Liz replied indignantly. "I just don't like them very much."

Jake finished his margarita and let the silence build for another 30 seconds (that felt more like 5 minutes) before he spoke.

"Let me see if I have this right. You hate handicapped people – your words, and you dislike teenagers – again your words. Is that about right?" Jake asked her.

"When you put it like that and you mention them together you make me sound like a horrible person," Liz complained.

"This just in, Liz – that does make you a horrible person," Jake replied back with a laugh. He couldn't believe what he was hearing, and from someone with influence over the next generation.

"Well, it's not like I'm a racist or anything like that," Liz responded.

Jake could tell she was getting pretty worked up, but he couldn't stop himself.

"So, let me ask you this Liz -" but just before he could ask his next question, Pedro returned and asked if they were ready to order. Jake spoke for them both before Liz could reply, "Pedro, can you come back in a few minutes? We haven't quite settled on what we want yet."

"No problem sir," Pedro replied. "Just wave at me when you are ready."

Jake looked back across the table at Liz and resumed his question. "Now where was I? Oh yes – so Liz, how do you feel about handicapped teenagers?"

Liz had heard enough, she pushed her chair back abruptly and stood up. As she did her chair made a horrible squeal as it slid back on the tiled floor. She threw her napkin down on the table and stormed out of the restaurant attracting everyone's attention. Even the mariachi band stopped playing as she brushed past them on the way to the front door. Jake just smiled as he leaned over the table to grab what was left of Liz's Margarita and drank it in one swallow. He then waved Pedro to come over.

"Pedro, my good man – that was a fabulous Margarita. One of the best I have ever had."

"Thank you, sir," smiled Pedro. "Did your friend not like hers?" he asked.

"Let's just say it was not a flavour that she was used to," smiled Jake as he pulled out his wallet and left enough money to cover the bill and a sizeable tip. As he got up to leave, Pedro asked him if he had made a mistake on the amount of the tip.

"No, Pedro. That is all for you, and gracias."

"De nada, senior. Thank you, sir. That is very generous. Please come back again soon, sir!"

Jake stopped in the restaurant's entrance way and adjusted his scarf prior to pulling on his winter coat and buttoning it up. Even though the date had been a disaster he was quite pleased at himself for calling Liz out on her politically incorrect viewpoints. It troubled him that she was a teacher with the ability to influence so many young minds. He knew a few teachers and they were the exact opposite and that gave him hope that Liz was an anomaly to the profession.

He opened the door and walked up the street and around the corner to where he had parked. There hadn't been any parking spots close by, so he had circled the block a few times before he had found this one. He unlocked the door with his key FOB, opened it, and slid in behind the wheel. He started the engine and adjusted his iPod to his favorite playlist.

As the music started, he noticed a car with its signal light on, waiting for him to pull out so that they could take his parking spot. "Alright, alright," he said to himself in the car. He looked back again as he eased out and waved to the couple in the car. He almost did a double-take when he realized the passenger was the same beautiful women he had seen a few weeks ago at Starbucks. She waved at him and smiled as he pulled out; a thank you gesture for letting them into the parking spot. The driver, on the other hand, looked annoyed that Jake was taking so long. He was tempted to give the guy the finger, but he didn't want to offend the woman in the passenger seat.

CHAPTER 20

At first, Sarah was upset with Catherine when she realized that she had given out her home address to Geoff so he could pick her up Saturday night, but it was too late to do anything about it now. Catherine had reassured her it would be fine and that she would come over and look after Emma so Sarah wouldn't be alone when Geoff picked her up and dropped her off.

It was close to 5:45pm when Geoff arrived outside of Sarah's house. Catherine and Emma had spotted the car and yelled at Sarah that he was here. Catherine continued to peek out the front window to see if he was getting out of the car when Sarah's phone rang. Emma picked it up and handed it to her mother. Sarah read the message and then looked at Emma and Catherine with a puzzled expression on her face. She then looked at Catherine and said

"It's Geoff. He won't come to the door. Apparently, friends of his ex-wife live a couple of streets over and he doesn't want anyone to see him. This is not a good start, Catherine. I have a bad feeling about this guy."

"Don't be silly. Lots of people are starting over again and it's just easier to not deal with exes if you don't have to. I totally get that. Grab your coat, go have fun. Look, he has a nice car." She smiled as she peeked out the window again. Sarah reluctantly put on her coat, stopped in front of the hallway mirror to check her make-up and hair one last time before hugging Emma and heading out the door.

"You look beautiful, mom," Emma shouted as Sarah closed the door behind her and walked down the driveway to the sidewalk.

Geoff didn't get out of the car to open her door; instead he leaned across the front seat and pushed the door open for her. *A real gentleman,* Sarah thought.

At the restaurant, Geoff and Sarah drove around the block at least five times looking for a parking spot. Geoff was getting frustrated but refused to drive any further away to find a spot. Finally, they noticed a man getting into a car parked just around the corner from the restaurant and Geoff pulled over behind him, and turned on his signal light waiting for the driver to start the car and leave. As the car pulled out, the driver smiled and waved at them. Sarah smiled back and waved a thank you. She thought she recognized the man in the car but couldn't place him.

Sarah's doubts about Geoff were dissipated when he got out of the car after they were parked, came around to her side of the car to help her out, and then closed the door behind her. *Well, maybe he is a gentleman after all,* Sarah thought to herself as they walked to the Restaurant.

Again, Geoff held the door for her when they arrived and they both stepped inside the warm Cantina taking in the smells and music that greeted them. After Geoff confirmed their reservation with the hostess, their waiter Pedro seated them beside the fireplace. Pedro helped Sarah into her seat and commented to Geoff how beautiful his wife was. Geoff corrected him and said that Sarah was not his wife, but yes she was beautiful. Sarah smiled. This date was going much better than her previous dates, and much better than she had thought it would. As he placed napkins in front of each of them, Pedro asked if they wanted to hear the specials. Sarah, who had never been to the restaurant before, was about to say yes when Geoff interrupted her.

"No, we don't need to hear the specials and we don't need menus," Geoff told Pedro.

Sarah looked at Geoff and then turned to Pedro and said defiantly, "Actually Pedro, I would like to hear the specials and I would like a menu please."

Pedro placed a menu in front of Sarah, but Geoff reached across the table and took it from her, telling Pedro that she would like to have the chicken fajitas. Sarah, not amused, looked at Geoff and then back at Pedro, reached back across the table and grabbed the menu from Geoff.

"No, I don't want chicken fajitas, and yes, I need a menu."

"I've eaten here many times, Sarah, there is no need to hear the specials or see a menu. I'll order for both of us. We'll have two chicken fajitas, some tortilla chips and salsa to start, plus a couple of margaritas."

Sarah caved on the food, but insisted on water rather than a margarita. There was no sense in going back and forth with Geoff in front of Pedro, and maybe he did know the menu quite well.

A different waitress arrived with the chips and salsa, and as she set them on the table Geoff thanked her for giving Pedro a hand. He emphasized the "hand" part as if he was being funny. The waitress gave him a look that let Sarah and Geoff know that she wasn't amused with the comment directed at Pedro's physical disability. After the waitress had left, Sarah also let Geoff know that the comment was rude and offensive.

"How could you make fun of someone with a physical disability?" Sarah asked.

"Oh relax," Geoff replied, "I have been coming in here for years. Pedro is cool with it." Sarah didn't believe him. She could see the waitress talking to the hostess and looking back at their table. She was embarrassed. Sarah excused herself, telling Geoff she had to freshen up. Once she got to the bathroom, she called Catherine and told her what had happened. Catherine calmed her down saying it was quite possible that Geoff and Pedro had a long history and it all sounded quite innocent. Sarah wasn't so sure, but agreed to go back to the table and finish dinner. When she returned to the table, Geoff had already devoured the chips and salsa. She had only been gone 3 or 4 minutes, but he had eaten them all.

The food arrived a few minutes later, so they ate as Geoff started to talk about his ex-wife and every other girl he had ever dated. By the end of dinner, Sarah knew every ex-girlfriend, one night stand, and crush that Geoff had ever had. On top of that, Sarah also learned that he had a gas problem when eating beans-which just happened to be a generous portion of his meal.

By now, Sarah was pretty much done with both Geoff and dinner, as were the tables beside them. Not only had Sarah heard Geoff's dating stories and gas issues while he drank two more margaritas, but so had the customers sitting at the tables next to them. Two of the dining parties had asked to be relocated and Geoff hadn't even noticed.

When the time for the bill came, Geoff told Sarah that he had recently been laid off from his job at Boeing, and asked Sarah if she could pay. Sarah wouldn't have minded so much if Geoff had not had three drinks plus dessert – that he ordered to go, but at this point in the evening she didn't hesitate to pay so as to spare herself any further embarrassment.

Geoff was again a perfect gentleman as they left; helping her put her jacket on, opening the door for her as they left the restaurant, and again at the car. It was beginning to rain as they started the drive home. Geoff was making small talk and Sarah was half listening and half thinking about how she was going to reply if he asked her out on a second date. She knew he was going to ask. Her gut was screaming *No*. He had acted like a gentleman for the most part, and was rather good looking, but something didn't feel quite right. They were about five minutes from her house when the decision was made for her. Geoff loudly and unapologetically broke wind several times. Then he questioned why she cracked the window despite the fact that it was raining.

Sarah couldn't get out of the car fast enough. She had tried to hold her breath the last few minutes, but it was impossible. The car hadn't even pulled to a complete stop before Sarah was trying to open the door. Unfortunately, the doors wouldn't open until the car was at a complete stop and in park. Sarah didn't wait for Geoff to come around to her side to open her door. *Not that he would anyways,* she thought as she remembered he didn't want to be seen in her neighborhood. As she ran up her driveway, Geoff shouted out that he would text her later. Sarah didn't look back. She felt like she needed a shower.

Catherine and Emma were cuddled on the couch watching a movie when Sarah burst through the door. She was laughing at the thought of how obvious Geoff's farting had been and yet he hadn't acknowledged it. Surely he could smell it, and if you knew that beans gave you bad gas why would you have them when you are out on a date? Catherine and Emma had paused their movie when Sarah came through the door.

"What's so funny?" Catherine asked.

"Make a pot of tea while I change and I'll tell you all about it," Sarah said with a smile as she took off her jacket and hung it up in the hallway. "I'm going to have a quick shower first. Emma, you need to go to bed."

"Mom, it's Saturday and I want to hear about your date, too," Emma moaned.

"OK, but its bed after that," Sarah replied as she made her way down the hallway to her bedroom and a hot shower.

The three of them sipped their tea and had a good laugh as Sarah took them through the evening's events. When she was finished, Emma went off to bed while Catherine and Sarah picked up the dishes and took them into the kitchen.

"You can't give up Sarah," Catherine quipped as she picked up her sweater and scarf. "We'll find a man that's worthy of you yet," she smiled.

Sarah handed her the red touque that was sitting on the kitchen counter and Catherine put it on. "I know there's somebody out there somewhere, but why does it have to be so hard to find him? Was Michael really one in a billion?" she asked.

"There will never be another Michael – he was one in a billion. But maybe there's someone else who gets you and can give you what you need," said Catherine as she hugged Sarah.

"Maybe, and I hope so. He better not have gas though. That is a deal breaker," Sarah laughed as she walked Catherine to the door at the back of the kitchen.

Catherine hugged Sarah again and then started through the door. Half way down the back walkway she turned and looked back at Sarah and shouted, "Don't forget to read the book summary I sent you before tomorrow night, and come over early so we can plan your next date!" With that, she was gone into the fall night.

CHAPTER 21

The week had gone by quickly and Jake's plans to pick up snacks for the poker night had been pushed to Sunday afternoon. He sent a text message to Darryl to see if he planned to bring anything over that evening. He waited half an hour, and when he still hadn't heard back from Darryl, he decided he would go on his own and pick up what they needed. He poked his head into Mathew's room to see if he wanted to tag along, and found Mathew on his computer as usual. Jake looked around Mathew's room at the empty glasses, plates, bowls, and discarded candy wrappers.

"How can you stand to be in a room with all this shit everywhere?" Jake asked him.

"What? It's not that bad."

"Are you blind? Can't you smell it?" Jake said with disdain.

"I'll clean it up today. Sunday is my cleaning day," he smiled up at his dad.

"What about your laundry? You should do that today, as well. Darryl and the guys are coming over tonight for poker so make sure all your stuff is cleaned up," Jake added.

"They're not coming in my room, so that shouldn't matter."

"It matters to me. It's not healthy having all these dirty dishes in your room. Get off the stupid computer, clean everything up and run the dishwasher after you load it. I'm going to the grocery store to get some things for tonight. Do you want to come or do you want me to pick anything up for you?" Jake asked.

"Can I play? I need another hundred before I can buy the new Xbox," Mathew asked with a mischievous smile. "Uncle Darryl is usually good for losing 20 or 40 bucks."

"No you can't play, and I don't want you staying up to late tonight either. Plus you have school in the morning and I don't want you eavesdropping on the conversation. The guys forget your here sometimes, and they get a little carried away with their language."

"It's nothing I haven't heard before dad."

"I don't care. Clean up your room, do your laundry and run the dishwasher. I'll be back in about an hour," Jake ordered and then closed the door.

It was a beautiful Sunday afternoon and everyone was outside taking advantage of one of the last nice fall days before winter blew in. The traffic was busy at the grocery store and it took Jake a few minutes to find a parking spot. As Jake was turning off the car, he finally heard back from Darryl who hadn't picked up anything for the poker game yet. Jake sent Darryl a message letting him know that he was at the grocery store and asked him if he wanted anything. Darryl replied that he was only a few minutes away, so he would meet him

IN A RELATIONSHIP

there and they could grab some stuff together. Jake got out of the car and made his way into the coffee shop by the bakery. He ordered a coffee, took it over to the table where he added some cream and honey, and then grabbed a seat along the window to wait for Darryl. Jake enjoyed people watching. It was one of his favorite things to do, especially at airports. The grocery store wasn't bad – not as entertaining as Walmart, but still entertaining. Between sorting through different profiles on his phone's dating app, Jake watched customers come and go. After a few minutes he noticed a woman and her daughter leaving the store. It was that same woman that he kept running into when he was out on his dates. He was deep in thought while he watched her and the little girl walk across the parking lot to their car when he felt someone tap his shoulder.

"What's up with you, dude? I've been trying to get your attention for a couple of minutes," Darryl stated.

"Sorry, I was just thinking," Jake replied.

"I can see that, what's on your mind?"

"Do you see that woman over there getting into the Volvo? I've seen her a few times now when I've been out," Jake explained.

Darryl looked in the direction that Jake was pointing and watched the woman get into her car and close the door.

"Yeah, she's ok. She's driving a Volvo, though. Probably another teacher," he joked. "The last teacher didn't work out so well. Come on, let's grab some snacks – I have a coffee date in an hour."

"Speaking of dates, I've only got three left to go and then we're done right?"

"Three to go," Darryl nodded his head in confirmation. "I see you've been checking your matches," Darryl acknowledged as Jake started to put his phone in his pocket. "I have your next one set up. You'll like her. Here, give me your phone and I'll show you her profile," he added as he snatched Jake's phone from his hand and sorted through the dating app until he found the profile he was looking for. "Her name is Kristen. Here, check her out."

He handed Jake his phone back. Jake looked out the window and across the parking lot but the woman and her daughter had already left. Disappointed, he held the phone up and scrolled through the profile Darryl had opened. Kristen looked okay – not super tall or too short, had a career not a job and her pictures were recent and included a full body shot. Jake looked up from his phone at Darryl who was smiling like he expected a high five.

"Well, what do you think? She's great right?" Darryl beamed.

"That is yet to be seen," Jake smiled back not returning the hi-five. "When's the interview? Or, should I say date?"

"Wednesday at lunch, at the new wine bar down near the library," Darryl volunteered as he picked up the grocery basket beside Jake's chair.

"Let's get these snacks. I gotta roll soon. Hot date, you know."

Sarah and Emma had been up since early Sunday morning to clean up the house and do their laundry. They had a ritual on Sundays that included chores and going out for breakfast, followed by picking up groceries. Sometimes they would be more adventuress and look to find someplace new to try, but usually they went to the same old diner they had been going to since Michael had died. It was located in the same shopping plaza as the grocery store, so it made things a little more convenient for them.

When Michael was still alive and before Emma was born, Sunday mornings were quite different. It was the one day of the week that she would sleep in. Michael would be up early – it didn't matter where they were or what day it was, he just couldn't sleep in. He used to always quote Leonardo Da Vinci, "you can't expect to be successful if you don't get out of bed." While Sarah would sleep in, Michael would get up and make coffee. While it was brewing, he would cut up fresh fruit and throw some toast in the toaster. The smell would always wake up Sarah and she would stroll into the kitchen where she and Michael would listen to music and talk about whatever came into their heads. It was magical. Those memories were one of the main reasons she liked to get out of the house Sunday mornings – it was a nice distraction from bittersweet recollections.

While she and Emma sat in the restaurant drinking their tea and waiting for their order to arrive, Tony, the owner of the restaurant came over to say hello. He was a sweet old man who had been running the little dinner for over 30 years. He had developed a real affection for Sarah and Emma.

"Good morning, beautiful," he said to Sarah in his Italian accent.

"Good morning, Tony," Sarah replied looking up at the portly man in his stained cooking apron, returning his smile with one of her own.

Tony turned to Emma with a big smile and said, "Good morning, princess. I am so glad you came in today. I have a surprise for you in the kitchen if it's okay with your mom?"

"Go ahead, Emma. I'm going to stay and drink my tea," Sarah told them both.

As Sarah watched Emma and Tony disappear into the kitchen her mind wandered back to one particular Sunday morning with Michael. It was the same memory that always came back to her – one of the last Sundays they had before he passed away.

Sarah had dropped the tea bag into her cup of hot water and then stared at Michael across the table. He had been engaged in something on his phone and tapping his foot to the Motown song that was playing in the background. She remembered thinking that the war against time and the elements had been good to him. Sure, his face showed signs of too much sun, and he had a few scars from his years of playing sports, but those things had made him even more attractive to her. The lines by his eyes, the creases from smiling, they gave depth to his character and added to his presence.

She had cleared her throat to get his attention over the music that was filling the kitchen. She remembered him looking up and smiling back at her, as well as every word of the conversation that followed, like it had happened yesterday.

"What's up, beautiful?" he asked.

"I was just thinking," she paused and then slowly spoke so as to draw his interest into where she was going. "Have you ever thought about what life would be like without music?"

He paused and let the smile slowly leave his face. "Life without music," he repeated. "No, I can't say I have. I'm not sure that's a world I'd want to live in."

"Let's play a game," she said with glee and a sparkle in her eye as she got up and turned the music down.

"Oh, I hate it when you do this," he said, the smile back on his face. He picked up his coffee and took a sip. "Ok, you first."

"Life without music would be like a life without a sunrise. Where it was dark all the time," she said.

"Or, it would be like life without a sunset. A world that was forever bathed in sunlight," he replied back. "No beautiful orange and pink sunsets to light up the skyline".

"Can you imagine a life without summer? A world that only existed in a blanket of winter snow, where everything is covered in a frozen veil of white?" she stated as she got up from her chair and made her way around the table to stand behind him. "You would have to keep me warm," she whispered in his ear and wrapped her arms around him so she could feel the heat from his body.

"Well," he coyly murmured back as he turned to hold her, slipping his hand inside her robe to running his hand down the small of her back, "what if it was always sunny, it never rained or snowed and the heat was constant and stifling? You never got a chance to dance through a spring rain shower; or walk holding hands down a tree lined path with all the colors of fall captured in the leaves and falling on you? Or you never had a chance to lie in the snow and make snow angels? How would you like that, little Miss 'I love all four seasons'? What if there were never puppies or kittens or baby pandas? Or babies? What if everyone and everything was born into the world as adults?" he continued.

"Oh, I don't think I would like that," she quietly whispered as she pulled herself away from him, a tear slowly rolling down her cheek as she imagined a world without puppies.

"What if there were no butterflies?" he sadly asked.

"What if there was no coffee?" she smirked as she stood up wiped away the tear and filled his cup. When it was full she put in a splash of cream and stirred it for him.

He picked up the cup to take a sip and then pulled her close so she could feel his body tight against her. He breathed in her smell as he ran his hand through her hair and whispered into her ear.

"I could live without a sunrise or a sunset, babe. I could live without summer or winter, snow or rain. I could live without puppies, *babies and butterflies. I could even live without music."* Then he paused and looked intensely into her eyes, *"What I couldn't live without is you."*

Sarah could feel a tear running down her cheek as Emma ran up to the table holding a plate with a pancake made in the shape of what vaguely looked like a puppy.

"Look what Tony made for me, mom!" Emma exclaimed. Sarah wiped the tear off her cheek and smiled at Emma, hoping she wouldn't notice it or the faraway look in her eyes.

"Oh, that is so cute," Sarah answered as she pulled herself together. Tony had made his way back to the table by now; he was getting older and didn't move quite as fast as Emma did. "Tony, that was so sweet of you."

"Always a pleasure to make the Princess happy," Tony chuckled. He then realized that Sarah was a bit off.

"Are you okay, Sarah? Maybe you would like a puppy pancake as well?" he asked.

"No thanks, Tony," Sarah smiled as best she could, "I'm fine with my fruit and yogurt."

"That's okay, mom. You can have some of mine."

"Thanks, sweetie, but I'm good. Eat up so we can go grab some groceries and then get home. We need to finish the laundry," Sarah replied as she used her spoon to play with the yogurt, having lost her appetite.

"Thanks again, Tony. We'll see you next Sunday."

"Maybe you'll have pancakes next Sunday," Tony smiled back at her. "Don't forget, you two promised to work at our Christmas dinner for the homeless," Tony added.

"It's written in our calendar, Mr. Patrelli. We'll be here, right mom?" Emma responded with a mouthful of pancake. Tony chuckled, rubbed the top of her head and then put his hand on Sarah's shoulder.

"We'll see you next weekend," he smiled and then walked back to the kitchen.

CHAPTER 22

The vacuum cleaner is as old as Mathew, thought Jake as he unplugged it from the wall and wrapped the cord around the base of it before putting it away. Mathew poked his head out of his room and asked what time the poker game was.

"It's at 6, but the guys will start arriving around 5:30 when the Sunday night football game starts," Jake replied. "Did you clean up the bathroom?" he asked Mathew.

"Most of it, but I left the toilet. It's gross. Can't we get a maid or someone in to clean the bathrooms and the kitchen?" he complained to his dad.

"Sure, we could do that. If you want to stop buying video games we can use that money for a maid," Jake smiled back. "That won't help us today, though. You use that washroom so you need to clean it, and you need to do it now before the guys arrive. The cleaning supplies are under the sink." With that said Jake threw a rag at Mathew and walked back down the hall towards the kitchen.

"Why don't you take a portion of the poker money and use that towards a maid?" Mathew shouted at him down the hall, and then reluctantly picked up the rag and went into the bathroom to clean it.

Jake grabbed a few bowls from the cupboard and filled them up with pretzels and chips. As he was cutting up the carrots and peppers he saw the headlights of Darryl's Jeep as it pulled into the driveway. He looked up at the clock as he made his way to the kitchen door and turned on the outside light. Darryl opened the door without knocking and walked in with a case of Moosehead beer and set it on the table. Their friend Steve was right behind him, and he also had a case of beer and set it on the table.

"Ready to lose some money?" Darryl smiled at Jake.

"You can only dream," Jake smiled back.

"Hey Steve, how are you?" Jake asked as he shook Steve's hand and leaned in for the bro hug.

"I'm good, thanks. You know, living the life," he said sarcastically. Darryl interrupted the two of them as he opened the fridge and asked Jake if he could make some room for the beer.

"Don't put it in there. I made room in the beer fridge downstairs," Jake explained.

As Darryl and Steve made their way to the stairs, there was a knock at the door and Jake walked back and opened it. Jason and Trevor squeezed past Jake so he could close the door and keep the cold out.

"Boys," Jake greeted them and conducted the same hand shake man hug he had given Darryl and Steve. "Glad you could make it gentleman – and I use that term loosely. Hang your coats on the rack behind you, and then come on downstairs."

"Nice neighborhood, Jensen," Jason proclaimed as he looked around the kitchen and headed for the stairs.

"Thanks," Jake replied, "it's a little smaller than my last house but hey, that's what happens when you go through a divorce."

"Yeah, I hear you," Trevor chuckled. "Darryl was talking on the drive over about selling his place and getting something smaller now that he has alimony and child support to pay."

"I can hear you," yelled Darryl from the basement and they all laughed.

Jake had set up the poker table earlier in the afternoon, and as he walked down the stairs with the chips and veggies he could hear Darryl telling the guys to look for the remote so he could put the football game on.

"It's below the TV," Jake yelled over the guy talk as he set the bowls on the side table.

"Got it," Darryl exclaimed and turned on the game. The other guys had already sat down in chairs around the poker table so Darryl and Jake took the remaining two chairs.

Jason was sitting directly across the table from Darryl and couldn't help but notice that he was wearing sunglasses on his head. "What's with the sunglasses Darryl, you know it's dark out right?"

"That's his thing," Jake answered before Darryl could.

"What the fuck do you mean *his thing*?" asked Trevor.

"Don't bother explaining it to these simpletons. They won't have a clue what you're talking about," Darryl insisted as he took the glasses off the top of his head and put them on over his eyes. "I brought them to wear so you can't see my eyes," he added as he looked shiftily around the table at the rest of the guys.

Jake and Darryl had known Steve for years, while Jason and Trevor were friends of Darryl's that Jake had only recently gotten to know since his move back to Seattle. Steve worked at an Ad Agency that handled a lot of large local clients, including the Seahawks. He had moved a few client campaigns onto the TV station that Jake worked at, and at times had been able to get some game tickets for the guys including a pair that Jake and Mathew had used. He was married with a 3 year old and he and his wife were expecting a second in the New Year. Steve really enjoyed the poker nights; it gave him a chance to get out of the house. His wife's second pregnancy had been a difficult one and he wasn't getting any sex, a fact he wasn't shy about sharing with the boys.

Jason had taken over a very successful car dealership from his father and had divorced his first wife three years ago when she had caught him having an affair with the receptionist. He had two teenage children from his first marriage that lived with him halftime and twin 2 year old boys that he had conceived with the receptionist who he had married this past summer. Jason and Darryl usually tried to outdo each other with alimony and child support stories.

Trevor was the happily married member of the poker table. He had worked for a large local construction company for years but when the economy crashed in 2008 he had been laid off. He and his wife and three kids had sold everything they could to raise enough money to start their own company. At first they had just done small jobs, like decks and bathrooms, but things had gone well and now he had a crew of 12 guys, building and selling spec homes. Darryl had talked him into doing his kitchen reno and Jason, who had reluctantly agreed, was now regretting it.

IN A RELATIONSHIP
160

CHAPTER 23

"Tell me what this month's book is about, mom?" Emma asked as they locked arms together and walked down the last block to Catherine's house. It was a cool night again and Sarah could tell Mother Nature was preparing for winters arrival. The smell of wood burning fireplaces filled the autumn evening.

"It's about this woman whose husband cheats on her and she decides to travel the world to find happiness" explained Sarah.

"You would think she'd be happy that she wasn't with him anymore if he was cheating," stated Emma, with a very serious face.

"It's not always that easy," Sarah replied. "Sometimes, even when someone you're with is dishonest and does something to hurt you, you still want to be with them. I know that doesn't make sense to you, but it will one day. It takes time for the heart to heal," she added.

"It would be nice if there were Band-Aid's for the heart," Emma whispered to her mother as they reached the gate to Catherine and Peter's house. Sarah leaned down and kissed her daughter on the forehead just below the edge of her little red beret. She was so cute with her old school red hat, scarf and black Pea coat. Sarah was startled back to reality when Rex jumped up against the fence and gave an excited yelp when he realized it was Emma.

Sarah wasn't sure who was more excited, Rex or Emma. She opened the gate carefully so that Rex wouldn't get out, although she knew he wasn't going anywhere without Emma. They managed to both squeeze in past the gate and lock it behind them as Catherine opened the front door and yelled for Rex to give them a little room. That was pointless. Peter brushed past Catherine fully dressed for a walk and leash in hand.

"I got this," he told Catherine as he started down the sidewalk towards Sarah and Emma, then stopped halfway, turned around and walked back to give Catherine a quick peck on the cheek.

"Emma, how about we take Rex for a walk, and then we'll come back and watch a movie?" Peter asked as he tried to calm Rex down so he could put the leash on him.

"Sounds good, Uncle Peter. Here let me help," she offered and held Rex in her arms as Peter put on the leash.

"Can we watch The Walking Dead first? It's on at 6 and I need to see what happens this week," Emma asked excitedly.

"Yes, we can. I love that show," Peter smiled. "Thanks for the help with Rex. Here, you hold the leash," he said as he opened the gate. They waved back at Sarah and Catherine before closing it and heading down the street.

"Did you bring a bag?" Catherine yelled.

"Right here in my pocket," Peter yelled back. Sarah and Catherine watched them walk down the street for a moment and then went inside and closed the door.

Sarah pulled off her jacket and scarf and laid them over the back of one of the kitchen chairs. Catherine was standing against the counter just staring at Sarah but not saying anything. It was obvious that Sarah's mind was off in another world far away from Catherine's kitchen. A few minutes passed before Sarah realized that Catherine was staring at her.

"Fuck, I know," said Sarah, still a little distant. She then realized she had sworn and put her hand over her mouth.

"It's ok. The kids are downstairs, and it's not like they haven't heard that word before or worse," Catherine laughed. She came around to Sarah's side of the counter and gave her a big hug.

"It's ok to miss him. You two had a wonderful life together and it's completely ok to hang onto those great memories. It's ok. Now, give me a hand with bringing in the cheese tray, I picked up some new brie that the ladies are going to love and I also made some fresh salsa and guacamole. I know you didn't have any the other night when you were out for Mexican" she giggled.

"Oh, and I've been doing a little work on your next date. I hope you don't mind. I didn't know if we'd have enough time before the girls get here."

"I had so hoped that maybe you had forgotten," Sarah quietly muttered as she picked up the tray off the table and followed Catherine into the living room.

Sarah was impressed with the feast of snacks that Catherine had set out. As she was surveying everything on the table, it dawned on her that monthly book club meeting was becoming more lavish than the previous. *Not good news,* Sarah thought when she realized that it was her turn in January. She set the cheese tray down on the table next to the salsa and guacamole and then followed Catherine up the stairs to the bedroom. Catherine, the eager beaver, was already sitting down with Sarah's dating profile pulled up on the computer screen. She patted the empty chair beside her and motioned for Sarah to sit down.

"This fellow, Andrew, he seems really nice. Check out his profile, Sarah," Catherine offered as she turned the screen to face Sarah.

"I've exchanged a few messages with him and he's looking forward to meeting you for lunch on Wednesday. I thought lunch would be a nice change – not as formal and with a built in time limit. What do you think?" she eagerly asked Sarah.

"Hold your horses, girl," Sarah smiled up at her, "give me a minute to take a look."

"Alright, while you do that I am going to change and get ready. The girls will be arriving soon," Catherine smiled as she got up and walked into her large walk-in closet.

IN A RELATIONSHIP
165

"Oh, I poured us both a glass of wine. Yours is on the end table. I thought we'd get an early start," she quipped and then disappeared into the walk-in.

Soon Maroon 5 filled the air as Sarah browsed through the rest of Andrew's profile. He had decent pictures and was dressed impeccably in all of them. There were plenty of outdoor photos but none of him actually doing anything, which Sarah found a little odd. He was fit, had nice teeth and seemed well tanned. Either that or he had naturally dark skin. His profile stated that he was divorced and shared custody of a teenage boy. *Three more dates to go*, thought Sarah. *Why not Andrew?*

Sarah got up from the computer and walked over to the end table where she picked up her glass of wine and took a big sip. She smiled as she looked at the glass,

"I have a relationship," she told herself, "and it tastes great."

"What are you thinking?" asked Catherine as she stood behind Sarah.

"Sorry, I didn't see you there," replied Sarah with a mischievous little smile. "I was just saying, I have a relationship. It's with wine and we are going to have a good time tonight."

"You prefer wine to Andrew?" pouted Catherine.

"Yes, yes I do," answered Sarah, "and do you want to know why?"

Catherine was quite curious now, and enjoying the change in mood that had come over Sarah. Sarah sat back down in her seat and patted the empty one beside her.

"Sit down, my dear, and I will tell you," Sarah laughed.

Catherine sat for a moment and then realized she had forgotten her wine in the walk-in. She quickly jumped up, ran and grabbed it and then returned to her seat.

"Well, first of all," Sarah started, "a good bottle of wine is easier to find than a good man."

"Amen, I'll drink to that," laughed Catherine.

"Secondly," Sarah went on, "wine will watch whatever I want to watch. Even the Bachelor," Sarah and Catherine both giggled.

"Thirdly, wine never makes you choose between it and your friends," added Sarah.

"Oh, and wine never judges you," chimed in Catherine. They laughed out loud and clinked each other's glasses together.

"And lastly," Sarah whispered as she turned and looked back towards the door to make sure that no one with little ears was around, "a glass of wine lasts longer than 30 seconds."

Catherine almost choked on the sip of wine that she was taking. A little ran out of her mouth and some came out of her nose as they both fell back onto the bed laughing. When they had both calmed down, they looked to the doorway to see Peter and Emma standing there, looking at them like they were both crazy.

"Hey guys," Catherine managed to sputter out as she and Sarah scrambled off the bed and pulled themselves together. Peter was all smiles but Emma was a bit confused.

"We're going to head downstairs and watch some TV. Enjoy your book club," he added as he put his arm around Emma and they turned and headed down the hallway to the stairs. Catherine and Sarah giggled again and then started to make their way to the living room.

As they descended the stairs, Catherine turned to Sarah, "So, Andrew, you're good to go for lunch with him Wednesday right?"

"Yeah, I'm good to go, but I would prefer to date wine," Sarah replied still smiling.

It wasn't long before the other women started to arrive, and soon the conversation and wine were flowing smoothly. There were normally eight women who got together monthly for the book club, but two of them couldn't make it this time. Jenny, who had just had a baby, and Lindsay, who was out of town on business, were unable to attend November's get together. The other four members of the book club included Mary from Sarah's office, Peter's sister Jan, and two of Catherine's neighbors, Sheila and Sandy.

Mary was by far the youngest, and she was always the first to arrive and the last to leave. She had yet to enter the dating world again after breaking up with her last boyfriend, and enjoyed being around the older women, listening to them go on about their husbands and men in general.

Jan was pretty straight-laced, at least on the outside. She and her husband never had children and they spent a lot of time traveling. She tended to get a little crude once she had a couple of glasses of wine and it wasn't unusual for her to catch a ride to and from the meeting with Mary so she could drink more. Mary preferred to smoke weed over drinking wine and wasn't always comfortable smoking it in front of the ladies, so she was often in good shape when it came time to leave.

Sheila and Sandy were both neighbors of Catherine's, and had been living in the same houses for as long as Catherine and Peter had been living in the neighborhood. They both had two children – Sandy had two boys and Sheila had a boy and a girl, all roughly the same ages. Sandy had gone back to work at the local recreation complex, but Sheila had decided to stay home. She was more or less the mother bear for the block, and there wasn't much that went on in the neighborhood that she didn't know about. Sheila was also the founding member of the book club and the unofficial president. In other words, she ran the monthly social.

After everyone had a chance to say hello and catch up with some small talk, Sheila called the evening to order by tapping a knife on the side of her wine glass, urging the ladies to fill up their glasses and find a seat. Catherine and Sarah, who were a few glasses ahead of the others, sat down on the couch beside each other and waited for the ladies to top up their wine and sit down.

CHAPTER 24

The poker game had been underway for a little over an hour when Steve used a lull in the conversation to ask Jake about his online dating.

"Hey Jake, Darryl tells me you have been doing some online dating. What's it like out there in the modern dating world? You must have some good stories."

Jake looked at Darryl and gave him a death stare. "I can't believe you told him. Well, actually I can – but I asked you not to, asshole."

"It was an accident. I was on your profile on my phone in the car when I picked him up. Look, it's no big deal. Lots of people use dating sites."

"Yeah, don't worry about it," Jason added. "Do you have it on your phone now? Let me have a look, I want to see if I know anybody on there."

"See what you started?" Jake replied directly to Darryl.

"Come on, what's the big deal?" Trevor added and reached for Jake's phone.

Jake grabbed his phone before Trevor could reach it and put it in his shirt pocket. "Piss off, all of you," he smiled as he looked around the table. "If you want to look at something, look at Darryl's. He's the master of online dating."

"I read somewhere online that 50% of men on Tinder are married," chimed in Steve.

"What is Tinder?" asked Trevor.

"You don't know what Tinder is? Where the fuck have you been the last year?" laughed Darryl.

"Happily married, unlike the rest of you assholes," Trevor said with a big grin. "I don't need to go looking for love; I got all I can handle at home." The guys all booed Trevor and Darryl threw a pretzel at him. It bounced off his face and landed in his beer.

"Shit, look what you did. You ruined a perfectly good beer," Trevor responded as he wiped up the beer that had splashed out on to his cards.

"No loss. That's shit beer anyways," Darryl mocked him. "Here, have a real beer," he chided, as he reached into the beer fridge behind his chair and threw Trevor a Moosehead.

"Seriously, Jake," Steve started in again, picking up on his first question that still remained unanswered. "You must have some good dating stories to share, or maybe a few titty pics? Come on, just one?" he asked.

"I might have a few – stories that is, not titty pics – but I'm not sharing them with you assholes. That's all I need. Besides, who knows? Maybe one of them will turn out to be the next Mrs. Jensen, and I don't need you bastards knowing how I met her, and I certainly don't want to know that you perverts have seen her breasts."

Darryl could sense Jake's reluctance so he stepped in, "Look guys, I have been helping him out. He agreed to try a few dates and so far it hasn't worked out too well. But, we're not giving up. In fact, he has a lunch date this Wednesday."

"*We're* not giving up?" queried Jason. He then paused, put his hand on Jake's shoulder and went on in a romantic tone, "Are you two boys double dating? Aww, that's so sweet."

"You're a funny guy, Jason," Darryl laughed.

"Look," Jake added, "I've had three dates so far. One thinks all Muslims are terrorists, one was still in love with her ex and couldn't stop talking about him, and one made it clear she hated disabled people and kids. There, that's the story so far. Can we move on to a new topic?"

The table went quiet for a moment, and then Jason leaned into Jake and said, "I think I know what the problem is. You're letting Darryl help pick your dates." The entire table erupted in laughter. Even Darryl thought it was funny.

At that moment Mathew came down the stairs and walked up to the table. The guys each took turns saying hello to him. Of course, Darryl offered him a beer, to which he looked at Jake for permission. Seeing the stern look on his dad's face, he declined.

"What are you guys laughing at?" Mathew asked.

"Your dad was just telling us about his recent dates," Jason replied still smiling.

"Did he tell you about the night he came home from a date smelling like someone had pee'd on him?" Mathew asked with a smile, eager to be a part of the grown up conversation.

"What?" Jason asked. "No he did not, but I think he should. Come on, let's hear it. Give us the skinny."

"Thanks buddy," Jake said as he looked at Mathew and smiled. "I don't think so. You guys don't need any more ammo to make fun of me with. Mathew, you need to go upstairs, finish your homework, and get ready for bed, ok?"

"I did my homework. Come on, let me stay. I know how to play and I have my own money."

"You're not playing. Now go upstairs" Jake stated firmly and gave him a look like he was done with the conversation.

"Hey, before you go to bed, Mathew, can you run upstairs and grab my phone? I left it on the counter," Darryl asked.

"You lazy bastard, go get it yourself," Jason teased Darryl.

"Here's a buck, can you run up and get it for me?" Darryl asked again as he held out a dollar bill for Mathew.

"I can do it for 5 bucks," Mathew offered as he walked over to Darryl.

"5 bucks!" Darryl echoed. "Man, you're dad has taught you well." He then put the one dollar bill back on the table, grabbed a 5 and passed it to Mathew. "I thought we were buddies," he said with a mock sad voice.

"Business is business," Mathew smiled back and then bounced up the stairs to retrieve Darryl's phone. He was up the stairs and back in less than a minute. As he gave Darryl the phone it suddenly started to beep, and then at full volume the phone announced that Darryl had a new message from *Nurse Naughty*.

Darryl struggled to turn the volume down, but before he could accomplish that task, the sexy female voice read the incoming message out loud, *"Hey sexy. I'm lying in bed with no panties on and thinking of you."*

That was all that played before Darryl managed to turn off the phone. His face had turned a dark crimson and the guys were falling off their chairs they were laughing so hard.

"Mathew, you need to go upstairs and go to bed," Jake forced out between bouts of laughter. Mathew was laughing as he walked around to Jake's chair and gave his dad a hug before saying goodnight to the guys and heading off to bed.

Once Mathew was gone, the guys returned to their poker game. As they continued to deal the cards the conversation moved from online dating to other topics.

"Do any of you guys know a good orthodontist?" asked Trevor.

"Yeah, we used one a few years ago when Maggie needed braces. Fucking expensive, but they do really good work. Here, I'll send you the contact info right now," Jason told him as he used his phone to send the information to Trevor.

"Kids are expensive as hell," Trevor added as he opened his phone to acknowledge he had received the new contact. "See what you have to look forward to, Steve?" he added. "You're just getting started with the whole kid thing. It doesn't get cheaper dude. You need to be saving for this kind of shit, plus don't forget about University."

"I know. I used to be able to buy new clothes whenever I wanted to. We could go for nice quiet dinners or catch a concert, a vacation without having to worry about how we were going to pay for it. I haven't bought a new phone in 2 years. Do you know how far I am behind with phone technology? I have a blackberry for fuck's sake," Steve lamented as he pointed to his phone on the table.

"Well, at least you don't have that flip phone anymore," Darryl joked. "By the way, I picked up a slow cooker the other day. Oh my god, they are fucking amazing. I can put all the shit for a good stew into this thing in the morning, and when I come home, boom dinner is ready. I wish I had known about those things sooner. Why didn't you guys tell me?"

"My wife uses ours all the time," Trevor told the group. "When we were first starting the company, we didn't have a lot of money, so we became pretty good at keeping costs down by baking our own bread and growing our own veggies. Tracey even learned how to cut hair. She cuts all our hair."

"You can tell," Darryl told him, sparking another outburst of laughter from the group.

"Have any of you guys been in for a full medical exam recently?" Jason asked as he looked around the table. All of the guys shook their head. "I was in last week. I had to get it done for insurance purposes. By the way, Darryl, the story you told me about how they don't have to give you the old finger up the ass exam anymore? That's bullshit! I asked the doctor if I could have a blood test for it like you told me they have. You know what he said?" Darryl shook his head at the question. "He told me he wished there was a test because he didn't like shoving his finger in my ass any more than I did." The laughter again erupted around the table.

Jake was just sitting back and smiling as he listened to these grown men go on and on about their domestic challenges. When they paused for a moment after a big hand, he told them that they sounded like a bunch of women sitting around drinking wine, not a bunch of men playing poker.

"We are pathetic, aren't we?" Steve chuckled. "I wonder what the women talk about when they get together."

"Are you kidding?" Jason asked as he gave Steve a serious look. "They talk about women things like who does their hair, where did they get their new shoes, how cute their kids are and what happened on *The Bachelor* last week. They talk about boring shit, that's what they talk about."

CHAPTER 25

Sheila was having a difficult time keeping the ladies focused on a review of the actual book. It had started off ok, as they usually do, with Sheila giving her interpretation of the book and then going through a series of questions that at first the group had willingly participated in. But as they drank and the night went on, it became harder and harder to keep them on topic. The women had drank a few bottles of wine and the conversation was jumping all over the place, with no regard to keeping up the book discussion.

Catherine got everyone's attention, and then to Sarah's horror announced that Sarah was starting to date.

"Ladies, I have some news for you. Do you remember me telling you about the deal that Sarah made with me last year on her birthday? Well, our little Miss Sarah has been out on a few dates. She is back in the game." Sarah put her head down in embarrassment while the ladies all hooted and cheered.

"That's terrific, Sarah," Sheila offered.

"You'll meet someone nice, I know it," Sandy offered.

"Sarah, that is so exciting. Come now; tell us all about your dates. None of us get to date anymore so we need to live through you – and Mary," she added last minute, looking over at Mary. "But, young Mary here seems to have become celibate."

"There's not much to tell, really. I've had three dates, none of which I would classify as good. In fact, on a scale of one to ten I haven't had one that's made it past a 2," Sarah confessed.

"Come on, Sarah, give us some more details." Jan Insisted.

"Look, the first guy was a steroid monkey, the second one had never grown out of his high school self, and the third guy was broke and made me pay for everything. I know I agreed to six dates but after the first three, I don't have high expectations for the final three. Be thankful you're not single, girls. From what I've seen, there isn't a lot out there." Sarah didn't want to talk about it anymore, and went to the bar to fill up her wine glass. Mary was already standing at the bar pouring herself a coke.

"Is it really that rough out there?" Mary asked Sarah.

"Probably not for you, Mary. Don't listen to me. I don't know anything. Look at you – you're young and hot and you don't have a child. You'll be fine," she comforted her with a big hug that was interrupted by Catherine. Mary picked up her glass and left the two of them alone.

Mary decided she was going to take a break and sneak outside the backdoor to smoke a joint that she had brought. She had just finished lighting it when the door opened and Catherine and Sarah appeared in the doorway.

"Just as we suspected," Catherine smirked at Mary. "You went outside to burn one and didn't invite us."

"You two don't smoke weed and burn one. Really?" Mary laughed at them.

"Sssshhhhh," Catherine whispered, "We don't want the others to know. We'll have you know that we smoked our share of weed back in the day, young lady. We just don't do it very often anymore. We have children. We are responsible."

"You don't have to whisper. Marijuana has been legal in Washington State for a few years now," Mary replied with a lot of sarcasm.

"Just give us a drag," Sarah added as she reached out her hand. Mary smiled and passed her the joint. Sarah put it to her lips and inhaled deeply before passing the joint to Catherine. Sarah almost dropped it as she started to cough uncontrollably. Catherine took several hits and passed it back to Sarah, not Mary.

"Have one more, Sarah, and then give it back to Mary. We need to get back inside before the others come out to check on us," Catherine wheezed out as she too started to cough.

"Man, you two are amateurs," Mary laughed as she took the joint back from Sarah and continued to smoke it as Sarah and Catherine went back inside.

When Mary returned to the room, she could tell that the women had clearly abandoned any pretense of continuing with the book discussion. Jan, who had obviously hit the magic level of drunkenness she needed to reach to let loose her inhibitions, was now asking Sheila what hair style she had *down below*.

"That is none of your business," Sheila snapped back at her.

"Oh don't be such a prude, Sheila. It's just us women here, you can tell us. Does your hubby like a full bush – you know *Au Natural* – or do you shave it nice and smooth like a baby's bottom?" Jan teased her.

Mary, feeling the effects of the joint she had just smoked, decided she was going to wade into the discussion. She was curious as to what the older women did as far as womanscaping went.

"I shave it all," Mary said to Jan. "Always have. It just seems cleaner and I like the feeling."

"You like the Brazilian?" Jan smiled and then asked with real interest, "Do you get a full Brazilian or just a half? I get the full. I used to get just a half, but as you get older, you grow a lot more hair and you grow it a lot quicker."

"I get a full," Mary answered as she blushed in front of the group. "My ex used to really like it, and well, I just kept doing it even after we broke up."

With Mary's confession out in the open, Jan decided to go back at Sheila. "Well Sheila? Mary has no trouble talking about it. Come on now, what do you do down there?"

Sheila, not wanting to be shown up by Mary decided to play along. "I just trim a little, you know, so nothing pokes out when I'm wearing a bathing suit."

"We call that a bikini trim," Jan informed the group. "How about you two?" she asked as she looked over at Catherine and Sarah. The weed had started to kick in for them as well as they had moved over to the couch and were giggling at the conversation.

"I just have a little bit at the top," Sarah explained as she stood up and pointed to the area on her pants. "I think they call it a landing strip," she spit out, falling back into the couch while laughing uncontrollably as Catherine grabbed her glass of wine so she wouldn't spill it.

Jan got up from the table and came over to sit in the chair beside Sarah. "You should consider going with a Chaplin," Jan explained to her. "It's like a landing strip but it runs side to side. That way nothing will poke out from your bikini or thong."

"Why do they call it a Chaplin?" asked Mary.

"It's named after Charlie Chaplin," Sandy volunteered, "you know, the actor. It looks like his mustache," she continued. She picked up her phone and googled an image of Charlie Chaplin to show Mary as the ladies continued to laugh.

Catherine composed herself and waited for Sarah to do the same before she passed her back her glass of wine.

"Okay, I'm going to tell you guys something, but you need to keep it inside this group only," Catherine whispered. "Once, as a surprise for Peter, I shaved a lightning bolt just above mine, instead of a landing strip." She burst out laughing as soon as it was out of her mouth and the rest of them joined her. They were laughing so hard that tears were running down their cheeks.

"Why on earth would you put a lightning bolt there?" Sarah asked

"It was the night we went to the last Harry Potter movie and I wanted to give Peter a surprise," she managed to squeak out as she continued to laugh. The rest of them all burst out laughing again as well. Unfortunately for Peter, he appeared in the doorway to the room as the women were still trying to compose themselves. When they got a look at Peter, they all started laughing again. Peter faintly smiled, shook his head, turned and left. He didn't want to know.

Jan was on a roll now. She was past the point of caring what anyone thought of her, and she was Catherine's sister in-law so she kept pushing. "Catherine, what kind of penis does Peter have?" The room went suddenly very quiet, sure they had all had a bit to drink and some had smoked a little weed, but this seemed like too personal of a question. Catherine was used to this sort of question from Jan, though.

"He has a *Shape Shifter*," Catherine said with a little smirk on her face.

"What's a *Shape Shifter*?" Sarah asked Catherine, almost scared to hear the answer.

"It starts small, but it grows big," she squealed and the group lost it again. Once they all had a chance to calm down, Jan continued the penis discussion.

"My husband has a *Leaner*. You know, a little crooked," she smiled. "But he knows how to 'lean' into it," she howled.

"How about you, Sheila? What's your old man packing downstairs?"

Sheila was fully playing along now. She had dropped the prude role and was feeling no pain from the wine. "He's got a *Hoodie*," she told them with a straight face, anticipating the next question and waiting for it.

"You got us," replied Jan "What's a *Hoodie*?"

"He's uncircumcised," Sheila smiled. "It makes the head super sensitive and I can drive him crazy."

"I've never slept with someone who's uncircumcised," added Sarah. "Have you Mary?"

"Yeah, a lot of guys are uncircumcised now," Mary told the group.

"What other kinds of penises are there, Jan?" Mary asked.

"Hmm, let's see." Jan pondered for a moment. "There's the *Tear Jerker*. I love them but I hate them. That's the one that's so big you're either going to cry from the pain, or cry because it won't fit. Then there's the *Number 2*. Super slim like the number two pencil," she laughed before she went on with the last two she could remember.

"There is the *Stubby* – just as it sounds, and then finally there is the *Channing Tatum*."

Mary waited a moment for Jan to explain the *Channing Tatum* and when she didn't offer one, she blurted out "What is the *Channing Tatum*?"

Jan waited for everyone to focus on her before she answered, "It is the perfect penis. Dreamy and gorgeous."

No one laughed. They all seemed to be focused on a mental picture of the perfect penis.

The rest of the night consisted of more penis talk, a discussion on who would be the three men on their hall pass list, and what the best vibrators were. Finally, at around 11pm Jan and Mary decided it was time to leave, and started putting on their jackets and heading for the door. Mary said her goodbyes and went out to start the car and warm it up. Jan was having trouble standing in the doorway but was still intent on passing along some last minute advice to Sarah.

"It's called a *Magic Wand*, you have to get one Sarah," Jan slurred into her ear. "It is rechargeable and plug 'n' play. You can even charge it through a USB, like on your computer or if you need to, in your car," she winked sloppily. "And it comes with plenty of attachments. You can really pimp your ride, if you know what I mean," Jan smiled.

"Alright, Jan, time to go," Catherine said as she stepped in between Sarah and Jan, and then guided her out the door down the sidewalk to Mary's car. After she was safely tucked into the passenger seat, Catherine closed the door and walked back into the house where Sarah was sitting at the counter with a glass of water.

"Well that was fun. I haven't laughed that hard in a long long time," Catherine sighed. "Do you think it was the joint?"

"It probably didn't hurt," Sarah replied.

IN A RELATIONSHIP
186

CHAPTER 26

The week was flying by for Jake. It was always crazy during the weeks leading up to Christmas. He didn't mind. Since it was just him and Mathew, he didn't worry too much about putting up Christmas lights and decorations. Hanging the Christmas lights was one of the things he dreaded the most about the holiday season. If you didn't put them up early enough you were stuck hanging them up in the cold. He preferred to leave them up all year long and never did agree with his ex-wife that they had to be taken down in the New Year like the Christmas tree. The two of them had been through some heated discussions on the subject but he always ended up giving in and taking them down.

Jake unlocked the car with his remote as he walked across the underground parkade. He started the car, turned on his seat warmer and adjusted the volume on the stereo as his Bluetooth kicked in. He backed out the parking stall and headed to the exit. Once he was clear of the parkade he hit a button on his iPhone, "Siri, phone Mathew's mobile." He waited three rings before he heard Mathew answer the phone.

"Hi, dad."

"Hey, kid. How was your day at school?"

"It was alright, same same."

"Didn't you learn anything new today?" Jake asked.

"No, not really." Mathew answered

Jake wasn't up for this conversation. It was the same conversation pretty much every single day, and he decided that he needed to stop asking Mathew how his day at school was.

"I'm going to stop on the way home and pick up some Christmas lights, so go ahead and heat up the leftover chicken."

"Yeah, ok. Can you bring home something for me to drink? Buy some snacks too – we have nothing to eat in the house."

"There's lots of food, you have to cook it, though," Jake laughed into the phone.

"That takes too much time. I need to study for my science test tomorrow."

"Alright, but eat that chicken before it goes bad. I'll be home in about an hour."

"Yeah, I'll heat it up. Love you, dad."

"Love you too," Jake smiled and then hit the end call button. He never got tired of hearing his son say those words.

The home improvement store was a nut house. The Christmas decoration aisle had been picked clean and Jake had been lucky to find a few strands of lights that matched the ones he had in the garage at home. Once he was home and inside the garage he unloaded the lights and put them on the bench along the side of the wall.

I'll put those up on Thursday, he thought, *Thanksgiving*. It was going to be a quiet Thanksgiving this year as it was Mathew's turn to spend it with his mother. He was going to be flying to Vancouver Thursday morning and then returning Sunday afternoon. Jake planned to not only get the Christmas lights up while Mathew was gone, but he also planned to get all his Christmas shopping done. Mathew was sitting at the kitchen table eating the chicken he had warmed up and playing on his laptop when Jake entered the room.

"Hi, Dad. Did you pick me up a drink and some snacks?" Mathew asked.

"Hi, buddy. Yes, I got you some snacks and a drink." Jake pulled out a bag of chips and a carton of orange juice.

"Sweet! Dill pickle chips, my fave!" Mathew smiled.

"Are you doing your homework?" Jake asked as he grabbed two glasses from the shelf and poured the two of them some orange juice.

"I studied for a bit already. I'll do some more before I go to bed. I'm playing online right now."

"Let me guess: *Rudy2*," Jake guessed with a teasing tone and a smile.

Mathew blushed and then got up and put his plate in the dishwasher. He packed up his laptop grabbed the chips and his juice and then headed for his room. Still not acknowledging who he was playing with, he thanked his dad again for the chips and juice and left. Jake chuckled to himself, and then opened up the fridge and stared into it for a couple of minutes before he took out everything he would need to make a sandwich. He had been hoping on the drive home that Mathew had decided not to heat up the leftover chicken so he could eat it. A sandwich would have to do.

Jake settled into the couch with his sandwich and juice and turned on the TV to watch the Daily Show that he had PVR'd from the previous evening. When his iPhone started to ring, he looked down and could see it was a face time call from Darryl. He thought about not taking it and calling Darryl back after he had finished his sandwich and watched the show, but picked it up at the last minute. Darryl's head appeared on the screen but he was turned sideways.

"Yes, I know. I have lunch with Kristen tomorrow at noon," Jake stated as enthusiastically as he could.

Darryl turned to look into the phone when he heard Jake's voice. "Hey, Kristen needs to change it to 1pm. Does that work for you? She has a meeting or something. I told her it would be fine." He was almost whispering, and as he finished speaking he turned his head to the side again as if he was looking for someone.

"That works better for me," Jake replied. "I have a meeting at 11:30 and it could run long. What's going on with you? Is there someone there?"

"No, no. Everything's good. Umm, just a long day. I'm a little tired, that's all."

IN A RELATIONSHIP

"Whatever. You seem nervous. Who's there? It's the naughty nurse isn't it?" Jake laughed.

Darryl cut the conversation short, "K, I gotta go. Tomorrow, 1pm at the little wine bar by the library. Have fun."

Darryl dropped the phone but it didn't turn off. It was just lying on the bed, and Jake could see a woman enter the room wearing a sexy white nurse's uniform. As she crawled onto the bed sliding up next to Darryl, she asked him who he was talking to. Darryl told her it was just some telemarketing company, but before he could finish answering she started kissing him and telling him that she needed to take his temperature. Jake thought briefly about watching Darryl and the naughty nurse for a while until he remembered he hadn't eaten yet. He looked at his phone, then at his sandwich, and made the decision to turn it off before he lost his appetite.

IN A RELATIONSHIP

CHAPTER 27

Sarah opened the door when she noticed Catherine walking up the sidewalk to the house. The two women hugged for a moment, and then Sarah began to explain why she needed Catherine to sit with Emma for a bit.

"Thanks for coming over, Catherine. I know this is last minute, but I didn't know what else to do. Normally, I would take Emma with me, but she isn't feeling that great. I took her temperature but it seems fine."

"Anytime. You know that, sweetie. Go on, get out of here. I'll make some tea and hang out with her until you're back," Catherine comforted Sarah as she pushed her to the door.

"Thanks again. I shouldn't be too long. Mrs. Weller has been preparing for this, but I thought it would be helpful if I could make the trip to the vet with her."

As Sarah put her boots on, Catherine took off her jacket off and hung it up. She sat down beside Sarah to take off her boots. "I don't get you, Sarah. I really don't. You can comfort strangers when they lose a pet, but you can't bring yourself to let Emma get a dog. I just don't get it, honey."

"I know you don't get it. Nobody does, but that doesn't mean it's not the right thing to do for Emma and I. I can't explain it. Anyways, it's not forever, one day she can get her own dog, just not yet. I'll be back as soon as I can." And with that she was up and out the door.

Catherine locked the door behind Sarah, took the kettle off the stove and filled it with water. She put it on the back burner, turned the element on and then walked down the hallway to check on Emma. As she approached the door she could hear Emma talking to someone, but could only hear her side of the conversation. She stood at the door for a minute, pushing it slightly ajar so she could listen in. She felt a little guilty about it, but just a little. She had learned a long time ago with Jessica and Ben that being a parent meant that sometimes you had to be a wee bit sneaky. It was how she found out that Ben didn't want to play football. He was playing to make her and Peter happy, but he hated it. She had overheard him talking to one of his buddies from school when he thought she was out. She and Peter had no idea that he hated playing, so they discussed it before taking Ben aside and asking him what he would like to do if he could play any sport he wanted. He had surprised them by telling them he didn't want to play any sport – he wanted to learn how to play the guitar. So, they traded in the soccer cleats for an acoustic guitar and now he was hanging out with his buddies after school every day, hoping to become the next Carlos Santana – minus the drugs, they hoped.

"Thanks, Mathew," Catherine heard Emma speak into the headset she was wearing. There were a few seconds of silence as Catherine assumed whomever she was on the phone with must be talking.

"I know, but I don't want to wait. I've been waiting for what seems like forever already."

At that moment the kettle started to whistle, and it startled both Emma and Catherine. In an effort to cover up her spying, Catherine pushed open the door and greeted Emma like she had just arrived.

"I'll be right back, I put on a pot of tea. Well, your mom did. That's why it's ready so quickly and I was not standing here listening to you." Catherine stammered. "Okay. I was. I was standing here listening, but I didn't really hear anything," she continued. "Okay, I might have heard a little. Who's Mathew?" she finally asked before turning and quickly walking back down the hallway to turn off the stove.

When she came back into Emma's bedroom, she was greeted by a perturbed young lady.

"Auntie Catherine, you shouldn't eavesdrop on people. It's rude." Emma scolded Catherine but couldn't keep in a smile.

"I'm sorry, sweetie. I know. I wasn't listening for very long. Would you like some peppermint tea? Your mom said you weren't feeling well."

"I'm fine. I told mom I wasn't feeling well because I didn't want to go to the vet with her. I know why she was going – they were putting Mrs. Wellen's dog to sleep."

"You're too smart, missy. You are so much like your dad," Catherine told her as she walked around the kitchen counter and hugged her. After a good long hug Catherine let Emma go.

"Let's take the tea, crawl into bed, and you can tell me all about what's on your Christmas list."

"You know what's on the top of my list – it's the same every year."

Catherine poured the hot water into the tea pot and then dropped in the peppermint tea bag. She put the lid on, and then turned to Emma.

"You want a puppy," she smiled.

"Not just a puppy, Auntie Catherine. I want a Golden Retriever puppy. I don't know why mom can't get over it. She's being selfish." Emma said the last line softly; as if she was scared her mom would hear her.

Emma expected her aunt to defend her mom, telling her how hard it was considering how Michael had died. Instead, Catherine looked at Emma intently. She could feel Emma's sadness. She poured tea into one of the two cups and placed it in front of Emma. She picked up the other cup and put it back on the shelf. She opened the next cupboard, took out a wine glass, carried it to the fridge and then filled it with wine from a half full bottle in the side of the door. She turned back to Emma and told her to bring her tea into the living room. Emma sat in one corner of the couch while Catherine set her glass town on the coffee table and then picked up the blanket that was draped over the back of the couch. She sat down next to Emma, pulled the blanket over them and then reached out for her wine. It was then that she realized that the blanket was a picture of golden retriever puppies. She looked at Emma, then at the blanket and then started to laugh. Emma laughed as well.

"Sweetie, I understand how you feel. Peter and I both think you're ready for your own puppy. Rex won't be happy at first, but he'll come around," she smiled. "It's hard for your mom. Sure, she can help council people through the loss of their pets, but it's not the same as seeing a puppy every day and having that constant reminder of what happened. You need to be patient for a little while longer. I can tell your mom is starting to move past everything."

"How can you tell?" asked Emma.

"Well, you know she has been on a few dates right?"

"How is that helping?"

"It's making her realize that she needs to move on with her life. She needs to experience what's out there and she needs to let you experience things too. I can see a change in her the last few weeks, but this isn't something you can hurry. You just have to believe that it's all going to work out," Catherine explained.

"Do you miss my dad a lot, Auntie?"

The question caught Catherine off guard. She took a big breath and paused. She let her thoughts drift off to when she and Michael were growing up. Not a day went by when she didn't think about him. They were as close as a brother and sister could be growing up. Michael always had her back, and had bailed her out of trouble more times than she had ever had to do the same for him. She remembered how happy he was the day he asked Sarah to marry him. He had sold his motorcycle to buy the ring, and had begged Catherine to come with him to pick it out. She didn't think he could ever have been happier but she was wrong. When Emma was born, Catherine had been with them in the delivery room all day and night waiting for the big arrival. Everything had gone perfectly, and when Michael held Emma in his arms for the very first time he smiled the biggest smile she had ever seen on his face and it never left. He worshiped Sarah and Emma.

"I miss him every day, sweetie. We all do. Do you know what the happiest day of his life was?"

"Was it the day he met my mom?"

"He was pretty happy that day. But that wasn't his happiest day. I know, because he told me. The happiest day of his life was the day he and your mother held you in their arms." She pulled Emma into her chest and ran her hand through her hair.

"Oh, sweetie. You and your mom are two of the strongest and bravest people I know. Don't give up on her."

"I won't Auntie but I think she'd be happier with a dog than a boyfriend" Emma offered with a smile as she looked up at her aunt.

Catherine smiled back at Emma, "your probably right sweetie, you are probably right."

IN A RELATIONSHIP

CHAPTER 28

"Are you excited for your date today?" Mary teased Sarah.

"Not really, Mary. I'll be glad when I'm done with this whole online dating thing. I mean, it's been interesting and good to get out I suppose, but I'm just not sure it's the way to go for me."

"Maybe you'll meet a Channing Tatum."

Sarah picked up her pen and was just about to throw it at Mary when her cell phone rang.

"Saved by the phone," Mary smiled and then turned and left Sarah's office. She closed the door behind her, leaving Sarah to take her call. Sarah picked up her phone and saw on the display that it was Catherine calling.

"Hi, Catherine."

"Hi, sweetie. I wanted to call and make sure you hadn't forgotten about your lunch date."

"I haven't forgotten, and Mary was just in asking me if I was excited. If you were wondering as well, the answer is no! I'm really looking forward to being done with these dates." Sarah lamented to Catherine.

"Don't be so negative. You never know, this could be your Prince Charming."

"Sure, it could Prince Charming, or it could be the Prince of Darkness. That's far more likely."

"Open mind now, girl. Don't go there already convinced it's going to be bad. I called to let you know that he said he would be wearing a green scarf," Catherine informed Sarah.

"Is he not that bright? I mean I have his picture and he has mine. We should be able to recognize each other."

"I think it's cute. He seems excited to meet you."

"I'm sure he is. I mean who wouldn't be? I need to go now, though. I don't want to be late for the big lunch date," Sarah replied with as much sarcasm as she could muster. "I'll call you later tonight and give you the low lights." She ended the call, grabbed her jacket and headed for the door.

Rather than driving to the restaurant for lunch, Sarah decided to take the bus. It was only ten minutes, and it would save her the hassle of trying to find a place to park. The bus stop was at the end of the same block as the restaurant, and as the bus drove by she spotted Andrew out front waiting for her. He was dressed nicely in what looked like a suit and overcoat, and in his hand was a single red rose. Sarah smiled as she took the steps down from the bus and started walking up the block to meet him.

Maybe this will be ok, she thought. It was a rather long walk up the block to meet Andrew, but the street was empty and he was the only man standing out front. He was looking back and forth between his watch and down the street in the direction Sarah was walking. She smiled as she approached, and extended her hand to greet him. He hadn't noticed her until she was standing right in front of him and then when he did, he looked startled.

"Oh. Hi, you must be Sarah," he said and then turned and walked directly into the restaurant ahead of her. Sarah grabbed the door before it slammed, and then scurried in front of him as the waiter led them to their table.

Not the most gentlemanly gesture, thought Sarah as she took off her jacket, placed it over the back of her chair before she sat down, and then pulled it in.

"This is for you," Andrew spoke as he handed the rose across the table to Sarah.

"Thank you. That is very sweet," Sarah replied. "I hope you weren't waiting too long. The bus took a little longer than I thought it would," she explained.

"A few minutes," Andrew replied rather coldly. Then he smiled at her and added, "but it was worth the wait."

Sarah felt relieved. Andrew's smile removed some of the tension and they began a casual conversation about the weather and Thanksgiving until they were interrupted by the waiter who arrived with bread plates, a basket of warm rolls and butter. Andrew pulled the cloth covering the bread rolls back, picked up two rolls to place them on top of a bread plate, and then pulled it in front of him. He proceeded to butter both rolls with a lavish amount of butter, using up every little bit that was in the bowl. He was well into his third mouthful of bun and butter before he looked up at Sarah and asked her if she wanted one. Sarah watched in agony and amazement as he spoke with a mouthful of food. She understood him, but was slow to answer as her attention had shifted to a piece of bun that had fallen out of his mouth when he spoke. Unphased, he picked up the piece that had escaped and put it back in his mouth, continuing to chew while he waited for her to reply.

"No thanks," Sarah finally answered, "I'll wait for the waiter to come and take our order." Sarah didn't feel like eating after having watched Andrew's bread eating display, and he wasn't done. He continued to eat the rest of the buns in the basket until there were none left. As he was scrapping the remaining butter from the bowl, he waved at the waiter to get his attention and come over and take their order.

"I'm so sorry," Andrew apologized to Sarah. "I'm eating away and you must be starving," he added as the waiter approached the table.

"Good afternoon, and welcome to the Grape Vine," he greeted them with a big smile. "Have you decided what you would like for lunch?" he asked politely looking at Sarah first.

Andrew interrupted before Sarah could reply, and with his mouth full of food asked, "Could you bring us another basket of buns and some more butter?"

What is with this guy, thought Sarah? *One minute he's rude and the next he is polite.*

"Of course, Sir. I will have another basket brought out right away. And ma'am, what would you like for lunch?" he repeated looking at Sarah with a look that said *your date is a dick.*

Sarah returned a strained smile of recognized embarrassment, and then ordered a garden salad with chicken breast and balsamic vinaigrette dressing.

"And how about you, sir. What can we bring you?" asked the waiter.

"I would like your chili, but I don't want a small bowl. Can you Super-size it?"

"I'm sorry, sir. We no longer serve the large bowl, and it's only available in the small bowl as a starter or side dish," the waiter explained.

Andrew didn't respond, he just sat in his chair staring at the waiter who stood at the side of the table and stared back. The silence was killing Sarah. She wasn't sure if Andrew didn't hear the waiter, or if he was so disappointed that they no longer served the large bowl that he had gone into shock. Either way, it was very awkward. She felt terrible for the waiter. Andrew was not only not talking or looking at the waiter, he was staring off into space not moving or blinking, overcome with grief that there was no large chili.

The waiter broke first. "Perhaps, sir, you would like to order two bowls?"

This seemed to snap Andrew out of his misery and he agreed to order two bowls, and also threw in a reminder to bring more buns. Andrew's chili arrived first – two small bowls and a fresh basket of warm buns. Sarah smiled and laughed nervously, praying that he wouldn't make any further issue out of the fact that they no longer served large chili bowls. He didn't seem phased. In fact, he asked Sarah if she minded if he started without her.

"Fine," she said, and then sat for the next few minutes and watched him eat his chili.

If it had been difficult and gross watching him eat his bun, watching him stuff spoonful after spoonful of chili into his mouth was a new low. It was like driving by an accident – you don't want to look but you can't help it. She wished she could video his devouring of the chili so she could play it back for Catherine. At one point, there was so much chili in his spoon that it spilled out onto his chin and then back into the bowl. He didn't even notice the food on his chin until Sarah got his attention and pointed to her chin and then to him. He stopped long enough to wipe it off, and then went right back at it. Sarah was beginning to think she had been spared carrying on a conversation while he ate, but no such luck.

Her food arrived shortly after his, and then he started telling her all about his encounters with famous people through his job. He was a promoter, and quite often would have A-list celebrities that he would entertain while they were in the city for a show. Sarah found the conversation interesting, but every time she looked up at him, she could see his mouth full of food as he spoke. She swore she would never have chili again.

She made it through and skipped his offer of dessert for more reasons than the excess calories. The thought of watching him talk with a mouthful of chocolate mousse almost made her vomit. She finished her coffee and offered to pay half the bill, but Andrew would have nothing of it. *A partial gentleman*, Sarah thought to herself.

As they walked out the door, she started to panic a little inside wondering how she was going to tell him that he wasn't her type, but she didn't have to worry. Andrew's phone rang as they were starting to say goodbye, and after a few seconds he mouthed the words, "I have to take this," and then turned and walked away. Sarah was relieved.

What the hell! This guy is full of himself, she thought to herself as she turned and walked the opposite way down the street towards the bus stop.

While she was waiting for the bus, she pulled up the back collar of her jacket and repositioned her scarf to stay warm from the wind and the light rain that had started to fall. It wasn't long before the bus pulled over to the curb and the passengers started to disembark. She stepped up onto the first step thinking everyone had gotten off, but there was one more straggler and she had to squeeze to the side to let him out. She recognized him as the man she had seen at Starbucks a few weeks back. He was on his phone and seemed to be in quite a hurry as he offered an "excuse me" and "sorry" as he made his way down the stairs and onto the sidewalk.

Sarah was able to find a seat along the side of the bus that faced the street and pulled her scarf down as she made herself comfortable. She took out her phone and checked to see if she had any messages. There was only one, and it was from Catherine. No doubt, she wanted the dirt on the lunch date. Sarah was about to reply when the bus stopped suddenly as a Black BMW pulled out and cut it off. The driver hit the horn, pulled out, and kept going as everyone on the bus took a good look at the BMW to see who the asshole was that almost caused an accident. As the car passed by, Sarah could see Andrew in the driver's seat talking on his phone, oblivious to anything else on the road. She shook her head and opened her phone message from Catherine. Sure enough, she was curious as to how the date had gone.

How was the date?
On a scale of 1 to 10, let's go with a 3
A 3? ☹ Sorry
Lol don't worry, this guy actually paid for lunch ☺
Well that's an improvement. I'll call you 2nite
Ok

Sarah put her phone back in her pocket and smiled to herself as she looked out the window at a couple walking down the street sharing an umbrella. It was raining a little harder now, and yet they didn't seem to mind the rain at all. The bus was waiting for the light to change and Sarah continued to watch the couple as they window shopped. They stopped in front of a pet store and she knew they were discussing getting one. Sarah sighed and pulled her jacket in a little tighter. She was grateful they lived on the west coast and didn't have to deal with a lot of snow. She liked snow, but only on Christmas Eve and Christmas day.

Christmas, she thought, *I need to get some shopping done soon.*

CHAPTER 29

As he stepped onto the bus, Jake knew he was cutting it close for his lunch date with Kristen. His 11:30 meeting had gone longer than expected, and he had decided to take the bus so he wouldn't have to look for parking space. It wasn't an easy thing to find a free spot over the lunch hour. As the bus slowed down in front of the restaurant, his cell phone rang. He looked down and saw it was Mathew calling so he answered it. It wasn't like Mathew to call during the day, so his first thought was that something was wrong.

"Hi, buddy. What's up? Everything alright?"

"Yeah, everything's good. Mom was just wondering what time my flight gets in tonight."

"Why doesn't she just call me, or ask me? I sent her a copy of your ticket for crying out loud. You get in at 8pm."

"OK, thanks. I'll text her back. Where are you?"

"I'm downtown meeting someone for lunch. It's a business meeting."

"Whatever. I heard you and Darryl the other night during the poker game," he laughed. "You're on date aren't you?"

"What else did you hear?"

"Lots," Mathew laughed. "I have to go now. I'll see you at home after school. Oh yeah, what time are we leaving for the airport? I haven't packed yet."

Jake walked down the aisle of the bus as it had come to a stop and all of the passengers had exited except for him. He continued talking to Mathew as he made his way to the top of the stairs and had to squeeze out of the way of new passengers who were getting on. A few of them gave him rude looks as he continued to talk on the phone while he made his way down the stairs. When he was finally onto the sidewalk he hung up his phone.

"Do you have a reservation?" asked the hostess.

"I'm meeting someone. She's probably already here," Jake replied as he looked past her and into the restaurant.

"Why don't you go on in and have a look around?" smiled the hostess.

"Thanks," Jake replied, and stepped past her to survey the restaurant.

At first he didn't spot her. The restaurant was full, but a lot of the diners were finishing up and on their way back to work. He was about to give up when he spotted her sitting at a little table towards the back of the restaurant. She saw him looking around, and was smiling and waving at him to get his attention. Jake waved back and made his way through the exiting dinners. As he approached, Kristen stood up and moved out from the table to greet him.

Jake was always unsure as to whether he should shake hands or give a hug – it was a date but it wasn't like they knew each other. He extended his hand as she was moving into hug, and then had to step back awkwardly and shake his hand.

"Hi, I'm Jake. It's nice to meet you."

"Hello, Jake, it's a pleasure to meet you as well. I'm Kristen," she smiled and then moved back to her chair. Jake quickly stepped in behind her and helped push her seat in.

"A gentleman," she grinned as Jake sat down into his chair. He smiled back and then looked around the restaurant again.

"Have you been here before?" he asked her.

"Yes, I've had a few dates here."

A few dates here? I'm not sure I would mention that right out of the gate on a new date, he thought to himself. "It's nice. How is the food?"

"The food is wonderful. You're going to love the fresh warm buns they bring out – quite delicious," she added.

At that precise moment, the waiter appeared with a basket of fresh buns, whipped butter and two plates with napkins. He filled up their water glasses, encouraged them to help themselves to a bun and stated he would be back shortly to take their drink order. Jake reached into the middle of the table, took a plate and passed it to Kristen before putting one in front of himself. Kristen reached into the breadbasket to grab a bun and then passed the basket to Jake.

As promised, the waiter returned, took their drink order, and explained the lunch specials. While they were waiting for their food to arrive they started making small talk about the weather and the upcoming Thanksgiving holiday. Jake's food arrived first, but he patiently waited for Kristen's to arrive before he started eating. As Jake started eating, Kristen leaned over the table and quietly asked how his experience with online dating had been so far.

Jake was uncomfortable divulging too much information to someone he had just met, and the date seemed to be going well so far. He told her he had been single for a few years and had just recently begun dating again after his divorce.

"Oh, come on. Don't be shy, we're adults. How many dates have you been on?" she quizzed him.

"I've only been on three."

"Only three? My, my, you are fresh meat," she laughed.

"How about you?" Jake smiled back. "How many dates have you been on?"

Jake soon regretted asking the question. Kristen went on for the next 45 minutes recounting every single date she had been on over the past year. It was in excess of thirty, and she knew every single date's name, age, occupation, how many dates she had gone on with each person (the list included men and women) and how good or bad they were at sex. She was a serial dater. Jake made a joke that she should write a book.

"I am," she said.

He nearly choked on his chocolate mousse. Normally, he passed on dessert, but she had insisted they share one. Of course, that was before he found out that she was the female version of Charlie Sheen.

When the waiter returned to the table, Jake asked for the bill and informed Kristen that he needed to get back to work. While waiting for the waiter to bring the cheque, Kristen passed her business card to Jake and told him to check out her website that was listed on the back of the card. Jake flipped it over and read the name of the site: *kristenscatchoftheday.com*.

"Do you have a business card?" she asked Jake.

Jake didn't want to give out his business card, so he offered his cell phone number instead. At this point, she didn't know his last name or where he worked and he wanted to keep it that way. *I can always block her number if she became a stalker,* he thought, *what harm could it do?*

The waiter returned and Jake paid the bill. Kristen offered to pay half, which he thought was a nice gesture, but he politely refused.

"Can I walk you to your car?" he asked as he stood up from his chair.

"No it's ok. I'm meeting someone here in a few minutes," she answered.

"Oh, a friend?"

"Yes, a friend," she smiled meekly like she had been busted by her dad.

Jake could feel the weirdness as well. She had obviously set up another date right after theirs.

She's a piece of work, he thought as he turned and made his way to the front door. He put on his jacket and stepped outside. He walked down the street to the bus stop and reflected on the lunch date.

How could someone go on that many dates in one year? How many people had she had sex with in the past year? How many women had she slept with over the past year? He started to think about whether she had slept with a man and a woman on the same night or at the same time. As he stood there deep in thought, it started to rain again. It was at that point he remembered that he had left his umbrella at the restaurant. His bus hadn't shown up yet, so he ran back down the street to the restaurant to find his umbrella was gone. *Shit,* he thought. That was the third umbrella this month he had left somewhere or lost. The hostess noticed him staring out into the street at the rain, and asked him if he needed an umbrella.

"I brought one with me, but it seems to have vanished," Jake complained to her.

"Happens all the time," she told him. "Hang on, I'll check our lost and found and see if we have another one." She returned a minute later with a bright yellow and black polka dot umbrella that reminded him of a bee. "This is the only one we have," she said sheepishly as she held it up for him to see.

Jake looked outside at the rain that was now coming down even harder than before. "Ok, I'll take it I guess," he whined as he reached out and took the umbrella from her. She smiled and he smiled back as he opened it and stepped into the rain, making his way back down the street to the bus stop. As he left, the hostess ran to the window and snapped pictures of him as he walked down the street with his bright yellow and black polka dot umbrella.

The waiter walked up behind the hostess who was now taking a video with her phone and asked, "How many people have you done that to now?"

She giggled and told him it was the first one today but the third this week.

"What do you do with the pictures?"

"I post them to Instagram and Facebook. Depending on how busy it is I sometimes video them and then post that to YouTube."

"You're sick. But you're funny," he laughed and then went back to work.

Jake got a few strange looks and had a few young guys make comments about his umbrella as he stood at the bus stop. Whatever he thought, it was better than getting wet. The bus pulled up and everyone took down their umbrellas to board the bus. Jake found a seat near the back and took out his phone to see if he had missed anything. He had a text from Darryl.

"Dude, what's the word"

"Slut," Jake texted back.

"What's that mean? She's a slut?

"You asked what's the word? Her word is Slut. I'll tell u more ltr. I have 2 get back 2 work."

"k, I have a date ☺ I'll call u 2nite"

CHAPTER 30

At least the rain has stopped, thought Jake as he dragged the box of Christmas lights out of the garage and onto the driveway. It was a beautiful fall day. Not only had the rain stopped overnight but the sun was shining and everyone was taking advantage of the great weather. He looked across the street and waved at his neighbor who must have woke up with the same idea. Jake took his phone out of his pocket to see if Darryl had sent a text. He was supposed to be over at 10am with his step ladder to lend a hand putting up the lights. He had just finished putting his phone back in the pocket of his hoodie when Darryl rounded the corner at the end of the street. He pulled into the front of the driveway leaving room for the two of them to get the ladder that was strapped to the roof of the Jeep. Darryl climbed out and removed his sun glasses from his face to place them on the top of his head.

"Thanks for helping, and bringing the ladder."

"No problem. Have you got many lights to put up?" Darryl asked.

"No, I picked up a few new strings last week. I gave most of my Christmas stuff away when we moved back."

"Good. The sooner we get these up, the sooner we can get working on your next date," Darryl smiled. As they pulled the ladder off the roof of Darryl's Jeep a woman jogged by with her dog. Darryl stopped mid job and stared at the woman as she continued down the block.

"What about her?" he asked looking back at Jake.

"She's married"

"But is she happily married?"

"I don't know. Why don't you go ask her?" Jake replied slightly annoyed.

"Whoa, I'm kidding. You're awfully grumpy today. Its Thanksgiving, dude. You should be more thankful that I'm helping you with not just the lights but your love life."

They continued with the ladder towards the side of the house where Jake put his end down. Darryl walked the other end up so it was leaning against the house. He pulled his phone out of his jacket, and after spending a few seconds bringing up a web page passed the phone to Jake.

"Have a look, you're famous," he smiled as Jake held up the phone. It was a video of Jake walking down the street in the rain with the yellow and black umbrella to the music of Blind Melon's *No Rain*.

"What the hell is this?" Jake asked

"It's from a YouTube channel called *Seattlelovestherain*. Nice umbrella."

"Thanks. Someone took mine and that was the only one they had left. Whatever, I'm glad I could provide some entertainment," Jake grumbled and grabbed a string of lights and started up the ladder.

"It's had over 100,000 views, dude! You're famous! I think we should add this to your dating profile."

"Are you kidding me? Don't you dare!"

"Come on, it's funny, and let's face it, every little bit helps."

"No. I mean it Darryl. Not a bloody chance okay?"

"Alright, you're the boss."

The two spent the next hour putting up the red and blue lights along the front of the house. When they were finished, they secured the ladder back onto the roof of the jeep and put the boxes away in the garage. The sun may have been out, but it was still cool so Jake put a pot of coffee on and offered to make some soup while Darryl pulled out his laptop and set it up on the kitchen table.

"What kind of soup do you have?" Darryl asked.

"Tomato or cream of broccoli?"

"Cream of broccoli? Who has cream of broccoli?"

"It's good. Don't be so negative. Do you want to try some?"

"No thanks. Tomato sounds good. What do you have for sandwiches?"

"Look, this isn't a restaurant. You'll get what you get and you'll be thankful. It's Thanksgiving, right?" Jake lectured Darryl and then smiled and added, "How does grilled cheese sound?"

"That sounds perfect. Why don't I make the sandwiches while you have a look through your matches and see if any of them jump out at you?"

"Before we do that, check out this web site that the last date told me about. What was her name? Kristen? Yeah, Kristen gave me this card. Check out the website on the back," Jake told him as he threw the card at Darryl.

Darryl picked up the card, looked at the website domain on the back and then entered *kristenscatchoftheday* into his search engine.

"Is this a restaurant or something?"

"I don't know When I was leaving she told me to check it out."

Darryl's eyes opened a little wider as the site came up on his laptop. He looked at Jake and smiled as he stood up to take over making the sandwiches.

"You need to look at this. I can see why you called her a slut."

Kristen had created a website that had a running list of all the people she had met and dated over the past year on the dating site. Names, ages, where they went on the date, who paid, what they ate, if they had a second date, if they were still dating.

"Oh my god. She was serious about the amount of dates she's been on. I thought maybe she was joking."

Darryl had moved back over to the laptop, and was scrolling down the list of names until he came across Jake's.

"Look, there's your name. Well, at least you paid for lunch. Good thing," he chuckled.

"Shit, it says we're dating. What the hell? It was one date and we are not going out again. I need to get that changed."

"Don't worry about it, she's just a little delusional and no one you know is going to see this. Has she called you or sent you any messages?"

"She sent me a text last night but I didn't respond."

"Don't, just block her number and she'll go away."

"She better, the last thing I need is some crazy woman stalking me. You never gave her my address or told her where I work did you?" Jake asked nervously.

"No – I never do that, not even for my dates. No one needs crazy knocking on the door."

As he was talking the smoke detector went off. "Shit, I forgot about the grilled cheese," shouted Darryl as he ran over to the stove and picked up the smoking frying pan amidst the beeping from the smoke alarm. Jake opened the door to clear the smoke and reset the alarm.

Darryl held up the sandwich with one side completely black. "Shit, well, we can scrape the burnt part off."

"No we're not. Throw it out and turn the fan on. It smells like burnt toast and that just makes me think I'm having a stroke," Jake laughed as he got up and took more cheese out of the fridge.

"You make them, then. I'm obviously better at the laptop than the stove." Jake took over the sandwich making and Darryl went back to scouring through his matches.

"Here's what we're going to do – I'm going to read you a name and a little from their profile, and you are going to say yay or nay. No picture for you, just go with the profile. What do you think?" he laughed.

"Sure, I mean can it get any worse? Seriously?"

"Ok. First up, we have *Ravenmoon* – 39, divorced, kids are grown and do not live at home, athletic and toned, makes between 50 and 75k, hardly ever drinks, likes art, positive energy, yoga and does not own a TV."

"That's a no"

"Aren't you Mr. Picky? Here's number two. *Tallblondie65* – she's 41, no kids, social drinker, full figured, smoker--"

Jake stopped Darryl before he could continue.

"Why do they send me matches that say smoker? I'm sure they're super nice, but we ticked off *non-smoker*, not *trying to quit or sometimes*."

"I don't know, I'll skip those ones. Here's number three. *Tweetybird42* – she's 43, never married, no kids, wants kids--"

"Again, why do they send me matches with women who want kids? We were clear when we filled the stupid profile out that we do not want to have any more kids! If they already have kids, fine. What the hell?"

Darryl smiled, "I think the sandwiches are ready. You bring those over and I'll keep moving through these. Number 4. *Milunyang* – 40, never married, does not want children. Looking better right? 5'

1", curvy, never smokes, never drinks, never works out. Speaks Chinese and a little English and is looking for someone between 35 and 75."

"Are you serious? I'm going to date someone who doesn't speak English, can't see over the dashboard to drive, and is looking for someone between 35 and 75? I don't think so. Move over and eat your sandwich. I'll handle this."

Jake adjusted the screen so he could see better, and started scrolling through the matches. "Where do they come up with these names? Listen to these. *Snugglebug*. If you're going to post a name like *Snugglebug*, you need to post a picture that shows you're someone who a guy would want to snuggle with, right? Look at her picture – she's holding a deer she shot. I'd sleep with one eye open if I was with her.

"How about this one? *ucanthide*. What does that mean, *ucanthide*? Does that mean she's a stalker?

"Listen to this one, *worththewait*. First off, with this picture she has, it actually looks like she's been waiting forever.

"But it gets better. *This* is the woman I have been waiting for? 43, divorced, 5 kids that live at home, smokes (well trying to quit), drinks daily, never exercises, has cats and is self-employed. What is she self-employed at? Yes, I have been waiting my whole life for her."

Darryl laughed so hard the tomato soup sprayed out of his mouth and all over the kitchen table. "Hey, there's someone for everyone! Don't be so mean!"

"I don't mean to be. I'm sure they are all nice in their own way. I'm just trying to figure out why they ask all of those questions when you sign up if they don't use that information to send you matches you have something in common with? It's stupid," Jake added as he continued to go through the matches.

"Hold on a second, here's one I like. At least her picture is intriguing. *TinaTina11* - 38, never married, no kids, non-smoker, social drinker, and exercises five times a week, loves dogs, cats and horses. This one may have potential."

Darryl put his bowl in the sink and wiped the counter where he had sprayed his soup. "Let me see," he asked as he pulled the screen over. "You might be right. I think *TinaTina11* has potential. Her pictures look good, nice body, good teeth. Look at this picture of her with some of the Seahawks. Obviously a football fan as well. If you don't date her I will," he smiled as he clicked on her pictures and enlarged them on the screen.

"Fuck off. Don't you dare! After the last few dates you picked, I'm due for a good one. The law of averages has got to start balancing out for me."

"Don't get your panties in a knot – I'm just kidding. I'll send her a message for you later and see if I can set up a date for next weekend. I have to go, I'm going to drop by and see my kids before they have turkey dinner. You're still coming over to watch the late football game, right?"

"You bet. I've got a few more things to do around the house and then I'll come over. Are you cooking a turkey?"

"Damn right. It's in the oven cooking as we speak. All the trimmings as well so bring an appetite."

IN A RELATIONSHIP
228

CHAPTER 31

Emma was standing at the door, ready to go. She loved Thanksgiving. Truth be told, she loved all holidays. Any chance to get together with family made her feel good. Every Thanksgiving that she could remember they spent at Aunt Catherine and Uncle Peter's. It was a tradition that she never wanted to end. Even when she grew up and had her own family she was going to come to Aunt Catherine's.

"Mom!" she yelled down the hallway. "Let's go."

"Hold your horses, I'm coming. Can you grab the bottle of wine from the fridge and the cupcakes we made last night?"

"Why are we bringing the cupcakes? Auntie Catherine will have lots of desserts."

"You always have to bring something when you're invited for dinner. It is the polite thing to do," Sarah instructed as she walked to the door.

"We always bring the same thing, though. Can we bring something for Rex?"

"Sure, give him one of your cupcakes," Sarah joked as she sat on the bench beside Emma and put her boots on.

"Rex can't eat cupcakes, mom. He'll get diarrhea and also they have chocolate in them and you know chocolate is bad for dogs."

"I was kidding, silly. Of course he can't. Go look in the cupboard in the garage. I think we have some treats left from last time we dog sat Rex for Catherine."

"Oh yeah, I forgot about those. Good idea mom," exclaimed Emma as she bounced up off the bench, gave Sarah the bottle of wine and cupcakes and darted into the garage to get the dog treats. Sarah finished putting on her boots and jacket, and then grabbed one of their shopping bags from under the bench to put everything in for the walk over to Catherine and Peter's. When Emma returned from the garage, she put the dog treats for Rex in the bag and then offered to carry it for her mother. It was a beautiful afternoon and the two enjoyed the walk, with Emma skipping every now and then. As they rounded the corner onto the final block they almost ran headlong into a couple out walking their puppy. It was a chocolate lab and Emma had to stop and ask if she could pet it. As she bent down, the puppy jumped up at the same time and the momentum carried the two of them over onto the sidewalk. Emma was laughing and the puppy was busy licking her face as the puppy's owners started to apologize and pull back on the leash.

"It's ok. He's not hurting me. He's just giving me puppy kisses," Emma giggled between licks to her face.

"How old is he?" Sarah asked.

"He's three months old," the woman answered. "His name is Theo."

Sarah bent down beside Emma and Theo, and gave the puppy a scratch behind the ears. "He's gorgeous. If you ever need a dog walker or dog sitter, Emma is your girl. I'm Sarah, by the way," she added as she held out her hand to the woman who shook it and introduced herself as Anne and her husband William. William shook Sarah's hand as well, and then introduced himself to Emma.

"You can call me Will, and we may take you up on that one day, Emma."

"We live in the little blue and white house on Oceanview Drive," Emma told them. "And you can call me anytime to dog sit. I'm very good at it, right mom?"

"Yes, she is very good at dog sitting and pretty much anything to do with animals," Sarah echoed.

"We'll keep that in mind," Anne smiled as she pulled Theo away so they could continue on their walk. "Happy Thanksgiving."

"Happy Thanksgiving to you as well," Sarah returned the sentiment and smiled back. "Alright, Emma the dog sitter, let's get going. We don't want to be late."

Emma looked up at her mom as they walked the last block to Catherine's. "Theo was so cute mom. See? You were good with him. You gave him a pet and everything. I think you're ready, mom."

Sarah smiled back at her. *It had been ok,* she thought to herself. *Maybe it is time.*

When they reached the gate to Catherine's, Ben was outside playing with Rex and they both came to greet them. Ben held Rex down so that the two new arrivals could get through the gate. Rex, of course, could smell the treats and cupcakes in the bag and was busy trying to get his nose into it. Sarah held it up little higher, but Rex wasn't fazed as he stood up on his hind legs and continued to sniff the bag.

"Looks like Rex likes whatever you brought in the bag, Aunt Sarah" Ben laughed.

"He recognizes the smell of the treats Emma put in there. He's had those before. Emma, maybe you should give him one now?"

"Sure. I don't think we'll ruin his Thanksgiving dinner. Is it ok if I give him one, Ben?" she giggled as she reached in and took one out. "Sit, Rex."

He sat patiently and waited for Emma to give him the treat. She held it out in the palm of her hand. He gently took it and then ran into the back yard as Ben and Emma chased after him. Sarah watched Emma and Ben chase Rex around the backyard for a few minutes and then let herself in the front door.

The house was warm and filled with the smell of turkey. Catherine and Peter hadn't heard her come in so she took off her boots and jacket, hung them up in the hallway closet and then wandered down to the kitchen with her bag full of wine and cupcakes. As she walked down the hallway she could hear Michael Buble playing in the kitchen. She quietly turned the corner to see Peter and Catherine dancing. It was so cute – it was like they were in their own little world oblivious to anyone and anything else. Sarah didn't want to disturb the moment so she just stayed partially hidden around the corner and let them continue. She would have let them dance forever but just as the song was ending, Jessica came in from the other side of the kitchen.

"What are you doing?" she asked with a disgusted look that only a teenage daughter can give her parents.

"We're dancing, what does it look like?" Catherine explained. Then she pushed Peter away and bent over at the waist and attempted to twerk. "You like that better?" she smiled at Jessica.

"OMG, mom! That is the funniest thing ever! Don't stop, I want to video this for YouTube."

"Sure, film away, Jess," Catherine laughed. She noticed Sarah standing in the other doorway and waved her to come join in, "Come on Sarah! Let's show the kids how to do this."

"I think you got it handled all on your own, Catherine. Peter, you should join her."

"Not a chance. I don't even know what twerking is, and I think I'm going to keep it that way," he laughed.

"Whatever. You guys are just jealous. I'm done though. Jess, can you help your dad with setting the table? Sarah and I have some catching up to do, don't we, sweetie?" Catherine took a second to catch her breath before refilling her wine glass and then filling a second for Sarah. The two women left Peter and Jessica to set the table and headed up the stairs to Catherine's room.

"So tell me all about Andrew. I can't believe you said he was only a 3."

"Andrew. Right, the chewer."

"The chewer?"

"He ate a basket – no, make that two baskets – of buns. I had the pleasure of watching him eat those while he carried on a conversation."

"That is so gross. I can't believe it."

"Oh, believe it, alright. On top of that, he also ordered two bowls of chili because one wasn't enough, and then he proceeded to eat both bowls while he tried to carry on a conversation. Have you ever looked into someone's mouth while they were eating chili? It reminded me of changing Emma's diapers."

"Enough! Stop! I don't need to hear anymore! I am so sorry you had to go through that. What is wrong with people?"

"I know. It's rough out there, Catherine. Don't make me go back out," she begged sarcastically. "Oh, I almost forgot. Remember that fellow I told you about that I saw a few weeks back at Starbucks? I saw him again. He was getting off the bus when I was getting on."

"Did you talk to him?"

"I couldn't, he was the last one off and he was talking on his phone as he left the bus. I don't think he even noticed me. He probably talks with his mouth full or has bad gas anyways," Sarah laughed as she took a sip of her wine.

"Come on, there are some good ones out there, you just have to kick a lot of tires. Here, you sit and go through your matches, and I'll run down and check on Jess and Peter, plus grab the wine. You pick this one, and then I'll work on setting up a date."

Sarah moved onto Catherine's chair and started searching through the matches. *There has to be someone on here that's normal,* thought Sarah. After several minutes of looking through profiles, she still hadn't found anyone she was interested in. Catherine returned with a full glass in one hand and a half full bottle in the other hand, and informed Sarah that dinner would be ready in about twenty minutes.

"I can't find anyone interesting on here. They all look or sound the same," Sarah relayed to Catherine without looking up from the computer screen. "What is with the shirtless selfies in the bathroom? Do they not look at the pictures before they post them? Look at this guy, he takes a selfie, no shirt, but doesn't realize his laundry is in the background. Look, his underwear is lying on the ground!"

"I know. It's so funny, and a little bit sad. Here, fill up your glass and I'll read you a few and you pick one. We'll eliminate the pictures from your decision making and maybe that will help." Catherine got comfortable, reset the search parameters and then hit *Go Search*.

"Here's number one, are you ready?"

"No, but let's do it anyways."

"First up is *Toyguy*."

"Next" Sarah interrupted.

"What do you mean, next? I haven't even read you his profile."

"*Toyguy*? I don't need to hear anymore" Sarah laughed.

"Humor me ok? He's 38..."

"Too young," Sarah cut Catherine off again.

"Look, missy, let me at least read you their profile before you nix them," Catherine scolded and then continued. "*Toyguy* is 38, non-smoker, average body, animal lover and he loves to go off-roading in his truck."

"I have to see the pics. You might have been able to talk me into this whole personality only shit on the first date, but now that I've had a few, no way. Bring them up," Sarah demanded.

"He has 5 pictures. Let's see, his dog is in three of them, he has a hat on in 4 of them and one is a picture of him with no shirt standing in front of his truck."

"Aww, that is so sweet – he loves his dog and his truck," Sarah howled. "Why does he not have any pictures without his hat on?"

"He's probably bald."

"So what? Be proud of it. I don't mind bald guys – it's better than a comb over like Donald Trump. Now that is unattractive. He's a *no* though, regardless. Next."

"Oh my god," Catherine laughed. "You'll love this guy. *Fishbonker* – he's 42 so a little bit older than the last one, he is a nonsmoker, athletic, no pets, unfortunately, and he's not divorced – only separated, so there could be some drama there. He's has four pictures, so let's have a look at those. Humm, it appears he does not own any shirts."

Sarah and Catherine both laughed. *Fishbonker* had four pictures; he was shirtless in all four and wore sunglasses in all four. "He does have a nice body. I wonder if he has eyes. Maybe he's an alien and that's why he refuses to take off his sunglasses. The light from the sun is just too bright" Sarah wondered out loud.

"Next!" Catherine added as she clicked on the next profile tab. "Here's one for you, *69ismyfavorite*."

"Is that really his profile name? Why would you do that? I mean what kind of woman is going to respond to someone whose profile name is *69ismyfavorite*?"

"It takes all kinds, sweetie. Let's see what he's all about. He's 48, nonsmoker, no pets, it says he's single but it doesn't say whether he's divorced or separated, but bonus points because he's 420 friendly." Again the two women burst out laughing.

"Well, with a name like *69ismyfavorite* I have to see the pictures," Sarah added as she wiped the tears from her eyes. *69ismyfavorite* had long hair in a ponytail, full beard, dark sunglasses and every picture was a selfie taken from inside what looked like an old camper van. The two burst out laughing again.

"Can we just stop now?" Sarah asked as she got up and went into the bathroom to get some toilet paper for both herself and Catherine to wipe away the tears.

As Sarah re-entered the bedroom, Catherine turned to her with a smile, took the toilet paper and told her she found a good one. "Look at this guy," she invited Sarah. "He's 45, divorced, no kids but loves them, has a dog and an average body. He is an entrepreneur/business owner who has lots of free time, and is looking for someone to enjoy the journey with. He would like to meet a positive outgoing girl with a sense of humor. Look at his pics – no hat, no sunglasses, he is wearing shirts. I think you should go on your next date with him."

"What's his profile name?"

"*Bigdavid29.*"

"Well, that could mean a couple of things," Sarah laughed. "Let me see," she asked and clicked on the pictures making them larger. "Alright, whatever. It could be a lot worse I suppose," she sighed. At that moment Emma came into the room to let them know that dinner was ready.

"Perfect timing, Emma" Catherine stated as she got up from the chair and picked up the empty bottle of wine from the desk and headed for the door.

"I'm going to use the washroom and then I'll be right down," Sarah told Catherine as Emma sat down beside her.

"Were you helping Uncle Peter and Jessica?"

"A little bit – they had everything pretty much under control. What are you doing on the computer?"

"Your aunt and I were looking at some of my matches from the dating site."

Emma smiled at her mom. "Did you find anyone nice?"

"Maybe. You never know. I'll be glad when this online dating experiment is over. I think I would prefer to find a date the old fashioned way."

"Like how you met dad?"

Sarah laughed and then turned serious as she remembered that first time she had met Michael. "Sort of, although I don't think I want to go back to University."

"Maybe you could take some night classes, mom? You could learn something new and meet some new people at the same time."

Sarah pulled Emma close and kissed the top of her forehead. "That is a great idea, kiddo. When this online dating thing is done, I might just do that. Let's wash up and go eat. I am so hungry I could eat a horse."

"Why do people say that?"

"Say what?"

"Say they are so hungry they could eat a horse? People shouldn't eat horses or any animals. I know they do in some countries but they shouldn't be allowed."

"Let's not start that conversation today, Emma. Let's enjoy Aunt Catherine's turkey and be thankful we have a delicious meal and amazing family to share it with. Now go wash up." Emma set her phone on the desk and went into the washroom to wash her hands. While Emma was gone, her phone pinged to indicate a new message so Sarah picked it up. There was a Happy Thanksgiving message with an emoji of a turkey from *Seahawk17*. Sarah started to put the phone back down when a second message came across the screen.

Hope u get your new puppy soon ☺

What is she up to? Sarah thought to herself as she put the phone down on the desk.

When Emma came out of the bathroom, Sarah told her that she had a message. Emma picked up her phone and read the two messages from *Seahawk17*. As she was replying, Sarah asked her what the new puppy message was all about. Emma, not wanting to get into the puppy issue again with her mother – especially with everyone waiting downstairs at the table – scrambled to think of a good answer.

"Oh, that's nothing, mom. Just a friend. He knows I really want a puppy," she told her mom. It wasn't a lie but it wasn't the whole truth. She could live with it.

"One day, princess. One day. Now let's go eat. I could eat a turkey." She laughed.

CHAPTER 32

When the grey sky and winter rain became a regular daily occurrence it meant time to start looking for sunny vacation destinations. Jake always felt closed in when sunny fall days were replaced with winter rain storms. It had been an entire week of the same thing, day after day. Along with the dreary weather, it felt like every single person he worked with had watched the video of him hurrying down the street with the yellow and black polka dot umbrella. It had been a week from hell. Jake had been so busy at work that he hadn't been able to spend a lot of time with Mathew since he had returned from spending Thanksgiving weekend with his mother.

"Hey, dad, can we go and do a little Christmas shopping this weekend? I need to buy a couple of things."

Jake turned away from the window he had been staring at the city skyline through, dreaming of sunshine and beaches. "Sure, who do you need to buy presents for?"

"Mom, of course. Plus I want to buy something for grandma, and you, and a friend."

Jake smiled to himself and sat down at his desk. "Who's the friend?"

"No one, just a friend."

"Whatever. Is this friend a girl?" he teased.

"Forget it. I don't need to if you're going to ask a million questions," he muttered and left the room.

"Hey, come back. I was just kidding. Of course we can go. I need to pick up a few things too. Let's plan for Saturday." He hollered after Mathew who was long gone from the room. Jake's attention shifted to his phone sitting on the desk as it was flashing a new message from Darryl.

Have a fun night tonight with Tina ☺

Right. Fun. Like the last 4 dates.

Don't b so negative. This could be the one

Where is this place I'm supposed to meet her?

The Comedy shop. Its downtown near the space needle. We went there once remember?

Oh yeah. 7pm right?

Yeah, the show is at 8, meet her in the lounge at 7 for drinks

Got it

She seems nice, keep an open mind. I'll call you later

Jake decided to take a cab rather than the bus downtown to meet Tina so he could leave the house later and wouldn't be as rushed. He stripped off his clothes, stepped into the bathroom and turned the shower on. While he waited for the water to heat up he linked his iPhone to the blue tooth speaker, cranked up the Foo Fighters, shaved and then hopped in the hot shower. When he stepped out of the shower, the bathroom had become a steam room. He dried off, put on some deodorant and then walked out into his bedroom to get dressed for his date. He did a double take as he left the bathroom when he spotted Mathew sitting at his desk on his laptop.

"Whoa, dude, what are you doing in here?" he asked as he quickly scrambled to cover himself up with a t-shirt he picked up off the floor. He ran back into the bathroom, grabbed a bath towel to wrap around his waist and then went back into the bedroom.

"My computer is going to be a while downloading new software, so I thought I'd use yours."

"Right. Well why don't you take it to your room? I need to get dressed."

"Big date tonight?" Mathew asked with a slight smile as he packed up the computer and power cord.

"I wouldn't say big, but yes, I have a date tonight. Number 5."

"Maybe you should take an extra pair of pants, dad, you never know," he laughed as he left the room.

Jake walked to the bedroom doorway and shouted down the hall at Mathew, "It could happen to anyone!" He closed and locked the door, and went to his closet to pick out some clothes for his date with Tina.

The cab ride was uneventful, allowing Jake to arrive at the Comedy Club a few minutes early. Normally the traffic on a rainy

Friday night would have been hectic so he had purposely left early, and now found himself with some time to kill. He went into the club and made his way to the lounge where a few other couples were sitting having a drink before the show.

There was an empty table at the back that allowed him to sit and watch people enter. He was confident that he would recognize Tina. She had long brown curly hair, big brown eyes and from her profile pictures she looked extremely attractive. He was surprised that she had agreed to meet him – he typically stayed away from girls that were this good looking. Darryl didn't share his surprise – he had been telling Jake that he was a great catch and not to be intimidated by attractive women.

"You have lots going for you dude," were his exact words. "You have a great career, you're in good shape, and considering your age you look pretty good."

He was right, Jake thought, and compared to some of the guys they had looked at online he was a damn good catch he told himself.

"I'll have a vodka soda tall and a shot of tequila please." He may be all those things Darryl had said, but a little liquid courage wouldn't hurt.

Jake managed to throw back two shots of tequila before Tina arrived, and was nursing his vodka soda when he spotted her walking in along the side of the lounge. There was a half wall separating the lounge from the lobby entrance so he could only see her from her neck up. She spotted him as well, and waved across the lounge. Jake smiled and stood up to help her into her seat.

She's more mesmerizing than she had been in the pictures, he thought as she floated around the corner and walked over to his table. Jake moved around to her side and offered to help her with her jacket. She turned her back to him so he could slide the jacket off her shoulders, and then she stepped forward to free her arms and turned around. Jake's smile turned to a look of shock as he took in her full view. She was either pregnant or had a stomach tumor the size of a basketball. He just stood there, holding her jacket and staring at her stomach. Tina was first to break the awkward silence.

"I mentioned I was 8 months pregnant, didn't I?" she laughed as she took her jacket from Jake's hands and hung it up on the coat rack against the wall beside their table.

"No, I don't think you did. In fact I'm positive you didn't," he stammered, but then thought maybe she did in her messaging with Darryl thinking that it was him.

"Oh. Well, I am," She smiled and then asked with a little girl pout, "Is that going to be an issue?"

Jake had recovered from the initial surprise, and rather than be rude decided to at least sit down and spend a little time with her. After all, maybe she had told Darryl. He would deal with him later. They spent the next 45 minutes having a great conversation about Seattle, the rain and sunny destinations. Eventually the subject of past relationships came up and she confessed that she used to date a football player from the Seattle Seahawks. It hadn't been a long relationship, but they did date for a few months. Jake mentioned that he was a big Seahawks fan and asked who it was.

"Oh, I have a picture. Do you want to see?" she asked as she pulled out her phone. She took a few minutes scrolling through her pictures until she found the one she was looking for. "Here it is. We took this at Pike's Market," she explained as she passed her phone over.

Jake's eyes went wide for the second time that evening when he looked at the picture of her kissing Marshawn Lynch, the star running back for the Seattle Seahawks.

"You dated Marshawn Lynch?" Jake asked in complete disbelief.

"For a few months. I met him when I was a cheerleader a few years ago. He's super nice. This isn't his baby, though, in case you were wondering. We broke up a while ago. I wish he was the father, and not the deadbeat who knocked me up. It's almost eight – we should go get a seat for the show. I'm so glad we came tonight. I love this comedian – he's one of my favorites."

Jake was still coming to terms with the fact that Tina had dated Marshawn Lynch for several months and that she was a former Seattle Seahawk cheerleader. In his mind he was thinking she most likely slept with Marshawn Lynch and God knows how many other football players. What the hell was she doing out on a date with him?

"Do you still want to go to the show?" she asked, snapping Jake back to reality.

"Yeah, sure, why not? I mean, we're here, we have the tickets, let's do it."

Jake paid the tab and escorted Tina into the venue. The show was close to starting as they were ushered down the stairs to their seats. Their table was at the very front and in the middle so they had to walk by everyone in order to get to their seats. It was a little difficult for Tina and her baby belly to squeeze through, but it also meant everyone was super polite. *Who's going to give a beautiful pregnant woman a hard time?* thought Jake.

Once they were seated, the waitress came and kneeled by the table to ask them if they wanted anything to drink before the show started. Tina asked for water, and Jake ordered a double vodka soda along with another shot of tequila. *What the hell,* he thought; *I might as well enjoy this.*

The enjoyment was to be short lived.

The lights dimmed and the house announcer's voice boomed over the PA introducing the featured comedian. He came onto the stage and started his routine, talking about his childhood growing up in Jamaica. Everything was going smoothly. Jake was enjoying the comedian and his drinks, as were Tina and the rest of the audience. About 15 minutes into his routine the comedian started making penis jokes.

"This fellow was so deeply in love that just before he was married, he had his bride's name tattooed on his love muscle. Normally, only the first and last letters were visible, although when he was aroused, the tattoo spelled out W-E-N-D-Y. Now they're on their honeymoon at a resort in Montego Bay. One night, in the men's room, this fellow finds himself standing next to a tall Jamaican at the urinal. To his amazement, he notices that this man, too, has the letters W-Y tattooed on his penis. 'Excuse me,' he says, 'but I couldn't help noticing your tattoo. Do you have a girlfriend named Wendy?'

"'No way, mon, I work for the Tourist Board. Mine reads, *Welcome to Jamaica, mon. Have a nice day.*'"

Tina started to laugh so hard she was snorting. This not only got the attention of everyone at the show – who were now laughing at the joke and at Tina – but it also garnered the attention of the comedian who decided he would come and stand in front of Jake and Tina's table.

He looked at Tina and asked where she was from. After she told him she was from Seattle, he asked her when she was due. She told him she was expecting a New Year's baby. He asked her if she had ever seen a Jamaican newborn. When she told him she hadn't, he went into a story about a proud Jamaican father that he knew.

"A Jamaican man bought a round of drinks for everyone in the bar, announcing that his wife had just given birth to 'a typical Jamaican baby boy weighing 20 pounds.' Congratulations showered him from all around, and many exclamations of 'Wow!' were heard. A woman fainted due to sympathy pains.

"Two weeks later, he returned to the bar. The bartender said, 'Say, you're the father of the Jamaican baby who weighed 20 pounds at birth. How much does he weigh now?'

"The proud father answered, 'Fifteen pounds.'

"The bartender was puzzled. 'Why? What happened? He weighed 20 pounds at birth?'

The Jamaican father took a slow sip from his beer, wiped his lips on his shirt sleeve, leaned into the bartender and said, 'Had him circumcised.'"

The crowd erupted in laughter, led by Tina who once again went into snorting fits that only encouraged the audience and the comedian. Jake was trying to be as invisible as he could, praying that the comedian would not switch his focus to him, but it was all for not. He asked Jake where he was from and what he did for a living. After several sales jokes he moved even closer to their table and thanked them for being good sports.

"Just one last thing before I get back to the rest of the show," he told the crowd. Then he leaned into Jake with the microphone and asked, "What do you call a woman who loves small dicks?"

Jake shrugged his shoulders and then replied into the mic, "I don't know. What do you call a woman who likes small dicks?"

"Your girlfriend," he answered. The place lost it, as did Tina. Jake sunk as low into his chair as he could, picked up his double vodka and soda and downed the rest. The remainder of the show went by in a blur, and eventually Jake forgot about the humiliation that had been had at his expense.

He and Tina waited for everyone to leave before they left their seats and slowly walked up the stairs and out the front door. The rain had let up but it was still a little chilly out. He thought about offering to share a cab with Tina but decided against it. He just wanted to get home as fast as he could. He waved down a cab, gave Tina a hug as he held the door and helped her in, and told her he would call her, although he knew he never would.

The cab pulled out and Jake waved for the next one to drive up. As he reached for the cab door, a short little man beat him to it. He was going to say something, but he saw that the man was with a woman so he stepped back and let them take it. The man held the door for the woman, who slipped into the back seat. He closed the door and went around the other side to get in. As the cab pulled out, his eyes met those of the woman in the back seat, and he recognized her as the same woman he had seen several times before. She smiled at him as the cab drove away.

CHAPTER 33

Sarah was grateful that she had found a parking stall in the underground parking lot. She reminded herself that even though it had been raining all week it was better than snow. She hit the *Unlock* button and the *Open Trunk* button on her key FOB and laid the dry cleaning down carefully so that it wouldn't get wrinkled during the short drive home. She started the car, backed out of her stall and then found the nearest exit to start her commute home. There was a fair amount of traffic out, and it was moving extremely slow with the heavy rain falling. As she waited in line to merge, she pressed the Siri button on her iPhone and asked Siri to call Catherine.

"Hi, sweetie, are you almost home?"

"I'm about 15 minutes away as long as traffic keeps moving."

"You're not leaving yourself a lot of time to get ready. Don't forget you need to meet David at 7:30pm at The Comedy Shop."

"I know, don't worry, I'll be there on time. Hey, can you do me a favor, please? I'm going to be tight on time so do you think you could get Peter to swing by and pick up Emma?"

"Not a problem. He needs to take Rex out for a walk anyways, so he can swing by then."

"Perfect. Thanks, Catherine. I'll have her ready around 7pm, ok?"

"Are you excited about tonight?"

"Not at all. I just want to get this and the next one over with so I can get back to my life."

"It hasn't been that bad has it?"

"You haven't had to go on these dates," Sarah laughed as she turned off the freeway. "I could write a book."

"Well, keep an open mind about tonight's date with David, and try to have fun. You're going to a comedy show so that should be good for some laughs at least."

"I'm going to cab it so I'll be able to have a few drinks. Let's hope David doesn't forget his wallet."

Catherine laughed into the phone, "Take yours, just in case."

"I'm almost home, I'll let you go. And tell Peter thanks!"

"I will. Have fun, sweetie. Come over in the morning for coffee so you can give me all the gory details. Love you."

"Love you too. Thanks again."

The smell of teriyaki greeted Sarah as she struggled in the front door with her arms full of dry cleaning piled on top of her purse. Emma was busy at the stove but noticed her mother needed some help, so she rushed over to take the dry cleaning and hung it up on the coat hanger against the wall.

"Hi, mom. How was your day?" Emma greeted her mother as she gave her a hug.

"It was good. How was yours?" Sarah replied as she sat down on the bench and took off her boots.

"I had a fabulous day. We had a field trip to the Pacific Science Center and watched an IMAX movie on climate change. Did you know that in the Netherlands they have a solar highway that melts the snow so you never have to plow it?"

"No, I did not know that. Seems like a pretty smart idea though. What are you cooking? It smells delicious."

"I'm making a teriyaki stir fry. Do we have any tofu?"

Sarah laughed at the question. "No, we don't have any tofu. Have you ever had tofu before?"

"Chelsea brought some to school today in her lunch and let me try it. I liked it and I was thinking we could eat tofu instead of meat."

"We'll have to pick some up next time we're at the grocery store. How's that sound?"

"I'll write it down on the list," Emma told her mom and then took the magnetic pen stuck to the fridge and wrote *tofu* on their shopping list. "What time am I going to Auntie Catherine's?"

"Uncle Peter is going to come and get you at 7 when he takes Rex out for a walk. I thought you'd like that."

"Yay, I'm going to take a few of the treats from the garage with me."

"Make sure you ask Peter if it's ok to give Rex the treats, and pack a change of clothes for tomorrow because you're going to stay over."

"You're not going to be out all night, are you?" Emma asked her mom with a concerned tone.

"Don't worry, missy. I'm a big girl. But no, I won't be out super late, but you should be asleep by the time I get home so I thought it would be easier to come and get you in the morning. You like Uncle Peter's breakfasts anyways."

"That's true, I do like Uncle Peter's breakfast, and Rex can sleep with me. Dinner is ready mom." Emma proclaimed proudly.

Sarah was loading the dishwasher when she heard Peter knock on the front door. She rinsed her hands off in the sink, dried them with the hand towel and then opened the door to let him in.

"Hi Peter," she greeted him with a kiss on the cheek and a pat on the head for Rex who was doing his best to try and jump up at Sarah.

"Hi Sarah," Peter smiled. "Is that what you're wearing out on your date tonight?" he asked as he took in the Christmas apron she had put on when she had started to clean up.

Sarah laughed. "No, but it is my fanciest apron. The Christmas edition," she added as she did a little twirl.

Emma came bounding into the kitchen with her backpack and ran up to Peter giving him a hug and then doing the same to Rex. Rex of course was more interested in sniffing at the backpack sensing that once again Emma had treats.

"No, Rex," Emma scolded him. "Those are for later."

Peter pulled Rex back by his leash and told him to sit. "Are you ready to go Emma?"

"Sure am, Uncle Peter. Can we take the long way to your house though?"

"I'm sure Rex would appreciate that," he chuckled.

"Go get you other jacket if you're taking a long walk," Sarah told Emma.

"Ok," Emma grumbled and then left the kitchen to find her jacket.

"Sarah, I hope you don't mind but Catherine has told me about some of your dates so I picked up something for you that I want you to keep in your purse," Peter explained as he passed her a small plastic bag that he had in his pocket.

"Pepper spray? Do you really think that's necessary?" Sarah replied as she took the bag and smiled at Peter.

"Yes, I do. There are a lot of creepy guys out there, and you're better to be safe than sorry as they say. I gave one to Jessica as well, and you should think about getting one for Emma."

"I will put it in my purse and thank you for worrying and thinking about me. I think we can wait a bit on picking one up for Emma, though."

Emma had returned to the kitchen with her jacket and boots on and ready to go. "Pick up one what for me?" Emma asked

"Nothing you need to worry about right now, kid," Peter told her. "Let's get going. Rex has some business to take care of."

"Did you bring a bag to pick up his poo?" Emma enquired enthusiastically.

Peter pulled an empty bag out of his pocket and showed it to Emma before he put it back. "Always prepared, Emma." He smiled and then opened the door for her and Rex as Sarah came around the table to give Emma a kiss and Peter a hug.

"Have fun you two. I'll see you in the morning."

Sarah finished cleaning up and then went to her room to get ready for her date with David.

It had been a long time since Sarah had been to a live comedy show. She and Michael used to love going out for dinner and taking in some of the local comedians who were trying to make it. Sometimes they were horrible and sometimes they were really good. She could use a few laughs as this week had been difficult with several of her clients having suffered through putting their pets down due to terminal illnesses. It was terrible to lose a pet at any time, but with Christmas coming in a few weeks it made it even worse for the pet owners to be alone.

The cab ride had been quick with the rain letting up and rush hour having ended. Sarah sent a short text to David to let him know that she had arrived already. He replied that he was only a few minutes away, so she decided to wait outside rather than go in alone. She had seen his pictures online so she was confident she would be able to recognize him when he arrived. Her phone rang and it was David telling her he was walking down the street towards her. She looked down the street but could only see a young boy walking towards her so she turned and looked the other way and there was no one on the street at all. Confused she looked back up the street at the young boy who was close enough now that she could see he was on his phone. He looked like David's picture but he was so much shorter than the 6 feet he had claimed to be on his profile. He was more like 5'2" and he wasn't nearly as attractive in real life as he had been in his pictures. He had acne scars on his face and was wearing glasses that mad his eyes look huge.

He must have a pretty strong prescription for them, she thought as her body froze there on the sidewalk.

Her first instinct was to pretend she wasn't Sarah and run, but by the time feeling returned to her body, it was too late. He was standing in front of her, extending his hand. Sarah put her phone into her jacket pocket and reached out her hand to give his a firm shake.

"I thought you would be taller?" Sarah spoke first. "Your profile said you were 6 feet."

"Yeah, sorry about that. No one wants to date a short guy so I put down that I'm 6 feet. If you don't want to stay I totally get it, but look, I'm a nice guy and I really just want to make some new friends. What do you say to a drink and then if you want to skip the show, cool?" David explained to her.

Sarah looked at her watch and then back at David. He was just staring at her with puppy dog eyes hoping she would throw him a bone. She was all dressed up, it was a Friday night and she didn't have any other plans. *What the hell,* she thought, *why not?*

"We're here, why don't we go in and take in the show. I don't know about you but I could use a good laugh after this dreary week."

You would think David had won the lottery. His face lit up and he eagerly opened the door for Sarah and they went inside.

"This comedian is supposed to be pretty funny. He's from Jamaica," David told Sarah as they stood in line to enter the venue. "I'm not sure how good these tickets are though. I won them on the radio."

The tickets turned out to be great seats. They were escorted to a table situated about half way down the tiered venue and as soon as they were seated they ordered a couple of drinks. They spent the next 20 minutes getting to know each other a little bit and then the lights dimmed and the PA announcer introduced the comedian. He was a large Jamaican man and was very funny. Sarah and David both found themselves wiping away tears from laughing so hard. At one point the comedian started to make penis jokes and there was one woman in particular located at the very front that was laughing and snorting so hard that it was making the crowd laugh even harder. It didn't take long for the comedian to start making fun of her and her date. Sarah was so thankful that their tickets were not in the front row. She would have died of embarrassment if that had been them.

When the show was over Sarah and David lingered a bit, allowing the crowd to filter out and to give David time to finish his drink. Considering how small he was Sarah was surprised at how many drinks he was able to consume. He had to have drank 6 beers to her 2 glasses of wine, but he had no problem picking up the bill. *A step up from some of my previous dates,* she thought.

Once the crowd was gone, they walked out to the lobby where David awkwardly helped her put on her jacket. It was a like a 14 year old boy was helping her. She smiled a little on the inside but realized how funny they must have looked together. David looked out the front doors and noticed a lineup of people waiting for cabs. He told her to wait inside and went out to the front of the line. He took the first cab that pulled in, and then waved for Sarah to come and get in. The fellow who was waiting for the cab looked a little perturbed, but he didn't say anything when he realized that David was holding the door for a lady.

She slipped into the backseat of the cab on the passenger side and David closed the door before walking to the other side and getting in. He gave the cabbie directions and they pulled away from the curb. Sarah looked out the window at the fellow from whom they took the cab and realized it was the mystery man she kept running into when she was out. She smiled at him as they drove away and he smiled back at her.

When they had driven a few blocks from the comedy club, David asked her if she minded dropping him off at the bus terminal and then she could carry on home in the cab. Sarah didn't have a problem with that plan; she actually preferred it because she didn't want David to know where she lived. During the short trip to the bus terminal, David kept hinting that he would like to see Sarah again, but she managed to stay non-committal and made some comments about not looking for anything serious.

They pulled into the bus terminal and David hopped out, closed the door on his side and walked around to Sarah's window where he motioned for her to roll it down. He leaned into the open window and asked Sarah if she had any change for the bus as he had spent all his cash on the bar bill. Sarah gave him a ten dollar bill that she had in her purse and politely thanked him for a fun night out. She couldn't wait for the date to be over, and ten dollars was a small price to pay. David leaned in to kiss her but Sarah had already pulled back out of his reach and started to close the power window. David had his eyes closed and jumped back as the window slid up across his lips. He seemed a bit embarrassed and annoyed, but didn't want to make a scene in front of the cab driver who was chuckling as he put the cab in gear and started to drive away. David was still standing on the curb trying to get Sarah's attention as he made the motion with his hand for her to call him.

Sarah sat in silence for a minute as they drove down the road. The cabbie looked at her through the rear view mirror and asked her where she was going.

"Nowhere it seems," Sarah told him with a heavy sigh, "nowhere."

"It's none of my business, ma'am," the cabbie told her, "but I think you'll be fine. He's not the guy for you. You can do a lot better."

"Sure, I could be with you right?" Sarah smiled back at the cabbie's reflection in the mirror.

"No ma'am. I have the most amazing woman in the world waiting for me at home. I stopped looking the moment I found her. You'll find yours too. I can tell."

"That is sweet of you to say--Bob." Sarah replied as she noticed his name tag on the dash of the cab. "But I found him and lost him already," she told him sadly.

"Lady, there's always more than one. Some of us never find one, some of us find more than one, sometimes we find two at the same time," he chuckled. "Love is the only thing worth chasing in life. Funny how elusive it can be though, like the Unicorn."

"Thanks, Bob, I'll keep that in mind. That is very sweet of you to say."

"Do you like Christmas music?" Bob asked.

"Yes I do, Bob. What do you have?"

"I put together a playlist of a few of my favorite Christmas songs. It helps me stay in the Christmas spirit. You know a lot of folks won't even say 'Merry Christmas' anymore? It's all 'Happy Holidays'. It may not be politically correct, but in my cab, it's 'Merry Christmas.'"

The two didn't speak the rest of the drive. Instead, Bob turned up the music and they enjoyed the sounds of the season – or as Bob would say, the songs of Christmas.

CHAPTER 34

When Sarah woke up in the morning, she could feel the warmth of the sun on her cheek as it streamed in through her bedroom window. It was the first sunny morning she had woken up to in nearly a week. She rolled over and looked at the alarm clock on the night stand beside her bed. The clock said 9:30am. Sarah sat upright, rubbed the sleep out of her eyes, and then reached for her phone to check her messages. She had one missed call from a blocked number and a text message from Emma. She was wondering what time Sarah was coming to pick her up, reminding her that they needed to go shopping.

She climbed out of her cozy bed and made her way downstairs to make a cup of coffee. While she waited for the Tassimo machine to finish brewing she sent a text back to Emma letting her know she would be over in an hour. She went through her phone calls again, puzzled by the missed call from a blocked number. There was no voice message so it couldn't have been that important. She tended to get annoyed when people would call and not leave a message. She shrugged it off, grabbed her coffee and headed upstairs to have a shower and get ready for a day of shopping with Emma. When she came out of the shower, she had another missed call on her phone from a blocked number, and again no message.

By the time Sarah showed up at Catherine's, they were finished eating breakfast and were putting the last of the dishes into the dishwasher. She didn't bother to knock and just walked into the front hallway where Rex greeted her with a wagging tail and wet kisses. "Some guard dog you make, Rex," she told him as she rubbed his head and walked past him on her way to the kitchen.

Ben was the first to spot her as she walked into the kitchen "Hi, Auntie Sarah."

"Hi, Ben," Sarah returned the greeting and walked up behind Emma who had turned to see her mom. "How was the sleepover Princess?" she asked as she hugged her from behind.

"It was awesome, mom. We stayed up until midnight watching *The Hunger Games* and made popcorn on the stove, not the microwave. It tastes way better that way and it's better for you. Jessica says we shouldn't use the microwave anymore."

"She does, does she?"

"Auntie Sarah, a study found that broccoli zapped in the microwave with a little bit of water lost up to 97 percent of its beneficial antioxidants. Also, toxic chemicals leak into the food from the packaging of things like pizzas and popcorn. When you microwave food in plastic containers, toxins are released and can get into your food. Microwaves are killing us. You should really try to eat only raw foods."

"She's really enjoying her science classes this year." Catherine chimed in.

"Is all that true?" Sarah asked

"Yes, and there's more. I'll send you a link to some recent independent tests. Did you know Russia has banned microwaves, Auntie Sarah? You should really think about getting rid of yours. I'm working on dad to get rid of ours."

"Don't get me involved in this," Peter declared as he stood up and put his coffee in the microwave to warm it up.

"What are you doing, dad?" Jessica yelled and then jumped up and stopped the microwave. "Didn't you hear anything I just said?"

"I've been warming up coffee and food in microwaves since before you were born. If I haven't died yet, I probably won't."

"Don't you want to be around to see your grandkids?"

"That's enough, you two," Catherine interrupted. "We'll figure out the future of the microwave later. Emma, you need to pack up you stuff so you and your mom can go shopping, and Ben, you need to pick up the dog sh--- poop from the back yard. Jessica, you can help."

"Mom, do you know how bad it is for my skin to be exposed to dog poop" Jessica complained in an effort to get out of helping Ben.

"Do you know how bad it is for your health to not do what I ask?" Catherine responded with a stern look.

Peter put his arms around both Ben and Jessica. "Let's go gang. Come on, I'll help with the dog--poop. Jessica, you can hold the bag and Ben and I will do the picking up with the shovel."

Once everyone had left the kitchen, Catherine poured Sarah and herself a cup of coffee, pulled up a chair to the table and then asked Sarah to give her a rundown of her date with David. Sarah gave her all the details; the lie about his height, how much he drank and that she had to give him bus money to get home. As she was finishing her story, her phone rang. When Sarah picked it up she saw it was another from a blocked number.

"This is the third call this morning from a blocked number," she told Catherine.

"You should answer it. It could be important."

"If it was important they would leave a message, don't you think?"

"I'm going to answer it for you."

"No, don't."

Catherine snatched the phone from in front of Sarah, hit answer, turned on the speaker, and placed it front of the two of them. Sarah didn't want to say anything and was shaking her head at Catherine who was mouthing the word *hello* so Sarah would say it. When she realized she wasn't going to, Catherine said it instead.

"Hello."

"Hi," was the reply from a quiet and soft female voice. "This is going to sound strange, but do you know a man named David?"

Both Catherine and Sarah looked at each other in shock. Sarah started shaking her head, but Catherine wanted to find out what was going on. "Yes. Why?"

"I'm his wife. He was out last night and wouldn't tell me where he was or who he was with. I found this number when I was going through his phone this morning."

She went on to explain that he had been cheating on her with numerous women for quite a long time. She couldn't understand why or how since he wasn't that good looking and he wasn't that good in bed.

Sarah and Catherine had to stifle a laugh when she revealed the secrets of his sexual prowess. For the most part, they were pissed at David and they felt bad for his wife. Catherine continued to pretend she was Sarah, consoling the woman for a few minutes, telling her that she wasn't going to see him again, and that she should leave his sorry ass. Unfortunately, they had 4 kids and she didn't have anywhere else to go. Catherine gave her the names of some women's support groups and programs and then excused herself from the phone call.

"She needs to leave that asshole. I can't believe he's online pretending to be single and out cheating on her while she's at home with his kids. That is fucked up," Catherine added.

"You see what I have to deal with? It's not easy out there."

"This shit has been going on forever, Sarah. It's not a new thing, men cheating on their wives, or women cheating for that matter. I am so lucky to have Peter."

Realizing what she had just said, Catherine came around the table and hugged Sarah. "Sorry, sweetie. I am completely stupid sometimes. You only need one good one. I'll find him for you, I promise."

Sarah finished off the last of her coffee and looked at Catherine with a big grin.

"Why are you smiling?"

"Because that was date number five and I only have one more to go."

"You're right. I better make this next date a good one. Leave it with me. No farters, no married guys, no short guys, no noisy eaters. Did I miss anything?"

"Sure, he must have hair, must have a job, must have manners, and if you can throw in that he must have a *Channing Tatum*, I think we'd be good to go."

"Let's hope he has pictures for all of those," Catherine winked at her, "especially the *Channing Tatum*."

CHAPTER 35

I knew I should have closed those blinds when I got home last night, Jake thought as he pulled the covers over his head to keep the sunlight out of his eyes.

His head hurt from all the alcohol he had drank the night before. As he reached for the large glass of water sitting on the table beside his bed, he started to remember the events of the previous night. Pregnant Tina, whose ex-boyfriend was Marshawn Lynch. That bastard Darryl had set him up on date with an ex-Seattle Seahawks cheerleader who not only used to date Marshawn Lynch, but was also 8 months pregnant. He would deal with Darryl later. Right now, he needed to drag his ass into the bathroom, take a piss, and get some painkillers into his body so he could shake his headache.

Jake stumbled slowly into the bathroom and rather than stand to piss, he sat on the toilet seat and rested his head in his hands. His head was pounding. Once he was finished he opened the cabinet above the sink and found a bottle of *Advil*. As he was prying off the child-proof cap, he accidentally dropped the open bottle into the toilet that he had yet to flush.

Great, he thought, *what else can go wrong?*

He thought about flushing everything, bottle and all, and then realized what a bad idea that was. The pills were a loss, but at least he could keep from clogging the pipes with the bottle. Turning his head, he reached into the toilet to retrieve the bottle and then flushed. He turned on the tap to wash his hand, trying hard not to throw up. Remembering that he kept a small bottle in his golf bag, he headed down the hallway towards the stairs. As he passed Mathew's bedroom he looked in and saw him already up and on his computer.

"Good morning," he croaked through the door into Mathew's room.

"Hi, dad. How was your date?"

"Memorable."

"Memorable good, or memorable bad?"

"I'll put it this way – you don't have to worry about her being your new stepmom."

"Are we going shopping today?"

"Yeah, we can go shopping, but it will have to be this afternoon. I have a killer headache."

"You shouldn't drink alcohol."

"You shouldn't eat candy."

"Haha, that's not the same. Candy doesn't give you a headache or make you say and do stupid things."

"True, but all that sugar is not good for you."

"You're deflecting dad. Alcohol is bad for you. Just admit it."

"You are correct."

"Where are you going?"

"I need to get some *Advil* out of my golf bag."

"Isn't there some in your bathroom?"

"There was, but there isn't anymore. Don't ask. Did you have something to eat for breakfast?"

"I had some cereal. We're out of almond milk, by the way. We should pick some up when we're out this afternoon."

"Good plan, along with some more *Advil*," Jake muttered as he turned and walked down the stairs and into the garage. He found the pills in his golf bag and then grabbed a bottle of water from the mini-fridge in the garage. He popped a couple into his mouth and chased them down with half a bottle of water as he made his way back up the stairs and into his bedroom. He closed the door and turned his blinds down so the room was shrouded in darkness, and then crawled back into bed.

He dosed for an hour or so before the sound of his ringing phone snapped him out of dreamland and back to reality. He rolled over and saw that he had missed a few calls from Darryl. No doubt he was looking for a recap of last night's date with Tina. He picked up the phone and called him back.

"Where have you been? I've been calling you all morning?"

"I was a little hung over."

"I thought maybe you had a fabulous night and had some unexpected company for breakfast," Darryl teased.

"Oh, you must be referring to Tina. Pregnant Tina."

"What? She's pregnant?"

"Yes, eight months pregnant. She said that she told me that when we were messaging back and forth. Of course, that was you and not me so how would I have known?"

"She never told me she was pregnant dude. I would have told you. Fuck. I wouldn't have sent you on a date with her, that's for sure. Did you just leave after you saw her and go get shit-faced or what did you do?

"She was cute and she was pregnant, so I didn't want to just tell her to piss off. We talked for a bit and then we went to the comedy show."

"That was awfully nice of you. It couldn't have been that bad a night then."

Jake laughed into the phone, "It got worse, believe me. It turns out Tina used to be a cheerleader for the Seahawks."

"How does that make it worse?"

"Oh, that's not all. She dated one of the Seahawks for a few months. Guess who?"

Darryl paused for a moment, "I don't know, Luke Wilson?"

"No, guess again."

"Fuck, just tell me already."

"Marshawn Lynch."

"Get out."

"No, you get out. I'm serious; her ex-boyfriend is Marshawn Lynch."

Now it was Darryl's turn to burst out laughing. "Sorry dude, I'm not laughing at you, but you have to admit, that is a pretty funny story. The guys are not going to believe it. Is she pregnant with his baby?"

"No, she said it's some other guy's. She and Marshawn broke up over a year ago, but they're still friends, apparently."

"I would have gotten shit-faced too. That is unbelievable man."

"It gets better. The comedian was this big Jamaican guy, and about 15 minutes into the show he starts making jokes about penis sizes. Of course, we were sitting right up front, and Tina was laughing so hard at his penis jokes that she started snorting. Everyone in the building could hear her. The comedian ended up coming over and started asking us where we were from, what we do, and then made a penis joke about me. It was embarrassing. I don't think I can ever go there again. God, I hope nobody I know was there."

"Now I understand why you're so hung over. I don't blame you for hitting it hard. Sorry, dude. I didn't know she was pregnant. Not something you think you need to ask when you're messaging someone on a dating site."

"I feel a little better now. I got up earlier and took some *Advil* and then went back to bed. That's why you couldn't reach me."

"What are you up to this afternoon?"

"Mathew and I are going to do a little Christmas shopping, and probably going to grab some dinner as well. How about you?"

"I have a date later. I'm going to check out that comedian you saw last night."

"Don't sit up front!"

"We won't," Darryl laughed. "Thanks for the warning, though."

"Have fun. I gotta go take a shower and then hit the mall. I'll talk to you tomorrow or Monday."

"I've got my kids tomorrow, so let's connect Monday. We need to find you another date. You still have one more to go."

"Great. Can't wait for that," Jake replied sarcastically and then hung up the phone.

CHAPTER 36

Sarah turned on the computer to check her schedule for the day when her cell phone rang. She looked at the phone and noticed it was Catherine calling. She thought about ignoring it, but she knew that Catherine would keep calling until she answered.

"No more dates," she answered without giving Catherine a chance to speak.

"Whoa, girl, hang on," Catherine replied."I found this nice guy last night and we exchanged a couple of messages. He seems perfect for you."

"Catherine, I'm serious. I don't think I can keep doing this. It's embarrassing."

"Don't be ridiculous. You made a deal, and damn it, you're going to stick to it. Besides, you need to get laid. How long has it been anyways? You know it will grow over if you don't use it, and you can't afford to keep buying batteries," she laughed.

"I have rechargeable batteries, thank you very much," Sarah laughed into the phone.

"Sarah, just stick with it. We'll find you a keeper. Login and check your favorites. His name is *the12thman*."

Sarah turned to her computer and logged into her account. She brought up *the12thman*'s profile and started to read it.

"He doesn't seem like a good match," she muttered to Catherine after a few minutes of perusing his bio. "He loves football and finds women who don't understand how the game is played annoying. He says he is a devoted Christian and a conservative."

"You like football, and you're spiritual," Catherine shot back.

"He said he finds you interesting and he'd like to meet you, so I set it up for you two to meet for a drink Thursday, 7 o'clock, at The Train Station Pub. His name is Chuck and he owns a couple of sporting goods stores. I think he used to be a semi-pro player."

"I don't think Thursday works for me Catherine," Sarah cut her off. "Thursday is laundry night and *Grey's Anatomy* is on."

"Nice try. Emma has already agreed to come over and hang with Peter and I, and she said you PVR *Greys*. I told him you would meet him there, though. I thought you might prefer to not be picked up, you know, watching out for your neighbors and all," she chuckled. "Got to go, catch you later." She hung up not giving Sarah a chance to back out.

Sarah looked at Chuck's pictures and agreed, he was good looking and a tad sexy.

CHAPTER 37

Jake was languishing through a long sales meeting the following afternoon when he noticed a text from Darryl with a picture attached. He turned his phone over so he wouldn't be tempted to look at it until the meeting was over. Once he finished up in the boardroom and everyone had left, he picked up his phone and opened the message. It was just a picture, but it was a picture of a very intriguing woman. She had dark hair and piercing green eyes. She was stunning. He sent Darryl a text back asking who she was.

That's Anna. She's from Hungary

Before Jake could reply, Darryl fired another message.

She saw your profile and sent you a text. I have been going back and forth with her all morning. If you don't date her, I will!!

Again, Darryl sent another message before Jake could reply, saying he had set them up for drinks at The Train Station Pub for Thursday at 6:30. Jake thought about making up some excuse, but he couldn't come up with one that he thought Darryl would believe. *OK* was all he sent back. He was nervous. This girl seemed too good to be true. He decided he better work out every night that week.

IN A RELATIONSHIP

CHAPTER 38

Sarah had been texting back and forth with Chuck all week and he seemed full of confidence, and had been quite the gentleman in all their communication. She was actually beginning to look forward to the date by the time Thursday evening rolled around.

Sarah put on the new green dress she had picked up that afternoon in anticipation of her pending evening out. She did her hair, put on her favorite perfume, and then applied a dark red lipstick. She normally didn't wear much makeup, but for some reason she found herself wanting to make a good impression on Chuck. She was standing in front of the mirror admiring herself when Emma walked into her bathroom. She sat down on top of the closed toilet and smiled at her mom's reflection in the mirror.

"You look amazing, mom," she said in a quiet voice. "I hope I look as good as you do when I'm 40." She hopped up and gave Sarah a long lingering hug.

"Thanks, princess," Sarah said smiling back at her. "You are the most beautiful girl in the world now, and always will be. Now let's get you over to your Aunt and Uncle's."

Sarah walked Emma to Catherine and Peter's door and rang the buzzer. They could hear barking inside as Rex came to the door to greet them. They could also hear Peter yelling at Rex to stop barking. They both laughed, listening to the chaos coming from inside the house. Finally, Peter opened the door, holding Rex by his collar. He was wagging his tail and trying desperately to get to Emma. Emma got down on her knees and hugged Rex, whispering into his ear. He calmed down immediately and sat still for Emma.

"How did you do that, Emma?" Peter asked her with a look of astonishment in his eyes.

"Rex and I have been working on his behavioral issues the last few times I've been over, Uncle Peter. He's getting better." Then she took a treat out of her pocket and gave it to Rex.

"Oh, I get it. You bribe him," said Peter with a chuckle.

"Yup," Emma replied, "it works well doesn't it? Mom does it to me so I thought it might work with Rex," she stated as if she had figured out some great scientific puzzle. Then she bounded down the hall to Ben's room with Rex in tow.

Peter looked at Sarah and whistled out loud. "Wow, Sarah. You look beautiful."

Sarah's cheeks turned a crimson red. She thanked him as he hugged her. "Tell Catherine thanks, I think," she smiled, "and tell her if I need a rescue I'll text her." She turned and hurried down the steps and onto the sidewalk.

As she was leaving, Peter yelled behind her, "you smell great too, and if he's a dick, text me and I'll come straighten him out! Or use your pepper spray!"

Sarah only heard the first part, and smiled to herself as she climbed into the car and started the engine. She felt good. Maybe this would be better than the last two dates.

When she got to the pub, she parked her car and then checked her lipstick in the rearview mirror one last time. It was a bit chilly out so she pulled her jacket tighter as she walked across the parking lot to the entrance. The temperature had dropped quite a bit now that it was getting dark earlier. It felt like winter was just around the corner. Fall was one of Sarah's favorite times of the year - the colors of the trees, the leaves blowing down the streets, the chance to wear coats and scarves. Yes, it was her favorite fashion time of the year.

She had been to the Train Station pub once before with Catherine and Peter. It was an old train station that they had converted into a pub. It was all the original brick on the inside, and it had a real old school charm to it. She was admiring the architecture when she opened the door and ran head on into a scantily dressed woman who was exiting. Her eyes were drawn to the woman's cleavage. She had the most magnificent breasts and they were pretty much all on show.

She couldn't stop looking at them, and apologized to the woman for not paying attention, but still hadn't really looked past her breasts. The woman told her not to worry, and kept going as she seemed in a hurry to leave with her boyfriend. As they passed, Sarah noticed at the last moment that it was the same fellow she had seen the last couple of times they were out. She was sure he noticed her as well, but he seemed to want to avoid making eye contact. Sarah continued into the pub and began to look around trying to spot Chuck. She spotted him sitting at the bar. He noticed her at the same time and got up from his seat and came to meet her at the door. They exchanged an awkward hug, and then he guided her over to the bar and waited for her to sit down before he took his seat.

He was a good looking man, a bit of a big fellow, and as they sat and got to know each other, he came across as intelligent, witty, charming and confident. He told her he had been married for five years, but recently divorced and had a four year old daughter. He seemed nice, but Sarah was looking for more than just nice. She was looking for a spark or lightning, and after an hour she began to find his self-assurance somewhat obnoxious.

After a couple of hours and a couple of glasses of wine, Chuck asked her if she wanted to go for hot chocolate. While part of her wanted to end the date and go home, another part of her was attracted to him so she accepted his offer to drive to the little coffee shop at the edge of the pier near the ocean.

They ordered a couple of hot chocolates and then drove down to the pier where Chuck pulled into the parking lot so they could chat and finish their hot chocolate. Sarah began to feel quite comfortable with Chuck as they sat and talked more about living in Seattle and some of the places they wanted to visit. Chuck had turned on some Christmas music, and when he attempted to kiss Sarah she let him. She knew it wouldn't work out with him long term, but it had been a long time since a man had paid this much attention to her and she felt herself getting caught up in the moment. As they continued to make out, she felt Chuck run his hand under her jacket and up towards her breast. It was at this point that Sarah came back to reality, and took Chuck's hand and pushed it away. She told him it was getting late and that he should take her back to her car. Chuck was revved up, and started whining and begging her for sex, saying she couldn't just leave him all turned on. At first Sarah just laughed it off as if he was joking but he grew increasingly desperate telling her he was about to explode.

"Can't you just suck it or at least give me a hand job?" he blurted out.

"Excuse me? Umm, no," Sarah replied, mortified at the thought, and shocked at how direct he was.

"I think it's time to go, NOW," She said firmly.

Chuck was frustrated and annoyed, like he was offended that Sarah had been willing to kiss but unwilling to give him any sexual pleasure. Sarah was starting to get really nervous. At that point, Chuck decided to whip it out of his pants, and then proceeded to masturbate, right there in the truck.

Stunned, Sarah turned and stared out at the ocean, trapped in a combination of horror and disbelief while he sat there stroking away like a mad man, moaning about how good it felt and how hot and sexy she was. Sarah pressed herself against the passenger door, trying to stay as far away as possible and looking around for potential help in case things got worse.

When he was almost finished, he asked her in a breathless voice, "Where do you want me to put it?"

When Sarah didn't respond, he continued.

It was at that moment that Sarah remembered the can of pepper spray Peter had given her. She opened her purse, took it out, and just as Chuck was reaching for her hand to place on his penis, she sprayed him in the eyes and then the crotch.

Chuck started to scream and yell as he put his hands up to his face and tried to get the spray out of his eyes.

"You fucking pervert!" Sarah screamed back at him as she opened the door and ran across the parking lot, not looking back until she was on the other side of the street.

Chuck had gotten out of the truck, but he couldn't see anything and was blindly stumbling around, yelling and swearing at her. He hadn't realized that his pants were still undone and they fell to the ground leaving him yelling with his pants around his ankles.

Sarah walked down the street until she could wave a taxi down. Once inside the taxi she calmed down and started to laugh, thinking about how ridiculous Chuck had looked standing outside his truck. Instead of being mad, she felt sad for Chuck. She gave the cab driver the address to where she had left her car and then sent Catherine a text.

You're not going to believe how tonight's date went ☹

CHAPTER 39

Jake was nervous about his date with Anna. She was without a doubt one of the most fascinating women that he had seen on the dating site so far. It had been quite a while since he had sex, and he was feeling very apprehensive about the night's potential – either he wouldn't be able to keep up with her or he wouldn't last long enough.

As he made the turn onto his street and got close to home, he could see Darryl's jeep parked on the street out front. He hit the garage door opener then rolled into the garage. He couldn't pull all the way inside as Mathew had left his bike lying on the floor at the back of the garage. He stopped the car and got out to move Mathew's bike to the side so he had room to pull all the way in. Once he had moved the car all the way in, he hit the *close* button for the garage door and went inside the house. He could hear Darryl and Mathew in the kitchen as he reached the end of the hallway. They were sitting at the counter and Mathew had his laptop open, explaining to Darryl how to play his online game.

"Teaching Darryl how to play?" Jake asked as he walked around them and opened the fridge to grab a beer.

"You know, it's not like Pong or Pac man," Darryl laughed. "These games are a long way from what we played. Remember Asteroids? I loved that game. We should try to find one online."

"Sure. While we're at it, let's see if we can get you a velour shirt," Jake joked back at him and then took a drink from his beer.

"So, you ready for your big date with Anna tonight?" Darryl asked with a slight smile on his face.

"Who's Anna?" Mathew asked looking up from his computer.

"Just a girl Darryl knows," Jake answered.

"Just a girl, dad? So, an internet date. Are you going to need to do laundry when you get home?" he chuckled.

"No, no more shower dates," Jake smiled back. "I better go get ready, though. I have to meet her at 6:30. Are you going to be ok here at home tonight?"

"Yeah. Darryl brought over some *Dorito*s and rootbeer. We're going to watch the football game while you're out."

"Shit, I forgot the game was on tonight. That sounds like a better time than my date. Maybe I should just stay home with you two."

"Oh no you don't," Darryl cut in, "You don't want to disappoint Anna. We'll PVR the game for you."

"Alright, already. I'm going to go change," Jake said with a statement of resignation knowing he was going to have to go through with the date. He finished his beer and headed up the stairs to get ready.

Jake stood in his walk-in closet staring at his shirts. He couldn't decide which one to wear. He really was a little freaked out about this date – a lot more than he had been with the first five. This one had the potential to end up with more than a kiss goodnight, and that's what was freaking him out.

His hair was still wet from his shower, and as he held a blue shirt up in front of himself he looked down at his groin and noticed that he should probably do some manscaping. He had read online that women liked a man to be a little less hairy down there. He grabbed his razor and starting to do some trimming. He was just about done when he realized that Darryl was standing in the doorway to his room, peering directly into his bathroom. He was about to snap a picture of Jake on his iPhone when Jake noticed he was standing there.

"Jesus Christ! Do you mind?" Jake yelled at him as he closed the door.

Darryl was laughing uncontrollably and from behind the door shouted, "Hey, don't get your balls in a knot. I keep the boys nice and trim, too! I've just never seen anybody actually doing it. I brought you a little something to take away your worries about performance. You'll be a super stud!"

Jake pulled into the parking lot at the Train Station Pub and was still feeling nervous about the possibility of having sex for the first time in almost 4 years. He reached into his pocket and double checked that the little blue pill Darryl had given him was still there. He had never used one before, but it gave him a little added confidence that if it came down to it, he would have some help. He unbuckled his seatbelt and opened the car door.

As he stepped out into the cool crisp autumn air he noticed a different smell. It wasn't anything he could put his finger on, but it reminded him of when he was younger and his father would say it smelled like snow. It was getting close to that time of year and he wasn't looking forward to winter. He disliked snow and everything about it. Well, except for Christmas. He did appreciate a nice blanket of fresh snow Christmas morning as long as he didn't have to shovel it.

He was standing at the door to the pub and opened it to step inside. The warm air from the fireplace, the smell of pub food and spilled beer filled his senses. He glanced around the bar and easily spotted Anna. She was wearing a tight little black cocktail dress that hugged her sleek body, and had a plunging neckline that didn't leave a lot to the imagination when it came to her breasts. There were men on either side of her, and she was intently conversing with the fellow on her right who was having a hard time making eye contact. She didn't seem to mind.

At that moment she looked up in the direction of the doorway and let out a little squeal when she saw Jake. She bounced out of her stool and ran over to meet him, wrapping her arms around him and giving him a huge hug. He could feel her breasts crushed against his chest and she smelled like cotton candy or something just as sweet. She told him he looked delicious and then asked the waiter to seat them in a booth. She babbled on about her day, but Jake was having a hard time listening to her as they made their way to the booth along the far side of the pub. Once there, Anna scooted up against the wall and tapped the seat beside her indicating Jake should sit next to her rather than opposite. The waitress came over and asked them what they wanted to drink.

"I'll have a cosmopolitan," Anna replied, "and he will have a double scotch on the rocks. You can bring us the bill at the same time; we're only staying for one." She smiled at the waitress and then winked at Jake.

They made small talk for a while, with Anna doing most of the talking and Jake trying to stay focused on the conversation rather than her breasts. She caught him staring several times but didn't seem to mind. Each time she would just smile at him and then carry on with her story. If Jake had any doubts about where this night was going to end up, they were quickly disappearing. After about 25 minutes, Anna suggested Jake pay the bill and then head back to her place for a drink. Jake didn't linger with the cheque.

Anna grabbed his hand and led him to the door as every man in the place watched them leave. Even those with their wives or girlfriends took the chance to sneak a quick look. As they were leaving, the door opened. As Anna stepped through, she walked straight into a woman entering at the same time. Jake, had been in a trance-like state, but snapped out of it when he recognized the woman that Anna had bumped into. It was the same woman he had seen on his previous dates. She didn't see him right away as she was also taken aback by the cleavage Anna was displaying. Jake felt a bit embarrassed by the show Anna had on display, and ducked his head down, moving behind Anna as they squeezed past Sarah and went out into the parking lot.

Anna told Jake that she had taken a cab and would hop in with him for the drive back to her place. She directed him to the main highway and head to the far side of the city. They had driven for at least 20 minutes, and were well up into the hills when Anna asked him to take the next right. They traveled down the poorly lit road further up into the hills and away from the city lights. Finally, after another ten minutes of driving above the city, they came to a stop in a quiet little cul-de-sac. Anna waited for Jake to come around to her side of the car and open her door.

"Why, thank you," she cooed, "such a gentleman." She leaned into him and gave him a passionate kiss on the lips.

It caught Jake by surprize and took his breath away. She was very forward, and he was feeling a little uncomfortable being all alone with a woman he had only met an hour ago, this far from his place.

They stepped inside the dimly lit entrance way of Anna's house and were greeted by a tall gangly teenager. Anna turned to Jake and introduced him to her 13-year-old son, Tyler. He was at least 5'10 – a big kid for 13. *His father must be a very large dude,* Jake thought

Jake shook Tyler's hand as Anna said to him, "Go to your father's house. I'll call you later." She then turned back to Jake, and with a seductive voice said, "Come follow me down the hall."

She walked him to the last bedroom on the right. There were beads hanging where a door once was. "This is my entertainment room. Go on in and get comfortable. I'll get you something to eat."

There were throw pillows scattered all over the floor and an entertainment center against the back wall. It was lit with a few candles and light jazz music was playing. Jake was feeling like an insect about to be trapped in the spider's web as he waited for Anna to return. She came back with a bowl of strawberries and whipped cream. Jake was thinking it was a bit unusual of a snack. In hindsight, he should have clued in, but it had been a long time since he had been in a situation like this. He was a bit daft.

"Strawberries, my favorite… thank you," he clumsily whispered.

She laughed. "You're welcome, Jake. Enjoy a few while I go and change into something more--comfortable."

Jake made himself as comfortable as he could on the throw pillows, and began to ponder the situation he found himself in. He had just met this woman and really didn't know much about her other than she had a 13-year-old son that was as tall as he was. *What if she laced this bowl of strawberries with drugs,* he thought to himself. He decided not to eat them, just in case.

He placed the bowl on a nearby table and then heard her coo, "oh Jake." He turned to see her in a matching black bra and panties and a see through sheer robe. A younger Jake may have reacted differently, but this Jake was now feeling like a fish out of water, and not at all comfortable with the speed at which the evening was proceeding.

"I-I-I think I need to go," Jake stuttered. "I've given you the wrong impression." He moved to go past her.

"Oh, please don't go. I'm sorry. I'm so lonely, please stay," she started to cry, dropping to her knees and wrapping her arms around his leg.

Jake now found himself in the hallway of a house on the outskirts of town with a scantily dressed woman whom he'd met just an hour earlier, who had a death grip on his right leg. He could see tomorrow's headline in the local paper: "Local Woman Assaulted in Home by Internet Date".

He moved down the hallway as best he could with Anna clinging to his leg and eventually made it. Her firm grip on his leg as tight as ever. At some point during his struggle to the front door, she had transitioned from a lonely, sobbing woman to one that defiantly insisted that he remain with her.

When he finally made it to the door he discovered it was locked. Jake thought she'd locked him in, but she had probably locked the door to keep them from being interrupted by her son. At this point, Jake was too caught up in the moment to think rationally. He looked around the room while Anna continued to insist that he stay and make love to her. He glanced at the kitchen table where his keys were lying next to the empty whip cream container, and hanging on the back of one of the chairs was his jacket. He grabbed them both and then looked at Anna.

"I'm counting to 3. You either let go of my leg or we're both going out this door."

She looked up at him with a disbelieving look, "You're too nice, you won't do it."

Jake counted out loud, "One….two……THREE!" and then he went through the door, Anna still clutching his leg.

The sight of a nearly naked Anna and Jake stumbling out of the doorway and him breaking free from her hold caught the eye of neighbours who were walking their dog in front of her house. Jake rushed to his car and Anna scurried back inside.

As Jake drove away, he reached into his back pocket. *Yep… still got my wallet*, he thought to himself and noticed that his shirt was soaked with sweat.

As he drove the 30 minutes back into the city he fumbled with the radio to end the silence and take his mind off of what had happened. He felt sorry for Anna – she was probably just lonely and looking for someone to make her feel better, but he wasn't in the right head space for what she was looking for. A younger Jake would have reacted differently, he was sure of that. Hell, Darryl would have spent the night and banged her until the sun came up or her son came home, whichever came first. He turned up the radio and smiled as Heart's

Barracuda played. Darryl would be disappointed when Jake retold the story of the night's events, but he wasn't Darryl.

Jake was still trying to digest the evening's events when he walked in the door to his place. He knew Darryl was going to want all the details. As he walked into the TV room Darryl and Mathew were glued to the TV and didn't notice he had returned. He was about to speak when they both erupted in a cheer and jumped up off the couch, high fiving each other. He looked at the TV and saw that The Seahawks had just scored to end the game. They noticed Jake at the back of the room.

"The Seahawks won in overtime, Dad!" Mathew exclaimed.

"It was an amazing game," Darryl added. "They tied it with ten seconds left and then won in overtime!"

That only served to add to the night's events for Jake. "Awesome," he replied, not hiding his disappointment. "Well, there's no use in me watching it now."

"You should still watch it, Dad. It was the best game they have played all season! Hey, how come your home so early?"

"I wasn't feeling it," Jake answered. He could tell Darryl wanted more details but he didn't want to get into it with Mathew in the room. "Hey buddy, it's late, you should get to bed. You have school tomorrow."

Mathew picked up his cell phone off the coffee table and high fived Darryl one more time, thanking him for the rootbeer and snacks as he left for his room. "No computer gaming either," Jake yelled at him as he and Darryl went into the kitchen with the empty chip bowl and glasses. Once in the kitchen, Darryl didn't waste a second.

"So, how was the date? You're home a little earlier than I expected. Come on, give me all the details."

"Man, I don't even know where to begin. I mean she was smoking hot, but she was totally into getting it on and was coming on so strong it freaked me out. When I tried to leave she literally threw herself at me."

"No way! That's fucking awesome! How is that a problem?"

Jake went on to tell Darryl every little detail and just as he had suspected, Darryl was clear that he would have closed the deal with Anna. He couldn't believe that Jake had rejected a beautiful woman who clearly wanted to get laid in a bad way. Darryl starting going on about the first girl he slept with after his divorce, and tried to make Jake feel better about not being ready yet. Jake tried to explain that it wasn't that he wasn't ready – he was – it's just that he wanted to have more of a personal connection first, and he wanted to get to know a woman before jumping into bed with her. It was no use arguing with Darryl about it, though. They were both looking for different things in a woman. In fact, he wouldn't be surprised if Darryl ended up calling Anna himself. They were probably a better match anyways.

IN A RELATIONSHIP
296

CHAPTER 40

Sarah was a creature of habit. Every weekday morning at 6:30 the alarm on her cell phone would kick in and she would wake up to the song *Best day of my Life*. The tune echoed through her bedroom as she fumbled with her phone that was sitting on the night table next to her bed. In her attempt to pick it up and turn off the alarm she knocked not only the phone onto the floor but also the glass of water she had brought to bed the night before.

"Shit!" she muttered out loud and then scrambled out of bed, throwing a towel from the laundry basket onto the area of her bedroom floor that was now covered in water. Using her feet, she moved the towel around on the hardwood until all of the water had been absorbed.

She sat down on the edge of her bed and recalled her date from last night, letting out a small giggle when she got to the part of the evening when she had pepper sprayed Chuck. She still couldn't believe that he was jerking himself off in his vehicle with her sitting right beside him. She wondered what Catherine would have done if that had been her in the truck. She checked the messages on her phone and then hopped into the shower. Sarah didn't have to worry about Emma – she had stayed overnight at Catherine and Peter's so she could just swing by their place on the way to work, pick her up and then drop her at school.

Sarah finished dressing and made herself a cup of coffee. It was quiet in the house without Emma. Checking her phone one more time before she walked out the door, she noticed a new message from Emma. She had forgotten her backpack with her school books and needed Sarah to grab it from her room before picking her up.

When Sarah went into Emma's room she noticed her computer was up and her Facebook was open. She knew she shouldn't, but she couldn't resist. It wasn't like she didn't have her password; she had just never gone on it. They had made a deal that Sarah would have all the passwords but would not check up on Emma unless she gave her a reason to. So far, she hadn't.

Sarah noticed a message from *Seahawk17* asking Emma if they were still on for playing that night, a couple of short messages from some of the girls in her class regarding a homework assignment, and some discussion of music involving *One Direction* and which band member was the cutest – nothing alarming. Sarah couldn't stop a slight grin from appearing on her face as she thought about how well adjusted Emma had turned out despite the trauma of losing her father at such an early age.

She spotted the backpack at the end of Emma's bed and swung it over her shoulder. It was a lot heavier than it looked. Sarah put it on the bed and opened it up to see why it was so bloody heavy. Inside she found text books for math and science and a book on how to train a puppy. It made her smile. *One day*, she thought, *one day soon we'll have to get a dog*. Emma was obviously ready.

When Sarah pulled into Catherine's driveway, Emma was waiting for her and came running down the walkway with Rex right on her heels. Jessica, Ben and Catherine weren't far behind.

"Do you mind dropping Jessica and Ben at school? It will save me a trip." Catherine asked leaning into the window of Sarah's Volvo.

"Sure, my pleasure," Sarah replied, her face lit up with a big smile. "Good morning, Ben. Good morning, Jessica," Sarah greeted them as they climbed into the backseat.

Emma was putting her seatbelt on when Rex jumped up onto her lap like he was going with them. Catherine shouted, "Rex! What are you doing? Get out of there!"

It didn't faze Emma – she laughed and pushed Rex out of her seat onto the driveway. "He wants to come to school Auntie."

Ben and Jessica laughed in the back seat as their mom struggled to get control of Rex.

Once Rex was under control, Catherine refocused on Sarah and in a much lower voice leaned back into the window and said, "I want to hear all about your evening with Chuck."

Sarah looked up at her, and then at the time on the dashboard clock, "Well, look at the time! Running late, gotta go!"

She put the car in gear and started backing out of the drive way.

"Watch out for Rex, Mom!" Emma shouted.

"Don't worry, sweetie. I have him," Catherine shouted back. "Sarah, call me when you get to work."

Sarah turned up the radio and pretended she didn't hear by putting her hand to her ear and shaking her head as they drove off down the street.

CHAPTER 41

"I love Christmas!" Mary beamed as she lovingly hung Christmas ornaments on the tree in the staff room. "I love all of it! The music, the food, the decorations and especially the Christmas parties!"

"Mary, Christmas is supposed to be more than music, food and parties. It's about spending time with family and friends, and giving to those who need it the most. You should join Emma and me; we volunteer at the homeless shelter on Christmas day."

"I'd love to. That sounds amazing."

Sarah unplugged the kettle that had started to whistle and poured hot water into her tea cup. She dipped the tea bag in and out of the hot water while she asked Mary if she had been able to get a hold of Nancy Weninger. It had been over a month and Sarah was starting to get worried about her.

"I called and left a message again this morning, Sarah. She hasn't responded to any of my messages."

"That is so unlike her. Can you look up her address for me and leave it on my desk? I think I'll stop by on the weekend and check in on her."

"Sure, I'll have it for you after lunch. Did you get the message from Catherine? She wants you to meet her for lunch at Barney's."

"I did, thanks. She's been trying to get me stick with the online dating thing. I'm done though, it's not for me. You should try it, Mary, I'm sure Catherine would love to help you."

"I signed up for one last week," Mary smiled. "I have a date tonight."

"Look at you, girl! Alright! That's awesome. I can't wait to hear all about it."

"Have you looked outside lately?" Mary asked excitedly. "It's been snowing for about an hour and the weather channel said it's not going to stop until tomorrow morning. They say it's going to be the biggest snowfall in years. I'm so excited. Maybe we'll have a white Christmas."

"Why are you so excited? It's going to be a mess on the roads later. I think we should close early so we have lots of time for the drive home."

"Yes, that's a great idea. Maybe we should close at lunch."

"I was thinking more like 2 or 3," Sarah countered.

"2pm it is," Mary said as if she was accepting the offer and then quickly left the room before Sarah could change her mind. Sarah smiled too herself as she sipped her tea and played with the Christmas ornaments that Mary had just finished hanging. She hadn't realized that Mary had hung dozens of different puppy Christmas ornaments all over the tree including the Golden Retriever ornament that Sarah was holding in her hand.

Sarah was lost in thought and failed to notice that Mary had re-entered the room. Mary watched Sarah play with the ornament for a few moments before she interrupted. "Sarah, I called you a cab, the buses are running really slowly with the snow and I didn't want you to be late. It should be here shortly."

Sarah released the ornament, turned back to Mary and thanked her. "Mary, I think we should close now. Why don't you lock up and head home after you put Nancy's address on my desk. It's a snow day!"

"Really? Oh, thanks, Sarah! I have a few things I need to do before I go home and get ready for my date. You're a Christmas angel. Thank you, thank you. Enjoy lunch and say hi to Catherine for me."

IN A RELATIONSHIP
304

CHAPTER 42

There were close to a dozen people waiting to be seated when Jake arrived at Barney's a few minutes before noon. He shook the snow off his umbrella before he collapsed it and fastened the snap. He stepped inside the door, appreciating the warmth of Barney's after having walked several blocks in the cold snow. The hostess offered to take his jacket and umbrella, but Jake refused. He wasn't going to lose another umbrella. She asked if he had a reservation and he told her he was meeting someone there. She told him to feel free to go have a look around but if he needed a table it was going to be at least a 20 minute wait.

As he scoured the restaurant he spotted Darryl sitting at the bar, chatting up the bartender. Jake made his way to the bar and sat down on the stool next to Darryl without him even noticing that he was there. It wasn't until the bartender put a coaster down in front of Jake and asked him what he wanted to drink that Darryl realized he had arrived.

"Hey, there you are. It's about time."

"I know, it's a winter hell out there. This city does not deal well with snow."

"That's because we don't normally get snow in Seattle. Were lucky if we get snow once or twice a year and it normally never sticks. This shit is crazy. It's been snowing since 9am and it's not supposed to stop until tomorrow morning. They say we could get upwards of around a foot."

"Great," moaned Jake.

"Come on, it's Christmas. Santa needs a little snow to help get around in his sled," Darryl joked.

"Right. Santa needs the snow," Jake added sarcastically as he adjusted his chair and pulled his jacket over the back of it. Once he had that all sorted out he reached into the jacket pocket and took his phone out and placed it on the bar. "Is this where we're going to eat or did you get us a table?"

"I forgot to make a reservation so we'll have to eat here at the bar. That's alright. It gives us a nice view of all the ladies coming in, so it's all good," he said with a smile as he looked at Jake and then at the female bartender who smiled back at Darryl.

"You told me you sat at the bar because I was working," the bartended replied with a look of mock disappointment.

"You, young lady, have a boyfriend," Darryl responded with his own look of disappointment. She changed the subject and asked Jake what he wanted to drink as she placed menus in front of both of them.

"You two should put your order in as soon as you can. The kitchen is going to be slammed shortly."

"I'll have a coffee," Jake told her.

Darryl gave Jake a look of disgust "A coffee? Let's have a drink, 'tis the season."

"I have to go back to work after lunch. We have a bunch of last minute orders to put through. You're still coming over for dinner tonight though, right?"

"You bet, I'm going to bring over Mathew's present as well."

"What about mine?"

"Do you think you've been a good enough boy this year?" Darryl teased him.

"A lot better than you," Jake laughed back. "I'm pretty sure you're on the naughty list."

"Being on the naughty list isn't all that bad," Darryl smiled back.

Darryl noticed that Jake's phone was flashing a new message from Anna. "Is that sexy Anna?" Darryl enquired.

"She's the only Anna I know," Jake replied.

"I wonder what she wants? Here let me check it," Darryl said as he reached over to pick up Jake's phone.

"I got it," Jake told him, picking up the phone before Darryl could, and opening the message. He took a moment and then started to laugh as he held the phone in front of Darryl so he could read the message. It was a picture of Anna wearing Christmas wrap across her breasts and around her waist, with a caption that said she would like to be unwrapped on Christmas morning under his tree. They both laughed.

"What are you going to do?" Darryl asked.

"I'm going to ignore her. What do you think I'm going to do?"

"Can you send that pic to me?"

"You're sick, dude. No."

"Come on, it's Christmas. Where's your Christmas spirit?" Darryl pleaded.

Jake shook his head in disgust as the bartender placed his coffee in front of him and asked them if they had decided on their order. They picked up the menus, ordered a couple of appies and then continued to argue over whether Jake should share the picture with Darryl or not. While they continued to argue, Jake noticed a beautiful woman enter the restaurant. The hostess escorted her to a table at the far end of the restaurant, against the window near the street. Jake recognized her right away as the woman he kept running into when he was out on his dates.

"That's her!" Jake exclaimed to Darryl as he watched Sarah sit down with Catherine.

"Her who?" Darryl asked.

"The woman I was telling you about! The one I keep running into when I'm out."

"She's real? I thought you were making that shit up."

"Does she look real to you? She's stunning."

"You should go talk to her."

"I can't do that, she's with someone. I don't want to be rude."

"You pussy! That's not being rude, that's being confident. Women love confidence. Do you want me to go and talk to her?" he added as he started to get up from his bar stool.

"NO. Just sit down. I'll do it, but not until after we eat, you know, in case she says no. I don't want it to be awkward having to stay and eat if she blows me off."

"She's not going to say no. Look at you, you're a catch dude."

"Thanks, but that's coming from you. Who knows, maybe she has a boyfriend? Anyways, I'll go over after we eat."

Sarah was grateful that Mary had called her a cab. It was still slow with all the snow and the unprepared drivers, but it was definitely quicker than taking the bus. Catherine was already at Barney's when Sarah arrived, and luckily had phoned ahead and made a reservation. The restaurant was crowded with everyone looking to stay warm and get out of the cold.

Catherine got up from her chair and gave Sarah a hug and a kiss on the cheek when she arrived at the table. "Can you believe this weather?" she asked Sarah as she sat down.

"I know. It's crazy. I was going to take a bus, but thankfully, Mary called me a cab at the last minute."

"I'm surprised you were able to get a cab with this crazy weather. I'll give you a ride back after lunch."

"Thanks, Catherine. I told Mary we would close the office early today though, so if you could give me a ride home that would be perfect."

"If you're not going back, why don't we go do a little shopping after we eat? I still have a few last minute things to pick up for Peter and the kids. Have you got all your shopping done?"

"I still need to find some stocking stuffers for Emma, but other than that we're done. Overspent as usual," Sarah smiled. "But sure, let's do a little shopping."

"What did you get Emma?"

"I got her a new Mac notebook. She's always on mine, so this way she can have her own."

Catherine reached across the table and took Sarah's hand in hers and slowly spoke, "Peter and I were thinking that maybe we could go halfers with you on a new puppy for Emma? What do you think?"

Sarah went quiet but didn't pull her hand back and didn't say no right away. She looked out the window at the snow falling on to the sidewalk and then looked back at Catherine.

"Soon, Catherine, soon. I know she's ready, and I'm almost there, but not quite yet. Maybe in the spring. It'll be easier to housetrain when the weather is better."

The waitress came and took their order as the two woman caught up on the week's events. Catherine still couldn't believe that Chuck had turned out to be such a freak. She and Sarah had another good laugh as Sarah took her through the Chuck Masturbation story.

"I can't believe that he just started playing with his penis, right there in the truck in front of you. That is so creepy."

"I know. Thank God I had the pepper spray in my purse that Peter gave me."

"You actually sprayed him in the eyes and then in the crotch?" Catherine asked with a wicked smile on her face.

"Hell yeah!" Sarah laughed and then turned serious as she looked intently at Catherine. "That was date six, so we're good now right. No more online dating."

"Are you sure? You still have another month on the membership and it would be a shame to let it go to waste. Maybe you can line up a New Year's date?"

"Not a chance," Sarah said sternly. "I'm done. I'll go back to trying to meet Mr. Wonderful in the produce department. It can't be any worse."

"Maybe Mr. Wonderful is sitting right here in Barney's having lunch," Catherine joked as both she and Sarah looked around the restaurant. There weren't any good prospects.

They did notice a couple of guys sitting at the bar, but their backs were to them. At that moment the waitress arrived with their food, and the two of them carried on with their conversation while they ate their lunch.

"How was your soup?" Darryl asked Jake as he motioned for the bartender to bring him another beer.

"It was good. The perfect meal for a wintery day. How's your beer?"

"It was so good I think I'll have another. The office is closed until after the holidays so I don't have to worry about work for 5 days. And don't worry, it's my last one and then I have a few last minute things to grab for the kids before I go home. In a cab."

"Good, I was just going to say you shouldn't drive if you're going to have another beer."

"Your mystery woman looks like she's done her lunch. You better hurry and ask her out before she leaves."

"Shit, right! I almost forgot." Jake started to get up when his phone rang. He picked it up and saw it was a call from Mathew so he answered it.

"Hi, dad. What are you doing?"

"I'm having lunch with Darryl. What are you doing?"

"I was wondering if you could pick me up from school right now? They're letting us out early because of all the snow, but only if we have someone who can pick us up."

"Yeah, sure. I'm downtown so it will probably take me 20 minutes or so. Just sit tight and I'll be there as soon as I can, ok?"

"Ok, I'll be in the library so text me when you get here and I'll meet you out front."

"Sounds good. See you soon."

"Bye."

"That was Mathew. They're letting them out of school early so they can get home before the roads become any worse. I gotta go."

"What about the mystery lady?" Darryl reminded him. They both looked over at the table along the window but she was gone.

"Shit," Jake said out loud and then realized the bartender had heard him. He looked at her and apologized. He looked to the front of the restaurant, but she wasn't there either. She was gone.

"I don't think I was meant to meet her," he sadly told Darryl. "I've had numerous chances now, and I haven't made it happen. I gotta go. Don't drink anymore, and try and get to my place before seven if you can. And plan on staying over, especially now with all the snow."

"Alright, get going. And don't worry about the bill, I got you covered. I'll see you tonight." Jake put on his jacket as he walked to the front door and heard Darryl yell after him, "Send me that picture."

IN A RELATIONSHIP

CHAPTER 43

Emma walked in the front door of the house, threw her backpack onto the couch and hung her jacket in the closet by the front door before she moved to the kitchen. She picked an apple out of the bowl on the counter before heading upstairs to her bedroom and turning on her laptop. She brought up her favorites and clicked on the SPCA website just as she had done every day for the past 12 months. She gasped out loud, almost choking on her first bite of the apple, when she saw that she had a new message in her adoption folder file. She sat down in her chair, took a deep breath and opened it.

Dear Emma;

We are pleased to inform you that a Golden Retriever puppy has arrived at the Shelter and your wait to adopt a puppy is over. The puppy is ready to be picked up and placed with you. With the holidays approaching, we need to place the puppies before we close this evening at 8pm. If you are unable to be here prior to 8pm, a backup family has been notified to adopt the puppy and you will have to go back on the waiting list. We realize this is short notice, but the shelter will be closed for two weeks and all our animals need to be placed before we close tonight.

The note went on to talk about the fees and address but Emma was wiping tears from her eyes. She had waited so long for this to happen and she couldn't believe that it was finally going to come true. She looked at the clock, it was 6pm already. That only left her two hours to get there – she would have to take the bus as the shelter was on the other side of the city. What if she didn't make it in time? She knew she couldn't wait another minute; she had to leave right away. Emma opened her drawer and removed the tin in which she had been storing her allowance. She popped off the lid and put the money into her pocket as her computer beeped. It was Mathew online and looking for her to play. She didn't have time, but she was so excited about the puppy that she had to tell somebody. She sent Mathew a message that the puppy stork had arrived.

Mathew wasn't positive what she meant and messaged back, "What?"

"My puppy has arrived at the shelter, but I have to be there before eight or another family will pick him up. I have to go. I'll message you later and send you a picture."

"You'll never make it in time," Mathew sent back. "You're on the other side of town and it snowed all day today. The bus will be slow."

"I know, I gotta go. Bye," she replied, and was off and running out the door towards the bus stop with her jacket in hand.

Mathew knew how important this was to Emma and he knew how upset she would be if she didn't get there in time. The shelter was a lot closer to his house, and he thought he would have a better chance of getting there in time than she would, so he brought up Google maps, typed in SPCA and got the directions. He grabbed his jacket and ran out the door, determined to get there before it closed in case Emma didn't make it.

IN A RELATIONSHIP

CHAPTER 44

Sarah closed the door behind her and leaned against it for a moment before she sat down on the bench just inside. She was relieved to be home and out of the snow. She pulled off her boots and went straight upstairs to say hello to Emma and find out how her day had been. That was their routine – every day she would come home, go upstairs, lie on Emma's bed, and spend a few minutes unwinding by discussing how school had gone. Emma would usually answer each question with a question of her own, asking how Sarah's day had gone. Then they would discuss what the options were for dinner. Depending on how they were each feeling they would either go downstairs to cook or pick up the phone and order in. This definitely felt like an order in day. Sarah had been feeling guilty about still not letting Emma get a puppy, so maybe ordering from her favorite Chinese restaurant would be a nice peace offering.

As she got near the top of the stairs Sarah began to feel uneasy. The house was a little too quiet. Usually Emma had the radio or her iPod on, and was either checking Facebook or playing online. Tonight, Sarah heard nothing, the house was silent. She opened the door to

Emma's room to find no one there and not a sound coming from the stereo or the computer. She went back out into the hall way and shouted Emma's name with no response back.

Sarah began to panic and quickly did a complete search of the house to no avail. Now she was really getting worried. It was so unlike Emma, and her mind began to think of all the worst case scenarios. She phoned Catherine to see if she had heard from Emma, thinking that maybe she had gone over to visit like she sometimes did when they had a disagreement. Catherine answered after four rings, although it seemed like a lot longer to Sarah.

"Is Emma there?" Sarah asked trying to not sound too panicked.

"No, what's wrong?" Catherine asked back, sensing something was wrong.

"Well, I just got home and Emma's not here", Sarah blurted out. "I looked all through the house and there's no sign of her. I'm so worried Catherine."

"Just calm down," Catherine said quietly. "She's a smart responsible girl. I'm sure there's a good explanation. Does she have any friends she could be visiting?"

"I don't know. I don't think so. I mean, she doesn't really talk about anyone that much," Sarah responded.

"When I want to know what's going with Jessica, I creep her Facebook. Have you got her password?" asked Catherine.

"Oh, that's a great idea," Sarah replied. "Let me run upstairs and check. I'll call you back."

Sarah ran upstairs and turned on Emma's laptop. It took a minute to fire up and work its way to the main screen. Emma's screensaver was the same picture of a little Golden Retriever puppy, with a big red bow around its neck like a Christmas present. Emma's online gaming account came up immediately on startup, and Sarah noticed that *Seahawk17* was also online. It was a long shot, but Sarah thought that Emma may have told him where she was going. Even if she didn't, he might have an idea. She quickly clicked on *Seahawk17* and opened a conversation.

She typed in bold capital letters, "HELLO? ARE YOU THERE?"

IN A RELATIONSHIP
322

CHAPTER 45

Jake had dragged his ass around the office all day. Everyone was in a shitty mood for a number of reasons, not the least of which was the non-stop Christmas programming they had been playing all day to go along with the heavy snowfall. Jake knew most people loved the holiday music and TV specials, but when you worked in a TV station you slowly became jaded and even resentful of all the Christmas shows and music. It was the same movies and specials pretty much every year, and with the first of December he knew he was in for twenty-five days of the same shit he had been watching since he was a kid. With the holiday season came the pressure of holiday sales, and the incredible work load that everyone had to grind their way through before they could take a break on Christmas Eve and escape into a bottle of Vodka – or whatever it was that they drank or smoked.

On top of it all, it had been snowing all day and the roads and traffic on the way home were brutal. As he pulled into the driveway to *Let it Snow* he had to step on the gas to get over the ridge of frozen snow the plow truck had left in front of the house. But he was home, and that meant no more work for four days. No more internet dates, and a full bottle of *Grey Goose* that he had wrapped for himself and put under the tree that could now be opened. *Yes, it's beginning to feel a lot like Christmas*, he thought.

Jake was about to start closing the garage door when Darryl pulled his jeep into the driveway. That thing may not have been the smoothest ride, but it could go pretty much anywhere in the winter. Darryl climbed out and followed Jake through the garage door with two Christmas presents in his arms. One was a Christmas wrapped box addressed to Mathew. The other was wrapped, but there was no mistaking the fact that it was a bottle, and Jake's guess was *Grey Goose*. Darryl and his wife alternated Christmases with their kids, and this year being her year, Jake had invited him to spend the evening with him and Mathew.

Jake was so caught up in Darryl's arrival that he didn't even notice that he had to turn the hallway light on when he got inside the garage door, or that there was no noise coming from Mathew's room. It wasn't until he had cracked open the *Grey Goose*, poured a couple of drinks for Darryl and himself, and was relaxing on the couch that he realized all was not right in the house. He yelled for Mathew twice before he got up off the couch and made his way to Mathew's room with his new favorite Christmas drink - vodka soda with a splash of cranberry. When he entered Mathew's room, he noticed the computer was still on. The screen was open to his online gaming account with a conversation between *Seahawk17* and *Rudy2*. It was the same question about five times in big bold letters:

"HELLO? ARE YOU THERE?"

CHAPTER 46

Jake typed back "Hello" and immediately a reply came back.

"Hi Mathew. This is Emma's mother, Sarah. Do you know where she is?"

Jake could sense the panic even through the computer screen, and he began to feel it as well. "No, this is Mathew's father, Jake. Mathew isn't here either."

"Damn it," she typed back. Then, "Sorry, I didn't mean to swear. Do you have any idea where they could be?"

Now Jake was starting to freak out. The weather outside was ugly and it was dark and late. "Not a clue," Jake sent back, "let me have a look around in his room."

Jake started going through Mathew's desk and backpack looking for clues. Meanwhile, Darryl had grown tired waiting for Jake to come back, so he came in and asked what was going on. Jake explained the situation to Darryl and as he was doing so he turned back to the computer and noticed that Mathew had another window open. He clicked on the icon at the bottom of the screen. It was a webpage with a Google map and address for the local SPCA animal shelter.

That's weird, he thought. Jake typed the information back into the computer for Emma's mom to see, and asked her if that meant anything to her.

"They've gone to the SPCA," she sent back. "I am going there now!"

"OK," Jake said. "I'll meet you there. I'm a lot closer."

Darryl, in typical Darryl fashion, mixed his concern over Mathew with the possibility that Emma's mom might be hot and that Jake should put on a different shirt and brush his teeth. He was always thinking of the bigger picture.

"You can't be serious?" Jake asked Darryl with a look that said he couldn't believe he was actually thinking he should hit on this girl's mother.

Darryl shrugged his shoulders, "Hey you never know."

"For Christ's sake Darryl, give it a rest. I am done the Darryl dates. No more."

Darryl flipped the jeep keys to Jake. "Here, take the jeep. It'll be quicker and its way better in the snow than your car. I'll wait here in case Mathew shows up."

CHAPTER 47

Mathew stepped off the bus and started running the two blocks up the street to the SPCA. He had only been there once as part of a field trip with his school class. He didn't remember too much about that trip except that he had felt really sad for all the dogs in the tiny cages waiting to be adopted. That and the smell.

He had asked his dad after that trip if they could adopt a dog but he had said no. Mathew remembered when he was younger that his dad and Ashley had two dogs, and his dad had to find them new homes when he and Ashley had divorced. His dad was depressed for a long time after that, so he never pushed him on the dog issue.

It only took a few minutes for Mathew to make it to the front door of the shelter, and without missing a beat he took the front steps two at a time, burst through the front door and ran up to the reception desk. He was right; he had made it there before Emma. It was 7:45pm, fifteen minutes until closing time.

The woman working behind the reception desk was on the phone and took her sweet time before she acknowledged Mathew standing in line. She waved him forward, and looking though her coke bottle glasses asked him what she could help him with. Mathew explained to her that he was there to pick up a puppy for adoption under the name of Emma Stone. As he stood at the counter waiting for her reply, he noticed her name tag said *Carol*. It was written in big bold black felt letters, and her name was surrounded by Dalmatian puppies wearing Santa hats. She seemed nice, but very official. She reminded Mathew of the librarian they had at school, except her glasses weren't as thick as Carol's, and she didn't have gray hair.

Carol looked down at Mathew from the other side of the counter and said, "You don't look like an Emma."

She seemed very stern and serious as she waited for Mathew to answer. When he didn't reply immediately she smiled one of those fake *can I help you?* Smiles and asked him for ID. Mathew started to explain the whole story about the snow and Emma being so far away to Carol, but just as he started they were interrupted by the telephone. Carol picked up the phone and answered the call in her official voice, asking the caller on the phone to wait a minute.

She turned back to Mathew and told him he would need $175.00 to pay for the licensing and shots for the puppy before she could let him take him home. Mathew hadn't thought about that when he left the house, so he didn't have any money on him. It was now 10 minutes to eight and he was running out of time. He remembered that when he had gotten off the bus he had seen a gas station on the corner and they usually had cash machines.

He left his gloves on the counter and ran out the front door, determined to get the money and get back before the shelter closed. He was in such a hurry when he ran out the front door and down the steps that he ran straight into an older gentleman who was walking up as he was running down. Mathew didn't have time to stop, so he yelled out an apology as he continued on his way down the street to the gas station.

IN A RELATIONSHIP
332

CHAPTER 48

Time was running out for Emma and she knew it. She was close to tears as the bus finally pulled up to the bus stop two blocks from the shelter. She stood up and pulled her phone out of her pocket to check the time. She had a sinking feeling in her stomach that it was too late. As she turned it on she saw that it was 7:55pm.

It seemed to take forever for the bus to come to a stop. Once she made it down the stairs and past the other passengers, she ran as fast as she could through the snow covered sidewalks. As the tears began to roll down her cheeks, she slipped and fell face first into a snowdrift. She was cold and wet but none of that mattered at that moment. She struggled to her feet and slipped again. As she tried to get her balance and pull herself out of the snow, she felt a hand grab her hand and pull her to her feet. Through a scarf and toque her eyes met two blue eyes that seemed to know her, yet she was at a loss as to who they belonged to.

"Emma?" the faceless eyes said. "I'm Mathew. Are you ok?"

For a brief second Emma forgot about the puppy as she stared back into the soft blue eyes and felt the warmth of his hand on her wet cold fingers. Reality clicked back in, and she said, "It's eight," and turned and ran towards the shelter.

Mathew raced after Emma, and the two of them ran up the stairs into the shelter as fast as they could. There was no one at the front desk when they got there, but Emma ran up anyways and started ringing the bell like she was sending out an SOS. No one came, and Emma slowly stopped ringing the bell, turned her back to the reception desk, and slowly slid to the floor in tears.

Mathew felt helpless and started ringing the bell, yelling out Carol's name. It took about 30 seconds of insistent bell ringing and shouting, but Carol finally came through the back door and put her hand over the bell.

"What is going on?" she said curtly.

"I have the money. This is Emma, and we want her puppy!" Mathew blurted out. "Please, Carol," Mathew shouted at her and threw the money on the counter. "Please, we need the puppy."

Carol picked up the money that had fallen over the counter on her side, calmly placed it in a neat pile, and pushed it back towards Mathew. "I'm sorry," she said, "but when you didn't show up by 8pm we gave the puppy to the alternate family on the waiting list. There's nothing I can do. The adoption terms were clearly spelled out. All of the puppies have been picked up so that the shelter can be closed for the holidays. Maybe in the new year."

"No, you don't understand! We would have been here, but the snow and the roads! Emma has waited so long," begged Mathew to no avail. It was too late.

IN A RELATIONSHIP

336

CHAPTER 49

Jake was cursing Darryl as he stood in the freezing snow, filling the jeep up with gas. He wasn't sure if Darryl knew it was almost empty when he threw the keys at him, but right now that didn't matter. It was taking far too much time to put gas into it, and it had taken forever to find a gas station that was open on Christmas Eve. Jake figured 10 bucks was enough to get to the shelter and back to the house. If Darryl ran out of gas on the way home, he didn't give a shit.

He jumped back behind the wheel, threw it in drive, hit the gas, and drove down the freeway towards the turnoff to the shelter. There were cars in the ditch everywhere, so he stopped cursing Darryl and was actually grateful he had the four wheel drive. It took longer than he had planned, but soon enough he pulled into the SPCA parking lot and rolled right up to the front steps.

Jake jumped out and started running up the stairs at the same time as a woman wrapped in a scarf and heavy winter jacket. She looked vaguely familiar. Jake felt like he had seen her somewhere before, but he couldn't be sure because of how bundled up she was. They reached the door at the exact same time and reached for the handle. Jake was just a second behind her, putting his hand on top of hers. They locked eyes, recognizing each other at the exact same time. There was a pause, but neither of them said anything for what seemed like an eternity. They had both pulled their hands back from the door, so Jake took the handle and pulled the door open. "After you," he offered.

Sarah ran through the doors looking for Emma. She spotted her sitting on the floor, leaning against the desk and sobbing uncontrollably. She picked her up and hugged her tightly as the tears streamed down their faces.

"I was so worried about you," Sarah whispered into Emma's ear softly. "What are you doing here sweetie?" She wiped Emma's tears away and continued to hug her.

Emma pulled away and tried to compose herself. She was a bit embarrassed, now mixed with the disappointment that she wasn't going to get a puppy. She looked at Mathew who was fighting back tears himself, and still looking at Carol hoping that she would change her mind. He pushed the money back towards her, but Carol just shook her head.

Sarah looked at Mathew and Jake and then Carol. She was confused. "Why did you come down here Emma?" Sarah asked.

"It doesn't matter, mom," she replied. "Can we just go home?"

Sarah turned to Mathew. "*Seahawk17?*" she asked.

"Yes," Mathew replied. "Actually, it's Mathew, Mrs. Stone."

Jake put his arm around Mathew and asked him if he was ok. "Yeah, I'm good dad."

"Are you ready to go home?" Jake asked.

"No, we can't leave without Emma's puppy. She has waited so long, dad. We have the money too, and we were only a few minutes late! I should have been quicker. I am so sorry, Emma. I was here but I didn't have any money so I went to get some from the bank machine but it took to long."

Emma walked over and picked up the money off the counter. She open Mathew's hand and placed the money in it. "It's ok. You tried, and that means a lot to me."

Jake looked at Carol who was starting to put things away and tidy up her desk. "Come on, Carol," he said. "It can't be too late. It's Christmas Eve. You have a little girl in tears. You could make this the best Christmas ever for her!"

"As I was explaining to the children," Carol stated matter-of-factly, "we have policies and rules which were clearly explained in the adoption waiting list agreement. I've already given the puppy to the alternate family. There is nothing I can do now."

"Oh come on! Be a Christmas Carol for once in your life!" Jake blurted out, raising his voice, getting a little pissed off at her lack of empathy for the situation and pointing at her name tag.

Sarah stepped in between Carol and Jake, realizing that his approach was not going to resolve the situation. She told Carol the entire story – how Michael, Emma's father, had died in an accident on his way home from picking up a puppy for her on her 7th birthday. How Emma had named the puppy Rudy. How they had built a dog house together, and painted it, and got everything ready for the big day the puppy was supposed to come home. Sarah explained to Carol that she had not allowed Emma a puppy ever since that day because it had been too painful. That recently she had realized that she was wrong and that they should actually do the exact opposite. That what she and Emma really needed was a puppy to celebrate life. The story had Jake and Mathew close to crying, and Jake could tell Sarah's story was not only moving him, but it was having an effect on "No Christmas" Carol.

When Sarah finished the entire story, Emma looked up at Carol and explained to her she had been on the waiting list to adopt a Golden Retriever puppy for 12 months. How she had saved her allowance for a year so she could pay for the puppy. How her mother hadn't known anything about it, and that's why she was late because she had to take the bus.

A tear rolled down Carol's cheek, but she told them that she had already given the last puppy to another family and there was nothing she could do even if she wanted to. They would have to put their name back on the waiting list.

Jake had been mesmerized by Sarah's story. She seemed like an angel as she stood holding her daughter and reliving the painful memories of her husband's death. He couldn't believe that she was the woman he had been continuously running into over the past few months through his internet dating hell. She was beautiful, thoughtful, vulnerable and strong all at the same time.

Jake pulled Mathew close to him and told him they should go. Mathew turned to say something, but he looked past both Jake and Sarah, distracted by something else. Jake turned to see what Mathew was looking at, and there, standing directly behind them holding the most beautiful Golden retriever puppy in the world, was the old man that Mathew had bumped into running to get money from the bank machine.

Carol looked over as well, causing both Sarah and Emma to turn to see what everyone was staring at. Emma's face lit up for a second when she saw the puppy, and then the tears started to run down her cheeks again. Sarah was speechless. She just stared at the man and his puppy, not knowing what to say. Jake started to ask the man his name, but he walked right past Jake and Mathew to stop in front of Sarah and Emma.

"You don't remember me do you, Miss Stone?"

"No," Sarah replied quietly, her face expressionless. She looked tired now, but still beautiful. You could tell that the emotional recollection of the events of five years ago had taken a lot out of her on this particular evening.

"My name is Frank Weninger. I only met you once, so you probably don't remember me, but you would have known my wife, Nancy."

Sarah's eyes brightened a bit as she recognized the name. Nancy had been a patient of hers for over a year. They would meet every second Wednesday at 10am without fail. Then a little over a month ago, Nancy had stopped coming for their sessions without any notice. Sarah had left her messages and sent her emails, but she had never heard from her after that last appointment. Nancy's dog of 14 years had passed away, and it had been very difficult for Nancy to move on after the dog's death. Sarah had helped Nancy work through the pain of the loss of her dog, and they had become good friends. They both looked forward to the sessions, and Sarah had stopped charging Nancy because she found she spent as much time talking about her husband's death and Emma as they talked about Nancy's life.

Frank reached out and put his free hand on Sarah's, holding it tight. "Nancy spoke of you often, Sarah," he said. "She so looked forward to seeing you and all she could do after each session was tell me how kind and good you were. She begged me to come with her and meet you, but I just couldn't." He looked down at Emma. "And this must be Emma."

Sarah nodded. "How is Nancy?" she asked.

Frank turned his attention back to Sarah and his eyes turned misty. "She passed away about a month ago," he said, softly fighting back the tears.

"I'm so sorry, Frank," Sarah said, and put her other hand on top of his.

"Nancy put her name on the SPCA Adoption list a year ago when she was diagnosed with breast cancer," said Frank. "I didn't know about it until today when they called to say that they had a puppy for her. There were six in the litter and this is the last one, the runt. I have been in and out of this shelter all day, trying to get enough courage to pick up this little angel. Nancy left me a note with the papers she had signed here at the shelter. She said she wanted me to have the puppy – to keep me company and help me move on without her. That was just like her, always thinking of other people."

The tears were now freely flowing down the strong, quiet old man's face, and you could tell it wasn't easy for him to share this with Sarah, or anyone for that matter.

Frank pulled his hand from Sarah's and knelt down beside Emma. He took the puppy and placed it in her hands.

"If Nancy were here, she would want you to have this puppy, Emma. Merry Christmas."

Emma hugged Frank so hard; Jake thought she was going to squish the puppy. Frank stood up, and Sarah hugged him and kissed him on the cheek, thanking him and wishing him a Merry Christmas.

Frank turned, shook Jake's hand. "You're a lucky man. Take care of those three," he added as he looked over at Sarah, Emma and the puppy.

Jake blushed and just nodded, not wanting to ruin the moment. Mathew smiled and had a little chuckle at his dad's expense. Then he apologized again to Frank for running into him earlier when he was running out to the bank machine.

"It's ok," Frank said. "Everyone is always saying slow down and enjoy life, but as you know, sometimes you have to hurry up so you can do just that."

After Frank left, Mathew and Emma both sat on the floor and played with the puppy. Jake walked over beside Sarah and held out his hand to her.

"Hi, I'm Jake Jensen, Mathew's father. It's really nice to finally meet you, Sarah Stone."

Sarah smiled back and put her hand in Jake's, "It's nice to meet you too, Jake Jensen. You look very familiar. Do you get out often?"

Jake laughed, "Not that often, and when I do, it's not always with the right people."

"Me too," she smiled back. "Maybe we should go out together sometime?"

"I think I would like that. I think I would like that a lot," Jake smiled back, realizing he was still holding her hand and let it go.

Sarah looked down at Emma and Mathew. "What are you going to name her, Emma?" she asked.

Emma looked up with a huge smile and said, "Rudy2!"

"THE END"

Manufactured by Amazon.ca
Bolton, ON